DANNY DECKER

and the
HORRIBLY UNLIKELY
SPACE ADVENTURE

JOHN ROBERT MACK
Tales of Mystery and Woe

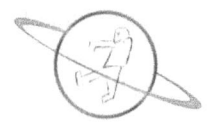

ZEN MONSTER PRESS

Available or forthcoming from John Robert Mack

Tales of Mystery and Woe
Supernatural / Sci Fi Universe
Tales of Mystery and Woe: a comedy
Tango with a Twist
Whiskey Tango Foxtrot
No Tengo Tango

A Consequence of Folly

Danny Decker and the
Horribly Unlikely Space Adventure

Superhero Universe
Call Me Angel
Übermen

Third Testament
The Gospel of John
The Acts of St. Michael
(Forthcoming)

Avalon Redux
Once a Future King

Several characters appear in both timelines of the TOMAWAC multiverse. Names like Elizabeth Turner, Morrison James, and Bobby Decker appear in both timelines. Rest assured that to avoid universal collapse, these characters may share names, but they are completely different people who never meet. All thanks go to Maestro who travelled from 200 years in the future to keep slavers from invading Earth in 1961. Unfortunately, time doesn't work like that. Now we have multiple timelines.

The Law of Narrative Causality

"So," Danny asked, "the evil alien insects that discovered this world in *your* timeline. . . do they even *exist* in this one?"

"Do they exist?" Maestro leaned against the railing. "Of course, they *exist*, but they should have discovered this world a hundred years ago. Since they haven't been here yet, they must have missed the boat for some reason." He shrugged and then spoke horrifying words. "I'm sure we're perfectly safe. There's absolutely nothing to worry about."

Danny cringed. "You did *not* just say that." He searched the moonlit landscape below them. "*Why* did you just say that?" Movement at the edge of the distant lawn caught his eye. "Spit."

Maestro scowled. "What's the big deal?"

With a withering sigh, Danny pointed at the landscape below, where a number of skittery shapes crested the hill from the beach. "Do you know *nothing* about the laws of narrative causality? You can't say something like, 'I'm sure we're perfectly safe. There's absolutely nothing to worry about,' without evil aliens appearing out of nowhere to attack you. It's an absolute *law*."

"That's just not bloody possible," Maestro muttered.

Danny rolled his eyes, grabbed Maestro by the back of the neck and pointed again. "Tell *them* that!"

Maestro shook off Danny's hand. "Are you sure you're only twelve years old?" He surveyed the approaching line of aliens for a second. "Drat." He hauled Danny over to the other boys while shouting into his Doohickey. "Babbage, get your manufactured butt back here on the double. We have company." He cut the feed before Babbage could respond and leaned in close to Danny. "I will do everything in my power to get you out of this. You have every right to hate me for this for the rest of your natural life."

After a moment, he added, "However long that may be."

Danny Decker and the Horribly Unlikely Space Adventure

This book is an original publication of Zen Monster Press.
Edited by Lauran Strait.
www.linkedin.com/in/lauranstrait

Visit the author at
www.johnrobertmack.com
email: john@johnrobertmack.com
www.facebook.com/johnrobertmack

Contact the author for information regarding volume discounts for classes, studios and other organizations. Bring the author to your live event, in person or online.

Jacket design by John Robert Mack.
Cover photo: Triston Penn as "Danny Decker." @tristonpenn
          Rory Mitchell as "Maestro." @roaryhtelion-fit

For Blake, Byron, and Finn (in alphabetical order).
If you hate it, just tell your Uncle Jack it's great,
and then quietly delete it from your tablet.

"Find a Penny. . ."

With an immense sigh of resignation, Danny Denton Decker turned onto the sidewalk of his sadly unterrifying middle school and almost completely failed to notice the coppery glint on the concrete at his feet. *Find a penny, pick it up,* said a little voice inside Danny's head.

Danny picked up the penny and, without really looking at it, stuffed it into his pocket.

Hopefully, Mr. Hinkens, Danny's science teacher, would tease him because he was the only boy in class who had *not* signed up for intramural football.

Someone had to tease Danny or torment him in *some* way if he were ever going to have an exciting adventure. He read adventure stories all the time, and he knew the score. Science fiction. Fantasy. All the heroes started out as tortured loners no one loved or cared about. Unfortunately for Danny, his parents loved him, and he loved them. Also, while they were too old (or perhaps too young) to use the word itself, he and his older brother felt the same way.

Danny was average height for his age but skinny, with bones that stuck out in more places on his body than a body ought to have bones. His hair lay straight and brown, and his eyes were green. If anyone googled "boring, average twelve-year-old" he'd undoubtedly find Danny's photo. He was, perhaps, smart for his age but not enough to make him an outcast. . . or even very interesting for that matter. He even liked his teachers and earned good grades. Yuck.

At one point, he'd learned Taekwondo from his dad, but he didn't need fighting skills, did he, since Bobby protected him? It was more fun mastering video games, reading, or playing laser tag with his friends in the woods near his house.

Oh, spit. That ruined it, too. He had *friends*. Real, fun, honest to goodness friends like Torch and TJ who slept over sometimes and surprised him with birthday parties at Lazer Quest, cool presents, and lots of cake and ice cream.

How in the world could he establish the necessary tortured soul on a stomach full of birthday cake and ice cream?

Real heroes needed ghastly, painful childhoods to forge in them the strength to brave terrible horrors in alternate universes and spaceships on the edge of the galaxy. So Danny would never steal a tremendous horde of gold from a blood-thirsty dragon, fight evil alien insects on a desolate planet, or hunt angst-ridden vampires, werewolves, or zombies in an under-saturated urban sprawl.

It was enough to make him scream.

Once, Danny had actually considered antagonizing Bobby so maybe his older brother would terrorize him. Hard to say. Might have helped.

Unfortunately, as Danny had stood in Bobby's bedroom with Socrates the snake coiled around one arm, ready to unleash untold dimensions of reptilian fury on his unsuspecting brother, he just couldn't follow through.

Two reasons.

One: Bobby lay so innocently and helplessly, face down on top of his Star Wars bed sheets in his Fruit-of-the-Looms.

Two: What if the ensuing debacle injured Socrates? Danny's mother would've perished from grief had her favorite snake been harmed.

Okay. . . Danny was doomed. His *mother* raised snakes. His *mother*. You never had fantastic adventures when your mother was cool enough to own twelve snakes. It just. didn't. happen.

Had Danny not preoccupied himself with the utter impossibility of embarking on any kind of adventure, he might have noticed the little voice inside his head when he'd picked up the penny.

It had not been, in fact, his own.

This is Why Danny Wears Shorts to Bed

Danny dreamed of strange things that night: a red-haired woman and Old West taverns, images and events foreign to his actual experience. Had he not been awakened by his bed jumping six inches in the air and a foot to the left, he might have wondered about the dreams' origins the following morning.

Instead, he assumed that being thrown into the air and dropped on the floor next to his bed had to be part of a weird dream. Then someone shouted his name so forcefully the only options were Mom or Dad, so he woke up as quickly as possible. How might he explain that the jumping bed could be in no way his fault?

As he forced open an eyelid, all the unusual moments of his dreams slid into obscurity, replaced by the puzzle of who had awakened him in the middle of the night and why. The voice seemed too high for Dad and too low for Mom.

Danny's one open eye spotted Bobby hurrying to the side of the bed in his trademark Fruit-of-the-Looms and black footy socks. His brother's voice packed a force Danny had only rarely heard from his brother. . . and his words made no sense.

"Get up, Danny! The house is on fire, and we have to get out." Bobby lifted him to his feet. "We have to get out!" Bobby looked scared. . . Okay, *terrified* was a better word for it. Bobby—Danny's big, strong older brother who feared nothing—was terrified.

Spit! In a great number of people, seeing the person you want to emulate cowering in fear would create a feeling of helplessness, but, strangely, in Danny, it had the opposite effect.

Well, Danny Decker said to himself, and it was his own voice this time, *someone better keep it together or we're doomed.*

"You're sure," he said out loud. "Fire? How?"

"There was an explosion... Didn't you feel it? I opened my bedroom door... It's an inferno out there... can't you hear it?" He still held Danny, and, while affection was not uncommon in their family, his grip seemed more a clutch.

Danny listened. Something roared in the distance. Then it happened: one of those moments where time stretched and allowed him to think faster than normal. He looked his brother up and down. What to do? What to do?

This is exactly why I wear shorts and a t-shirt to bed every night, Danny thought, *and if we both survive this ordeal and Bobby is humiliated by standing in the yard in his underwear in front of all our neighbors, I am soooo going to say I told you so!*

Only six seconds after his brother had asked the question about the audibility of the fire, Danny grabbed the comforter from his bed, snatched his robe from the floor, and dragged his brother into the bathroom they shared where he retrieved Bobby's bathrobe from the back of the door to *his* bedroom.

He pulled brother, comforter, and bathrobes into the shower, cranking the water on cold full blast.

Bobby sputtered and struggled. "What the—?"

"Put your robe on before it gets wet," Danny insisted, shoving it into his brother's chest and pulling on his own as the water poured over them. "If it's wet, the fabric will stick to itself and make it hard to pull on. The wet stuff will protect us as we dash through the fire, and your bathrobe will prevent the neighbors from learning details about your anatomy they don't need to know."

Bobby looked at his brother through squinty eyes. "*I'm* supposed to be saving *you.*"

Danny turned Bobby in the shower's spray. "You can save me next time."

They jumped out of the tub, huddled together so they could pull the soaked comforter over the two of them. They rushed from the bathroom and through Danny's room since his was closer to the stairs which would, hopefully, lead them to safety.

"Wait a second." Bobby touched the door with one hand. "It's not hot. We're okay."

Oh yeah, someone had done that in a movie.

Bobby yanked the door open onto a hopeless inferno. Heat washed over Danny, but not enough to hurt. Smoke filled the air, but not enough to choke.

The brothers stepped into the open hall that looked over a railing and down onto the first floor living room.

Two things seemed strange: one, the living room wall—which had always blocked the view of the street and been a pretty solid wall type of thing with a lovely fireplace—had vanished. Completely. Ah, that was why they hadn't already asphyxiated from smoke.

Two, a little dinosaur stood at the bottom of the stairs blocking the escape of Mom and Dad, who held one another on the stairwell. The dinosaur shouted in a language like a really annoyed grackle and gestured at Danny's parents with what looked like a silver banana.

A silver banana?

Dad held a table leg in one hand, as if it might actually be some kind of protection against a silver banana. Mom, inexplicably, brandished some sort of vacuum cleaner attachment.

Oh wait, the little dinosaur wasn't blocking his parents; his parents were preventing *it* from climbing the stairs. They shouted at the dinosaur with rather astonishing language. If so many lives had not hung in the balance, Danny might have laughed.

He experienced another time-condensed moment: the dinosaur at the bottom of the stairs wasn't, in fact, a dinosaur. It was how a dinosaur, specifically something like a velociraptor, would look if it had evolved for a few million years more without a giant asteroid cutting short its evolutionary path. A change in its food supply, over millennia, would cause a velociraptor to shrink. Its brain case would grow, as would its arms, and it would walk upright. Nothing like that could have evolved on Earth.

On Earth. . .

It was an alien. . . and it pointed a weapon at his parents. . .
Danny knew what came next. "Look out!"
. . .too late. . .

There wasn't a beam. No bright blue or red or green light from
the weapon to the hapless victims. The little dinosaur simply pointed
his silver banana at Danny's parents, squeezed the thing, and Mom
disappeared.

The alien pointed the banana at Dad, squeezed, and Dad was no
longer there.

No special effects, no glory. . . just gone.

A horrible noise erupted from Bobby's throat when his parents
vaporized, loud and horrified and high-pitched. It drew the attention
of the alien, who looked up at the brothers, huddled together under a
soggy blanket at the top of the steps.

It narrowed its eyes and waved its banana at them as it climbed
the stairs.

Briefly, a holographic screen appeared in front of the alien, said
something in grackle, and then winked out. Danny had no idea what
the device registered, but from the way the alien's eyes widened and
it licked its lips, whatever the dinosaur sought. . . it had found it.

In a weird parallel to human behavior, it threw back its head
and laughed in triumph.

That simple action saved the boy's lives.

While the dinosaur laughed, it raised its gun arm without really
looking at them.

Bobby grabbed Danny and put himself between his brother and
the alien.

Oh, heck no! Danny had read the novels! "Shielding someone
with one's body" meant one thing and one thing only: instant and
horrible, bloody death.

"You idiot." Danny grabbed his unsuspecting brother, pulled
him close, and spun them both. With his back to the alien, Danny
planted his feet against the stairs and pushed off as hard as he could.

The brothers launched down the stairs directly at the smug alien
who had just finished his triumphant laugh. The collision hurt, and

all three of them rolled down the last of the stairs and onto the floor below, but Danny retained all four limbs and no one had been vaporized. When his world stopped spinning and crashing, he found himself flat on his stomach. His brother sprawled across his backside, pinning him, and the alien was prostrate a few feet away.

More importantly, the alien's silver banana lay less than a foot from Danny's hand.

While his brother wriggled around as if trying to sort up from left, Danny regarded the banana and the dinosaur, who glanced around, smacked its holster then locked eyes with Danny, who had the weapon in arm's reach without a clue how to use it.

Just grab the stupid thing, a strange voice in Danny's head said.

Danny grabbed the stupid thing.

Point and squeeze, said the voice.

Danny pointed and squeezed.

The alien vanished.

Problem solved.

Oh. . . wait. . . the house was on fire and Danny's parents were dead.

Danny had just killed an alien that resembled a highly evolved dinosaur.

Brain. wouldn't. work.

Bobby grabbed Danny and pulled him out of the burning house into the yard where a couple of firemen dragged them over to the fire trucks.

"Are you okay?" The firemen gave them dry blankets. "Where are your parents?"

If you tell them the truth, they'll think you're insane, the voice in Danny's head counseled, so he grabbed Bobby by the lapels of the bathrobe he wore only at Danny's insistence.

"We don't know what we saw." Danny pressed his mouth against Bobby's ear. "They were there one second and then they were gone. We didn't see anything else."

Bobby held Danny with anger in his eyes. "But we saw more than that. . . that thing killed Mom and Dad."

And that's the moment it hit.

That thing had killed Mom and Dad.

They were dead.

Horrible pain and anguish are never fun or entertaining to read unless you're messed up in the head, so we're close to the moment we leave the boys. They turned to watch their home burning to ash, one entire corner inexplicably missing.

They were orphans. . .

Orphans?

Realization slammed Danny in the frontal lobe like a cement truck.

"No, no, no, no, no. . ." Danny's legs buckled. "I didn't mean *this*." He fell helplessly to his hands and knees. "I didn't mean *this!*"

He was an orphan.

His adventure could begin.

All it had taken was the death of his parents.

Danny's wails morphed into screams, and Bobby held him close. The fire blazed in the background and the two brothers fell to the ground clutching each other in grief and sorrow. . . and it's really time to let them deal with this on their own.

We'll check in on them again the next day.

The Next Day

Danny dreamed about a beautiful red-haired woman he'd never met. She wore a white, flowing dress and floated in the deepest reaches of space, her hair blown about by an impossible wind... impossible because there is no air in the deepest reaches of space, but, no doubt, you knew that already. She smiled peacefully at Danny and held her arms out to him.

Danny awoke feeling peaceful and calm.

For about five seconds. Then he remembered that other dream... the bad one about the house fire.

Something heavy draped across his chest. An arm... Bobby's arm. The older boy curled around Danny, holding him close. They'd crawled into bed together, too afraid to sleep alone.

The bad dream hadn't been a dream at all.

Their home was gone.

Their parents were dead.

Danny pushed closer to his sleeping brother. If only he could be a little kid again when such things didn't happen.

They're not dead, a voice in Danny's head said.

I saw it, Danny replied. *They were vaporized.*

There'd been lots of confusion and screaming until Grandma and Grandpa Decker had appeared out of nowhere. The ambulance people said the boys were fine, so Grandma had bundled them in blankets of her own.

Grandpa stopped at the Walgreens where he bought sweatpants and t-shirts for the boys to change into to get them out of their cold, wet, smoky things. He'd apologized that the outfits matched, but what difference would it make?

Finally quiet, Danny had shambled like a zombie into Dad's childhood room and rooted through the Walgreen's bag. Grandpa had neglected to buy underwear.

"There's no underwear," Danny mumbled.

Bobby peeked into the plastic Walgreen's bag and shrugged. "Commando it is, I guess."

Danny smiled. It seemed almost naughty somehow.

Bobby had smiled back, but they were in Dad's old room and Dad was dead.

Both smiles had faded.

They weren't vaporized. They were teleported.

The boys had changed and climbed into bed as the curtains started to glow with the light from the morning sun. They'd held each other tightly, afraid of losing the only part of their lives that remained.

Seriously. . . They aren't dead.

Danny looked up at the digital clock. 8:54 p.m. He'd slept all day.

A Batman lamp in one corner shed the only light.

Bobby's steady breathing comforted Danny.

The faint, lingering smell of smoke disturbed him.

Hello? Are you paying any attention at all?

Quit it, Danny thought to himself. *This sucks enough at it is. I don't want to go crazy trying to convince myself they aren't really dead. I saw them die.*

He squeezed his eyes shut and held the tears at bay. He'd cried enough for one day. Why would his internal voice spout impossible rubbish?

Internal voice? Do I even sound like a twelve-year-old boy?

Danny opened his eyes. The voice in his head had a point. Of course, sometimes he talked to himself in different voices for the fun of it. . . but this seemed a *different* different, somehow. More like James Earl Jones than Danny Decker.

So. . . err. . . who are *you then?* Danny asked.

The silence stretched out.

Well? Danny demanded. Just how complicated would this be?

Remember the penny you picked up?

Danny touched the penny in the pocket of his sweatpants.

Why did you transfer a penny *when you changed clothes?* the voice of Darth Vader asked.

Why? It'd just seemed a good idea at the time.

Like a little voice told you so?

"Wait a minute!" Danny said out loud.

Shhhhhh. . .

Bobby muttered in his sleep. He rolled over but didn't wake up.

Danny took the opportunity to slip silently from the bed, through the glass door, and onto the balcony just outside the room. He pulled the penny out of his pocket and held it up for inspection under the light of a bright moon.

"It's not a penny at all." It was some kind of electronic doohickey. "Computer chip?"

Exactly. . . a chip with my memories.

"Your memories? Who are you?" Danny asked.

You don't need to speak out loud, you know. I can hear your thoughts perfectly well.

"Okay: one. . . *creepy!* And two: it's hard to tell who's talking if both voices are in my head. This way I know I'm the out loud voice and you're the inside-my-head voice."

Whatever pleases you.

"So who. . . what are you and how are you talking in my head?" Danny had several ideas on the subject but wanted to hear them in black and white. After all, a dino-like alien had vaporized his parents with a silver banana. A telepathic penny-sized circuit simply had to relate to the attack on the house.

You are more observant than most of your species, the penny told him. *My name is Babbage, and my ship was in a hidden orbit over your planet when the Saurians attacked and destroyed it. I expelled my memory core from the ship at the last moment, hoping it would reach the planet's surface where I might find a suitable native to aid me in acquiring another body and continuing my quest.*

"You said my parents are still alive?" He wasn't even going to touch the whole "quest" part of the explanation. The idea of adventure had recently worn thin.

Indeed. . . They were not vaporized. They were kidnapped. The Saurians are looking for me. They teleported your parents to their ship for questioning.

Did that mean—?

No, you did not kill the alien, Babbage said before Danny could ask. *You just sent him back to his ship. And I'm sorry, I will endeavor in the future to allow you to ask the questions before I answer them. . . Oooh. . . Oops.*

Danny surveyed his grandparents' backyard. A garden nestled in one corner, and a tire swing hung in the big, old oak. Bushes and shrubs and flowers surrounded the lawn, leaving plenty of room to play and a fence to keep out the neighbors.

The penny in his hand was a memory core that apparently belonged to some kind of alien AI who wanted him to search the galaxy for a way to return it to its robot body.

It didn't make sense.

Adventures didn't happen to kids like him.

The soft, bemused chuckling in Danny's head could only be described as smug.

"Yes?"

Sorry, the penny began, *but do you really think I want you to help me? You're a twelve-year-old boy with no battle training. Anyone who'd accept help from someone like you would have to be suicidal. No offense.*

Danny was, in fact, quite offended. "So why the heck did you ask me to pick you up in the first place?"

I need a pair of legs to carry me to the person I expect will be able to help me.

A courier, thought Danny, even more offended. *Great.*

Can we, for the moment, go back to the place where your parents are alive?

"Danny?" a familiar voice called from below.

Danny poked his head over the balcony rail.

The moonlight illuminated his two best friends, TJ and Torch, on the grass below. TJ was taller, as skinny as Danny, and wore his jet black hair long, wavy and messy. Torch wore his in a tight fade and was small for his age. They stood with their hands behind their backs as if hiding something, their dark faces and eyes as unreadable as the sphinx. In black t-shirts and jeans, they nearly melted into the darkness.

When Danny waved, both boys smiled. . . then lost the smiles. This wasn't really a smiling kind of visit.

"Hey, *mijo*," Torch said.

"Hey, *papi*," Danny replied. Torch was the oldest of the three. "Hey, TJ."

TJ waved one hand, keeping the other behind his back.

"Yer Gramps up there with you?" Torch asked.

"Nope."

The boys exchanged a puzzled glance.

"Who you talking to?" Torch asked.

"An artificial intelligence from another planet."

His friends exchanged another glance and thought that through for less than half a second before nodding acceptance. "Stellar," said one of them, and it could've been either.

"What are you doing out here?" Danny asked.

"Well, your Gramps kept telling us that you should be left alone right now," Torch explained with obvious contempt for all things grandparent-y. "We figured stuff that."

TJ nodded his agreement.

Danny glanced over a shoulder at the house in which his grandparents slept lightly with one ear apiece tuned in to that special frequency nearly deaf old people reserve for disobedient, sneaky grandchildren.

"If I let you in," Danny said, "there's no way my grandparents won't wake up."

"Only if we use the front door and the stairs." Torch gestured for Danny to take a few steps back. Such was the nature of their friendship that Danny complied without question.

We are on something of a timetable, you realize, Babbage complained. *There are several bloodthirsty extraterrestrial dinosaurs out to find me.*

Shut it, Danny sent back. *These are my friends.*

A short silence followed, then a brief "thwip-thwip-thwip" noise, and then two hooks hit the balcony railing at exactly the same time. A rope ladder now hung confidently from the balcony to the ground.

Danny smiled and leaned over the railing.

"So... are we coming up or are you coming down?" Torch asked with a grand gesture.

Grinning in a way that would have been impossible two minutes earlier, Danny glanced over his shoulder at the door that separated him from his brother, who still slept soundly. "You guys come up here. I don't want Bobby to wake up and find me missing."

"Thus sayeth the lord." Torch started his climb.

Babbage maintained a judicious silence while Danny awaited his friends. When Torch's head appeared above the railing, Danny helped him over.

As soon as his feet hit the wood of the balcony, Torch pulled Danny into one of those hugs that should have explained why Danny would never have an adventure, but, at some point, we need to stop beating that dead horse.

"Whatever you need," Torch muttered, holding Danny close.

"I'm good right now," Danny lied, but it was one of those moments when you said that sort of thing.

Torch smacked him on the back and both boys helped TJ over the rail. He hugged Danny as well.

All three boys sat cross-legged on the balcony.

A short, awkward silence ensued. What the heck should three twelve-year-olds discuss on such a night?

Torch smiled cryptically. "Tina Sanders totally kissed me when the announcement was made in school today. Not that I would ever try to benefit from your pain, *mijo*, but, well... It was *Tina Sanders!*"

TJ snorted.

Danny punched Torch in the arm.

Babbage psychically rolled his eyes.

"Oh... and Nax stopped by, too," Torch said. "You should tell Bobby."

"Nax? Really?"

Bernard Nackers, known as Nax, had been Bobby's best friend for years. They'd been sparring partners and pretty much inseparable until one day Nax stopped showing up. No amount of the nagging and pestering at which younger brothers so excel had wheedled any info on the whys and wherefores.

"He stopped by, what. . . two, three times?" Torch looked to TJ and shrugged.

TJ held up a hand with four fingers lifted.

Torch nodded. "He was ma-a-ad that Gramps wouldn't let him in."

Danny considered one face then the other. Wow. They must have hidden in the bushes all day waiting for a chance to see him.

"Guys. . . You are so cool. . . But I have to tell you something. . ." Danny's emotions jumbled up too much to separate them. He couldn't express his gratitude in words. . . except to tell these two the truth.

You're certifiably insane, Babbage said instantly.

Stuff it, was Danny's inevitable response. He glanced over his shoulder. Bobby needed to know the truth as well. *Can you talk to them, too?*

Can I? Yes. Will I? Doubtful.

I will flush you down the toilet.

If they're touching you, I can talk to them all at once. Can we just get on with it? Bloodthirsty extraterrestrials. Remember?

Torch cleared his throat. "Patiently waiting for the telling-you-something to commence?" He shrugged. "But no hurry. . ."

Danny pushed to his feet. "I need to tell Bobby, too. Let's go inside."

Dutifully, his friends followed him into the house. Huh. When your friends thought your parents were dead, they'd pretty much do whatever you asked them without question.

Oooh. Danny was evil for even thinking that. Although, since his parents *weren't* actually dead, the thought was almost funny. . . almost.

Torch and TJ held back as Danny climbed onto the bed, shaking his brother very gently to wake him. Bobby, after all, didn't know the good news.

"Bobby?" Danny called. "I'm sorry but I need you to wake up. TJ and Torch are here, too."

Bobby shifted and muttered a couple of indecipherable things before saying, "TJ? Torch?" He rolled over and rubbed his face, but let's fast forward a bit through the boring "Hey there, TJ. Hey there, Torch" stuff.

When Danny told his brother about Nax's visits, Bobby announced he had to pee.

Torch made a joke about the brothers looking cute in their matching track suits and eventually they all sat on the bed facing one another which is when the story gets interesting again.

Go-o-o-o-o TEAM!

Danny extended a fist with the penny gripped inside. "Everyone in."

Bobby sat on one side, Torch on the other, and TJ directly across.

"What is this, Danny?" his brother asked.

"Just do it, okay?"

Torch complied first, then TJ, and finally Bobby.

At first, nothing happened.

"Go team," Torch muttered.

TJ chuckled.

A tremendous *Go-o-o-o-o TEAM!* shouted in Danny's mind.

Three boys leapt back and even Danny jumped at the volume.

TJ tumbled off the bed but bounced to his knees, eyes flicking back and forth. "What the heck?"

"Holy *Frijoles!*" Torch shouted.

"How'd you do that?" Bobby demanded.

Danny shook his head. "I didn't."

Babbage chuckled and Danny worked hard, although only marginally successfully, to keep a straight face. It *had* been pretty funny.

Also: thank goodness. If the others had heard Babbage then he wasn't a psychotic delusion, something that would not have surprised Danny given the situation. He extended his fist again and gave the other boys pointed looks. "He won't be so loud this time."

"He?" Bobby asked.

"Babbage," Danny explained.

"Like the ancient computer guy?" TJ asked.

"Just do it, okay?" Danny jiggled his fist.

Slowly, the other boys crept forward, and this time Bobby seized Danny first.

Sorry about that, Babbage said in a much more civil tone. *I couldn't resist.*

The boys cast about frantically, as if trying to decide who was pranking them and how.

My name is Babbage, and I am an engineered life-form from another planet, stranded on Earth as a memory chip.

Briefly, Danny displayed the penny.

Bobby tried to take it, but Danny pulled away. "He can't talk to us unless we're all touching," Danny explained.

So Bobby put a fist forward and held out his other hand for the chip.

Danny passed it over and everyone reached into the middle again, passing the chip around for inspection.

"What's an engineered life-form?" TJ asked.

Torch nodded, apparently wondering the same thing. "Is that like an AI?"

I don't want to be petty. Babbage managed to sound sheepish. *But we really don't like your term. "Artificial" intelligence makes us sound fake. We have been engineered by scientists rather than born randomly by nature, but I am just as real as any of you. And we're more than just an intelligence, we have emotions and personalities, too.*

"Engineered life-form it is," proclaimed Torch. "EL."

Thank you.

"So you guys buy this?" Danny asked hopefully.

Torch and TJ nodded, grinning.

The penny made its way back to Danny, thank goodness. Letting it out of his possession rattled him.

Bobby met Danny's gaze. His expression showed that he knew Babbage was somehow connected to his parents "murder."

Danny touched his brother's knee. "But you buy it, right?"

Bobby nodded once.

Danny took a deep breath. "Tell them." The news would be more believable from the EL.

Your parents aren't dead.

Which created another uproar. Danny quickly quieted everyone for fear of waking his grandparents. He knelt on the bed facing his brother.

"This is real?" Hope filled Bobby' face, but uncertainty bled into the edges.

Danny nodded.

Yes, Babbage added.

Bobby seized Danny, and they cried a little more, but these were happy tears. While their home and everything they owned had been destroyed, those were just *things* and things could be replaced with *new* things. Parents were a lot harder to replace, especially *good* parents.

Danny's parents were the *best.*

After a bit, Bobby drew away without releasing Danny's shoulders. The strength of his grip proved his newfound fortitude. TJ and Torch each touched one of Danny's arms.

Babbage explained what he'd already told Danny then added new information. *The Saurians tracked me to your house and lasered it from space, vaporizing that entire corner.*

"Which explains why the fire spread so fast," Bobby tossed in. "It was like the whole house just caught fire at once."

Yes. They wanted to create as much confusion as possible so they could dash in, extract me, and be gone before the authorities showed up.

"If they could blast a house from space, why do they care about the authorities?" Danny asked.

Earth is a protected planet. Extraterrestrials aren't allowed to show themselves. You aren't ready for first contact.

But wait a minute. . . if aliens weren't allowed to contact locals. . .

TJ's scowl of confusion seemed to hold the same question.

Babbage, of course, heard their thoughts. *I know, I know. . . I'm breaking a hundred laws here, but I won't survive without help, and my mission is too important. It supersedes the Protection Pact.*

TJ and Torch exchanged wicked smiles at the word "mission."

And no, you will absolutely not *help me in my mission, and no, I will not even tell you what it is. I just need someone to bring me to the man who* can *help me.*

Another minor uproar followed, of course, this one essentially a wrestling match since everyone had to hold onto Danny to hear and be heard by the EL.

Finally, Babbage shushed them all. *You still have the Doohickey?*

"Doohickey?" The boys chorused.

The banana. . . the silver banana that transported your parents and the alien. Get it.

Danny snatched his discarded bathrobe from the bedroom floor. The others gathered around as he pulled out the strange silver banana.

"What the heck?" Torch tried a grab for it, but Danny held on.

"You kept it?" Bobby asked.

Danny nodded.

"What is it?" TJ asked.

"It teleports things," Danny explained.

Oh, it's so much more than that.

"Huh?" Danny asked.

As one, the other boys dropped a hand onto Danny.

It's called a Doohickey and the closest Terran equivalent is an iPhone with absolutely killer apps. It's a communicator, a weapon, a scanner, and about twenty other things as well. It isn't really a transporter but, connected to the transporter on the Saurian ship, it activated it remotely.

"Why's it look like a silver banana?" Torch asked.

It's a prehensile design, made for a species with a tail, activated by squeezing in different pulses to activate different features.

"Whoa, the alien dinosaurs can kill you with their tails?" Torch asked. "Stellar."

It's stolen tech. The Saurians steal most of their tech. They're actually fairly primitive for a space-faring species.

"Primitive. . . that's good, right?" Danny asked. "Not as intelligent then."

Not good, no. Primitive usually means violent. For a species to last long enough to develop an advanced culture, they have to avoid killing each other, so the most advanced societies are, usually, the most peaceful.

"This is all very enlightening," Bobby interjected, "but what do we do with it, and when do we get to the part where we rescue our parents?"

Danny, push the penny into the banana.

Torch chuckled. "That sounds naughty."

TJ chuckled, too, and elbowed Torch in the ribs for good measure.

I can't wait until I have eyes to roll.

As soon as the penny touched the Doohickey, the device made a friendly "ping" sound and a small slot opened in its side.

Insert the penny into the slot and no cracks from the peanut gallery.

Danny trembled. What would happen?

Everyone stared. They held their breath.

"GO-O-O-O-O-O TEAM!" the banana bellowed.

Spit! Danny almost dropped it.

Torch shrieked.

TJ yelped and grabbed Danny, pointing at a tall Black man in jeans and a white tank top. Where'd he come from? His skin was so dark; it was almost literally black. He looked to be somewhere in his late twenties, had lots of muscles, long braids, and stood peacefully with his hands behind his back.

The boys bunched up near the glass balcony door.

"Sorry again." Babbage's voice emanated from the Doohickey, but the stranger's mouth moved with the words. "That was just too much fun to pass up."

"Babbage?" Danny asked, glancing from the Doohickey to the man.

The man, Babbage, nodded.

"It made you a body?" Danny asked.

"Hologram," Babbage explained. He stepped forward and waved his arm. It passed through Danny and Bobby. Yikes!

"Wait a moment," Babbage said. He glanced at the ceiling then smiled. "Better?" His voice sprang directly from the hologram now. "The sonics on this model are pretty advanced."

"Okay," Torch said, "tell me that thing has, like, a million gig of alien music on it."

"A million terabytes," TJ corrected.

"Oh, man, what's bigger than a terabyte? I bet he has a *gajillion* of those." Torch bounced up and down on his heels.

Babbage seemed very pleased that he could effectively roll his eyes.

Merely Human

The man known simply as Maestro excelled at watching, waiting, and listening. He crouched behind some shrubbery across the street from a decidedly middle-class house, eavesdropping on the radio chatter of four uniformed officers who observed the house from their own cover.

"What, you've never seen a house burn before?" one man asked. "Wiring problem my butt."

"Whenever the Feds get involved," a woman said, "it means trouble."

"You think someone's really after the boys?" The third voice held indeterminate gender. "Will they try again, you think?"

Maestro adjusted his coat and settled in. The streets were deserted, so he couldn't just mosey by for a closer look. Too bad. He excelled at blending in. With brown hair, green eyes, average Caucasian features, and an age anywhere from thirty-five to fifty, he disappeared into almost any crowd.

Well, almost any crowd of human Caucasians. He'd have stood out like a sore dractyl on a Rapsoloid world.

The sun set, as was its habit at that particular time of day.

Sometime later, the boy named Danny Decker appeared on a balcony, apparently speaking with the EL Maestro had been sent to recover. Unless the boy suffered from schizophrenia and spoke with voices in his head.

Two other boys, friends of Danny's from the vast quantity of selfies the trio regularly uploaded, broke their own pathetic concealment and joined him on the balcony before retreating into the house.

"The bogies have entered the coop," one cop said. They'd been commenting on the boys all day out of boredom.

"Bogies?" The woman scoffed. "I still say they're little more than bog-lettes."

And the conversation sidelined into the best nickname for little bogies.

If Maestro said *bogitas* into his Doohickey, they'd discover his surveillance.

Drat. Bored, fidgety cops caused problems. They made mistakes. Of course, they didn't have the tech or the psychic ability to eavesdrop on the interior of the house the way Maestro could.

Wait. The EL mentioned Saurians.

Drat. Maestro fidgeted. Other extraterrestrials were involved? And Saurians? Bad news. Vile and violent and not very apt to negotiate.

He'd agreed to check the situation as a favor to a friend in the Galactic Police. The cop had noticed the EL drop from the sky and asked Maestro to retrieve the chip and investigate the EL's reason for orbiting a protected planet. The Galactic Police were occupied elsewhere and needed someone to look into it before too many locals were compromised.

Ugh. When cops referred to humans as "compromised," it usually meant messy clean-ups and memory-wiping. The GP had a worse reputation than the Men in Black for a reason.

The moon sank below the horizon. The enfolding darkness provided an excellent opportunity to sneak into the house and retrieve the EL. Which side of the building was most vulnerable?

Brief flashes of light announced the arrival of the Saurian welcome wagon. On the three sides of the house Maestro could see, Saurian assassins teleported directly behind the cops hiding there.

Three bodies hit the ground at the same time.

"Drat!" Maestro broke cover and dashed across the street, all efforts at concealment ended. He couldn't help the cops, but the Saurians would *not* take out the civilians.

He aimed his Doohickey, disguised as an iPhone, at the nearest Saurian, the one about to burst through the front door. His device used a thin blue beam. Not necessary, but Maestro aimed better with something visible to point.

The beam struck the Saurian dead center, and she vaporized silently. The brightly colored beam couldn't be hidden, though, and the Saurian crawling into a window on the north corner of the house hissed at him as he crossed the lawn.

"Drat," he repeated, kicking in the front door, hoping the noise might draw the attention of the other Saurians. He rolled a sedative ball down the long hallway to the grandparent's room to keep them out of the equation.

To the EL hiding out in this house, he sent telepathically. *Three Saurians have entered the building. The Galactic Police have sent me to retrieve you.*

A tall Saurian leapt at him as he crossed the threshold.

He kicked her in the head and blocked the whip of her tail. Ow! His arm went numb from the blow. *Get the boys out to the balcony and down the rope ladder.*

She leveled a banana-shaped Doohickey with her tail, but he knocked it out of her grip and raised his own device between them.

The Saurian vanished without a sound.

"Two down, two to go," Maestro muttered. *The old folks are safe enough. Do not. . . I repeat* do not *tell the boys what is—*

"Gramps!"

Maestro groaned.

The oldest boy appeared at the top of the stairwell with the others piled up behind him and one Saurian facing them on the stairs.

The Saurian chuckled in her raspy, throaty voice.

Are you mentally deficient? Maestro screamed at the EL. He fired at the stairs to draw the alien's attention. "Hey, rodent breath!"

The Saurian turned and hunkered down.

"Move it!" Maestro shouted to the boys who, not surprisingly, didn't move.

Inwardly cursing all extraterrestrial species, Maestro centered himself. He couldn't shoot at the Saurian, not with the boys right above her. If she ducked at the wrong moment, he'd vaporize one or more of them. Mind you, it would serve them right for standing around like idiots.

The Saurian glanced from the boys to Maestro, as if trying to decide which item on the menu would taste best.

Oh, bother. A shadow moved in the hall beyond the boys. The fourth Saurian must have climbed the outside wall.

Maestro hit the stairs at a dead run. Wait. Bad phrase.

A knife slipped into his hand from his sleeve. He slammed it into the Saurian's tail.

She screamed and dropped her weapon as Maestro planted his hands, straight-armed her shoulders, and vaulted her, landing lightly on the steps just above.

Without a moment's hesitation, he barreled into Bobby Decker, using him as a battering ram to force the other boys into the nearest room. They'd be bruised in the morning, but, if all went well, they'd also still be alive.

Maestro slammed the door and shouted, "Get out of the house so I can save your grandparents." Just in case, he trained the Doohickey on the doorknob and melted it to lock them inside.

After one quick breath, he turned. Just how badly screwed was he?

One Saurian, call her Kristy since all Saurian warriors were female, crept up the stairs toward him with a cruel sneer aimed in his direction along with her Doohickey, now in one claw.

A second Saurian, call her Sabra, inched toward him along the hallway, her own Doohickey metaphorically itching to vaporize.

Fortunately, the fact that he crouched smack dab between the two of them made it a trifle dangerous for either of them to fire, since they'd hit each other if he jumped. While a common comic device in literature, in his experience, Maestro had never made it work.

Kristy and Sabra inched toward him and clicked their Doohickeys onto their belts, opting to draw knives from sheathes. Well, Maestro always thought that species who stole their tech from more advanced civilizations suffered from "pirate's self-doubt." The Saurians possessed perfectly serviceable razor-sharp teeth and claws, but, wanting the species they pirated to consider them civilized, they pulled out knives shorter and duller just to prove they weren't primitives who'd bite and claw their way through a battle.

Forget that. Maestro would chomp and scratch with the best of them.

His opponents launched themselves at exactly the same time.

They'd obviously trained together.

Well, this is going to suck, Maestro thought.

The short, vicious battle ended with two dead Saurians splayed out on the stairs, tongues lolling out of their mouths.

Maestro panted for a couple of seconds, getting his breath back and pulling a knife out of his shoulder. He wiped it on his sleeve and tucked it away. Had any local cops shown up to complicate his life?

Nope.

He pointed his Doohickey at the closest bloody corpse and tapped the screen. "By the authority of the Galactic Police and the fact that you are bloodthirsty vermin, I solemnly pronounce you dust." He vaporized Sabra and Kristy so the locals wouldn't find inexplicable corpses.

Drat. The boys were watching from above, weren't they? Yep. And he'd worked so hard to seal that doorway.

Without turning, Maestro said, "You boys are going to give me a *lot* of trouble, aren't you?"

No response.

He turned.

They huddled like puppies, wide-eyed and staring.

The EL's tall hologram stood a few feet away.

Maestro crossed his arms to hide his deep breathing.

Something about the hologram seemed familiar.

"Now this," said the EL, "is the kind of guy who can help me complete my mission." His voice came from the hologram itself. Hm. Saurian Doohickey? Better tech than they should have.

No one else spoke. Oh. They expected Maestro to say something? He sighed. "An EL with a mission," he said with as much disdain as possible. "Goody. I am never, *ever* doing Test another favor."

"Test?" the boy named Danny asked. Hmmm. He seemed far too calm in the face of what he'd witnessed.

"Peter Test," Maestro elaborated. "A friend with an organization called the Galactic Police. A friend who knows I'm a time traveler from two hundred years in the future and who asked me to check out the EL here."

"Peter Test?" Danny raised an eyebrow. "P. Test?"

"Extraterrestrial's suck at picking unremarkable names, Danny. It's a flaw." Maestro needed to keep an eye on this one. "An ET partner of mine thought she was doing a great job when she came up with Elizabeth Turner. Took her a couple of months to realize her mistake."

"You're from the future?" Bobby stepped forward impatiently. "You have to help us rescue our parents."

Maestro's gaze flicked to Babbage. *Parents?*

"The Saurians took the boys' parents for questioning," Babbage explained.

Maestro closed his eyes. "Drat." Was there any chance his sigh expressed the true extent of his disgust?

"We can *help* you find our parents," Danny Decker insisted.

"And then help with Babbage's mission," one of his friends added. The other boys chimed in with an assortment of other mindless words.

As if Maestro would ever bring a bunch of kids on any kind of mission. He'd been a father, grandfather, and great-grandfather. He knew just how quickly even the most sincere kid fell apart in a truly life or death situation.

"What would we tell your grandparents?" he asked.

The Decker boys' eyes opened wide.

"Oh my God," Bobby exclaimed, "we completely forgot. . ."

They hurried forward but Maestro grabbed Danny's arm, effectively stopping both brothers. "They're sound asleep and safe," he assured the boys. "I made sure they wouldn't accidentally stumble into the Saurian attack."

"How'd you do that?" Danny asked.

Maestro grinned and held up his Doohickey, tapping the screen. "Pretty much like this."

Danny groaned. "I walked right into that one, didn't I?" He crumpled to the floor, slowed by Maestro's hand.

The other three boys weren't as fortunate. They dropped like stones to the thick carpeting.

Hm. Babbage actually tried to grab one of them before remembering he was a hologram. Only a freakishly advanced EL could forget something like that. Shifter tech?

"Now what?" The dark face considered Maestro sheepishly, apparently embarrassed at the error.

Maestro shook his head. "Logic would dictate I wipe the boys' memories of any of this, put them to bed and get you back into space where you belong."

"But. . ."

"Yeah, there's always a great big 'but' somewhere causing me trouble." He ran a hand through his hair. "But you told the Decker boys that their parents are alive and that's not going to erase easily. They'll *remember* that their parents died, but they'll *know* deep down that they're alive, and that kind of cognitive dissonance causes what is known in the profession as 'seriously wacked out kids.'" He stared the EL in the eyes and hoped the Doohickey's sensors were sensitive enough to register the deep disapproval he shot. "Ten second version, what's going on?"

Babbage pressed his lips together, most likely trying to parse a complicated story into ten seconds.

"The Saurians want me dead and will stop at nothing to make it happen. I need your help to get back to my body so I can save my entire home system."

Maestro nodded. He liked it. The facts alone and no pointless pleading. "The Galactic Police hold a cruiser in orbit with a safe room," he said, "where we can stash the boys until the Saurians have been dealt with. I don't want innocent blood on my hands." He had too much already.

"What about the grandparents?"

"What about them?" Maestro asked. "They've had no contact. Even the Saurians will know they're useless."

The EL shook his head. "That's not what I meant. They'll wonder what happened to the boys. They'll worry. They just lost a son. . ."

Wow. Multiplex emotional processing.

Your god is a Shifter, am I right? Maestro asked.

One inky eyebrow raised in inquiry. *How could you possibly deduce that?*

Maestro shrugged. *Call me prejudiced, but as far as I'm concerned Shifter EL's are the only ones who deserve the name. The rest are just artificial intelligences.*

Babbage's eyes popped open. Well, everyone knew multiplex ELs had issues with their lesser relatives. It just wasn't discussed in polite society. Not that Maestro was polite.

It's like the Saurians, Maestro continued. *They're bright and they're good with the tech they steal, but when it comes down to it, they're just big lizards who can talk. They have all the emotional capacity of a gecko. There's nothing in their brain designed to feel anything, so, as far as I'm concerned. . . they're not really people. It's the same with AIs. I don't care how smart they are, without the emotional core you possess they don't have souls.*

Babbage settled back on his heels. *Are you sure you're merely human?*

Maestro laughed. *To tell you the truth, Babbage, my good man, I'm not sure what I am.*

Not What You Would Expect from the Galactic Police

Ugh. Angry voices. Ow. Danny lay on a carpeted floor or very fuzzy ground. Soft music played. The words "bossa nova" floated around for a moment. The sounds of an argument drifted in from the background. Should he open his eyes or just pretend to sleep until the quarrel ended?

"This *can't* be what an alien ship looks like!" That was Torch, always vocal, usually full of opinions. "Where's the gleaming metal? Where's the giant panoramic window showing a sunrise over the Earth? Where's the dang hologram with cool animated graphics? Why is there shag carpeting?"

Danny moved his hand. He did, indeed, lie on a bed of shag carpeting.

"How do you even know what shag carpeting *is*?" said a familiar voice. . . a man. . . nondescript. . . Maestro!

Danny's eyes popped open of their own volition, and he pushed to a sitting position that quickly returned to lying down as stars exploded in his head.

The events of the last thirty-six hours blitzed Danny's consciousness. Ouch. He held one hand to his forehead and looked around. The room appeared, for all intents and purposes, like his grandmother's basement before she'd redecorated it years earlier.

He pulled the silver banana out of his pocket. Yep, he still had it.

"Hey, boss, I watch the History Channel," Torch said.

"Ouch," Maestro rejoindered.

Danny groaned and rose to his knees.

All eyes turned to him.

"Danny!" Bobby exclaimed and grabbed his elbow, steadying him. "You're awake."

"Spaceship?" Danny muttered, pushing upright.

"Exactly my point." Torch appeared at Danny's side, nodding emphatically. "I keep telling him to turn off the cloaking device or hologram or whatever so we can see the real thing. It has to be a put on. He simply won't see reason."

Torch did have a point. Off-white, shag carpeting covered the floor. The walls were yellow and textured with sand. A gold, velvet living room set predominated the room, and the fattest TV Danny had ever seen created a focal point. Octagonal, plastic end tables textured to look like dark, stained wood held lamps whose bases could only be described as angel cages with dripping oil instead of bars. The golden baby angels imprisoned therein appeared rather blasé about their incarceration.

Speaking of bars, a rather large one covered in black vinyl and shiny silver buttons dominated one wall. The glass shelves behind it held bottles and decanters, including an amusing one shaped like a very young boy about to relieve himself, apparently, of brandy.

TJ stood to one side and shrugged.

Bobby, still holding Danny's elbow, did the same.

Babbage raised an eyebrow and shook his head. Apparently, he had no opinion, either.

Without speaking, Danny examined Maestro, who leaned against the bar holding a martini glass. His expression gave new meaning and depth to the word bemused.

"It's called a safe room," he explained. "It's where the Galactic Police bring humans they need to question or detain without ever knowing they've left the planet. It seemed the safest place for you while I sort out the Saurian dilemma and rescue your parents." He gestured at an orange, brown, and goldenrod painting of a covered bridge in the autumn. "Granted it could use a little updating."

"I don't believe him," Torch explained. "I'm *sure* it's a put on." He made a successful grab for the Doohickey in Danny's hand. "Hey Doohickey," he said into one end.

Time, as far as Danny was concerned, slowed down and crystallized.

"Turn off the cloaking device," Torch said, "and let's see what this ship really looks like!"

"All right, visitor," a soft male voice said.

Babbage blinked in complete and utter shock.

Torch smirked, but froze when he looked at Maestro, who stared at Babbage dumbfounded. When Maestro tuned his rigid gaze on Torch, the surprised face hardened into an expression of disgust and anger deeper than anything Danny had ever seen.

"Belay that order, Doohickey," Maestro shouted, "and for the gods' sake lock everyone out of the system but me and Babbage, authorization 34679193.2345236elizabeth38376." He glanced at Babbage as if contemplating locking *him* out as well.

Torch looked stricken. "But—"

Maestro pointed at him. "Shut it."

Time teetered on the edge of a very steep cliff. While Danny didn't really know how high the cliff might be, jumping off anything called a cliff, no matter how small it was compared to other so-called cliffs, had to suck.

Maestro's eyes flicked back and forth as if he waited for something.

"Why didn't you stop him?" he sniped at Babbage. "Aren't you linked into the ship's systems?"

"I couldn't. . ." The hologram stood immobile. "I couldn't believe he would do something so absolutely insane. I just. . . froze for a second. . ."

"*Mijo*. . ." In spite of the potential danger, TJ elbowed Torch in the ribs. "You totally Kirked the supercomputer."

"Doohickey. . ." Maestro glared at TJ. "Give me a screen."

A hologram appeared: a flat screen about four feet wide by three feet high. It displayed stars and, in one corner, part of the moon.

"Any activity?"

"A Saurian sniper ship approaches at two o'clock," said the male voice that must belong to Maestro's Doohickey. . . or the ship. . . or maybe both?

Torch glanced at his watch. Danny elbowed him.

His friend shrugged and shook his head as if he had no idea what was happening. How could he? Neither did Danny.

"Show it," Maestro ordered, and the screen changed, now presenting a pristine field of stars marred only by a growing silver shape in its exact center. "Drat. How long?"

"Twenty seconds."

"Head out!" Marestro drained his martini and darted to the back wall, waving as he moved. "Evasive maneuvers and feed the bloody fish."

"Coordinates?" the ship asked.

"Somewhere on the edge of the system. . . near a dense asteroid field in the Oort cloud."

A panel in the wall slid open to reveal a grey corridor beyond.

"Feed the fish?" Torch snorted as the boys moved to follow Maestro.

"You keep your mouth shut, little man." The angry man spun and pointed one outraged finger at the boy. "And I just may let you live if you haven't already killed us all." He stormed down the corridor and into a doorway on the right.

The boys stared at one another.

Should they follow? The wrong maneuver might be the last opportunity any of them had to make a mistake.

How much danger could they possibly face, though?

Maestro's wrath and a feeling in the pit of Danny's stomach said the situation was likely worse than he could imagine.

Torch shoved the Doohickey into Danny's hand.

"You might as well come ahead." Babbage appeared outside the door Maestro had taken and gestured for the boys to follow. "There's no way to keep you out of things now."

"What did I do?" Torch asked.

"You turned off the cloaking device," Babbage explained. "The one that hid this ship from the Saurians." He turned and walked through the door.

So the Saurians could find them now? Yikes!

Bobby and TJ followed the EL, both glancing at the unmoving Torch with their best expressions of "You are in *so* much trouble."

Torch didn't move at first. He stood there as if trying to wrap his head around the situation.

Even Danny couldn't do that.

How much trouble could they be in with a spaceship that had shag carpeting?

"How was I supposed to know?" Torch called out.

Danny darted through the doorway and plowed directly into TJ's back then Torch piled into Danny, who gazed into the room beyond.

Wow. After a holding tank furnished by rabid set designers from the Planet Brady Bunch and a boring grey corridor, the bridge of a Galactic Police cruiser took Danny's breath away.

This was how a spaceship should look!

Holographic viewscreens covered the walls of the circular white room with indecipherable charts, graphs, and symbols. A three-dimensional hologram of a massive starfield filled the center, with the Earth, the moon, and two ships in flight.

The lead ship twisted, darted, and generally evaded the laser fire of the chasing vessel while returning fire of its own. The incredible image filled a central arena lower than the rest of the room and surrounded by sections of railing.

Maestro leaned over a rail with Babbage at his side.

"Who's better at this?" The strange man pointed at the hologram, cursing under his breath. "You or the ship?"

"I am. . ." Babbage squirmed. ". . .however. . ."

Maestro shook his head. "If you're going to tell me you're a pacifist, I won't care. You got these stupid kids into this mess. It's your responsibility to get them out. You can wrestle with your conscience if we survive."

Babbage's face fell slack for a split second then his eyes darted back and forth. Was he seeing something completely different?

Why was everything so darn quiet and still? On the hologram, the Saurian ship hit them every few seconds. Where were the explosions?

"Are they missing us?" Danny asked. "Or is everything being absorbed by the shields?"

"What were you expecting?" Maestro scoffed. "Do you want the floors to shake so we can all lean dramatically from side to side?" He demonstrated how silly that would look. "That's just for the movies, kid. If the ship's stabilizers let a little laser fire push us around, what the heck's going to happen when we accelerate from standing still to a jillion miles an hour? We'd be crushed into Jell-O against the walls."

When he said it that way, it made sense, but how was Danny to know? He couldn't stop himself: "Can we really fly a *jillion* miles an hour?"

Maestro glared. Then his face softened. "I'm sorry. No. What we have is better." Louder, he said, "Babbage, tell me we're ready to get out of here."

Babbage's voice spoke over the com system. "Quantum flux will be generated in ten seconds."

Maestro glanced at the boys. "This might feel a little weird. . ."

"Three. . . two. . . one."

F-f-oom.

A heartbeat.

Infinite stars surrounded Danny in open space.

The Saurian ship raced past overhead.

The moon and the Earth hung suspended in the distance.

Maestro floated beside him, but the others had vanished.

It lasted less than half a second before Danny's insides pulled away faster than his outsides.

A flash of light, then he and the ever-present Maestro stood in a plain white room. . . but it wasn't a room.

It had no walls. . . just an endless white expanse. . . and then Danny inflated, filling up every atom of the white space and exploding like a balloon way too full of hot air.

The next heartbeat.

The ship returned.

Danny seized the railing as the effects of being an exploding balloon hit him full in the stomach, which emptied itself onto the pristine white tile at his feet.

He stumbled and fell to his knees, trying really hard not to fall into his own vomit.

Bobby held his shoulders as another spasm hit and Danny lost the rest of whatever his last meal had been.

"Danny! What happened to you?" Bobby dragged him away from the pile of sick as a small square box on wheels raced from a wall and cleaned up. "You. . . you went all blurry and CG and then, sort of. . . flickered for a second."

"Maestro did, too," Torch added.

Maestro seemed a little paler than usual but otherwise unaffected. He stared into the hologram which now showed the ship racing through an asteroid field.

What the heck had happened?

"Are we safe?" Bobby asked.

"Not by a long shot," Maestro replied. "I just needed to get us away from the Earth before someone there noticed the firefight." He pointed at the Saurian ship appearing in the hologram. It closed the distance and resumed firing.

Oh spit. Danny shrugged Bobby's arm away. They had more important things to worry about than a little nausea. He'd ask Maestro about the white room later. . . assuming they had a later.

"But this is a Galactic Police ship," Torch protested. "Shouldn't it be state of the art or something?"

Maestro scoffed. "You saw the safe room. This thing's been sitting in Earth orbit for fifty years." He favored Torch with a cold stare. "How state of the art is a fifty-year-old cop car?"

The two vessels exchanged fire, weaving in and out of the asteroid field.

Maestro's intensity was scary.

"Why'd your policeman friend leave it set so Torch could turn off the cloak?" Danny asked.

"Arrogance," Maestro replied. "It's like someone from New York who visits a podunk little village in the country and assumes it's safe to leave the back door unlocked because country folk look out for each other." He pulled a holographic screen closer and manipulated it. "Idiot. Just because we're nothing but ignorant little monkeys who don't know our backsides from our elbows doesn't mean we can't mess things up with the best of them."

Torch and TJ shifted around the hologram together, pointing and making noises of encouragement and dismay. Without feeling the impacts, they likely couldn't believe the damage was happening to them.

Maestro followed Danny's gaze then shook his head as if appalled.

"How much damage have we taken?" The sinking feeling in Danny's already tender stomach deepened.

"It's pretty bad." Maestro waved at the nearest hologram. "This ship is old and theirs is built to kill. See the red areas on our ship? Those have been compromised." He pointed his index fingers and pulled them apart. The image of their ship grew to fill the space. "Compromised means wrecked and open to vacuum. The purple areas are weak. The blue have been hit but are holding up."

Danny calculated. Half the ship had been hit. A quarter of it glowed red. At least Maestro was honest about it. Most adults would hem and haw and try to sugarcoat things. Maestro told it like it was.

"Is there anything we can do?" Danny asked.

"Do you believe in any kind of god? If so. . . start praying."

Another section of the ship blazed red, eliciting a sharp "Ohhhh" from the peanut gallery.

Enough was enough. "All right, you guys—"

A chime sounded. And the lights flashed red.

"Oh drat," Maestro said, "this is going to suck." He raced for a console built into one wall. "Get down! Get down! Get down!"

Boom! The console exploded in a massive fireball!

A white-hot light filled the room, and the floor dropped out from under Danny's feet as the heat hit him full in the chest. He flew backward—until a cool cocoon enveloped him in an instant and held him fast.

The white-hot explosion faded.

Was that death then? A cool, comforting cocoon?

Be Careful What You Wish For

Smoke filled the air, and an annoying klaxon woke Danny, forcing him to face a reality he'd rather avoid, thank you very much. The klaxon sounded like a bad Star Trek effect. He choked on bitter smoke.

"Make it stop," he muttered.

Something wet and sticky covered him. The air reeked of burned plastic and metal, like the odor of a fried motherboard. An unmistakable hint of charred barbecue hovered behind that, as if someone had left steaks on a grill too long.

Voices shouted in the distance. The one that penetrated belonged to Torch: "*Madre de Dios*, Bobby. . . Wake up."

That cleared the cobwebs instantly. What had happened to Bobby?

A flashing red light threw the broken room into sharp relief. Danny pushed to his feet and peered through the smoke. Where was Bobby? A butterscotch-colored sticky goo covered everything, including the huge hole where a wall had once been.

The holograms in the center of the room flickered with static, and all Danny could see was stars. The ships had vanished.

Torch sat in the middle of the floor beside an unconscious Bobby.

Danny crawled over broken metal to his brother's side. "What happened?"

Horror filled Torch's eyes. Where was his shirt? Oh, he held it against Bobby's head. Even though the shirt was black, the blood soaking it showed through.

"The wall blew up," Torch stammered, "and then the whole room filled with, like, foam. It freaked me out. . . it was like an air bag or something, I think. I couldn't move. I couldn't breathe, and then it just melted and turned to goo."

One side of Bobby's face was purple and distended, far bigger than the other side. The skin of his cheek had split and bled freely.

"He got hit by something," Torch said. "He won't wake up."

"Bobby?" Danny shook his brother gently.

He didn't respond. He just wobbled.

Bobby was hurt badly. Far worse than Danny could hope to fix. What would he see if he removed the t-shirt?

Acid filled his throat. When he spoke, he only managed a coarse whisper. "Where's Maestro? He'll know what to do."

Torch's face turned ashen as he looked across the room.

Danny followed his gaze. TJ sat beside the fallen man, staring blankly at him. Even from this distance, Danny could see it was bad.

Very bad.

Really, truly, completely horrible and bad.

Maestro's left forearm and hand stood at a right angle to the floor and his fingers were blackened, charred bone. Seriously. . . *bone.*

Most of the skin had been stripped away from his arm, as well. That whole side of his body from hip to shoulder was dark and red and vicious and his face. . . his face was half gone. The side nearest Danny was red and black. At least the heat had cauterized the wounds so he wouldn't bleed to death.

One empty eye socket and the other eye stared blankly at the ceiling above. His mouth was open wide as if in a scream. The hair on that side of his head smoked.

Without the ragged rise and fall of the stricken man's chest, he'd have appeared dead. How was he *not* dead? A tiny voice in Danny's head whispered in embarrassment that maybe Maestro would be better off if he *were* dead. How could he possibly come back from injuries like those?

TJ looked at Danny. Torch stared at him, too. Did they expect him to know what to do? Seriously?

Danny's heart raced for a moment, then inevitability poured over him like cold water. Somebody had to do something, and no one else seemed likely.

"Babbage," he shouted. "*Babbage!*" Maybe Danny didn't know what to do, but he sure as heck knew who did.

He pushed Torch out of the way and pressed the bloody shirt to Bobby's head, smoothing the hair away from his battered face. He glared up at Torch hoping to send a world of information in one glance: this was Torch's fault. All of it. If he hadn't grabbed the Doohickey, none of it would have happened.

Torch recoiled as if he'd been hit.

Danny *wanted* to hit him. . . hard. . . repeatedly.

It was all. Torch's. fault.

Static crackled over the PA system and Babbage flickered a few times before making a steady, if sputtery, appearance. "Sorry, boys. I'm stretched thin here."

"You're a computer," Danny shouted. "Learn to multitask. We have people. . . people are dying. . ." A horrible wad of bile tried to throw itself out of his mouth, but he forced it down. "Babbage. . . please. . . help us."

The flickering image turned to him. "Oh, shades. Hold on."

Danny's skin tingled and he abruptly knelt in a different room. The new room was bright and quiet with clean white walls. It smelled like a hospital. Stellar. He knelt beside an infirmary bed of some kind, which was exactly the sort of thing Bobby needed.

"Can we move him?" Danny asked.

"There's no spinal damage," Babbage said. "I think the only major injury is his head. The rest are superficial cuts and scrapes. He should be okay to move."

Suppressing an urge to ask, "You *think* the only major injury is his head? You *think?*" Danny looked over at Torch again, but his friend already crouched between Bobby's knees, one leg in each hand.

Danny called TJ over. They rearranged a bit then lifted Bobby onto the bed. Danny settled him as comfortably as he could. Moving an unconscious person proved much harder than it looked on video.

You're doing fine, Babbage's voice reassured him.

Oh yeah, the Doohickey was still in his pocket.

Babbage appeared beside them, and an array of weird high-tech stuff dropped from the ceiling and pointed itself at Bobby. "Take the shirt away and back off," Babbage suggested.

"But. . ."

"Please, Danny. Let us help him." So much empathy filled his voice, who could doubt that Babbage was a person and not just a fancy program?

Danny stepped back and a weird, sparkly glow enveloped Bobby. Blood gushed out of the head wound with the t-shirt removed. A flap of skin and hair hung loosely from that side of his head.

Danny swallowed a huge lump in his throat.

A dozen mechanized arms unfolded from the table and worked on Bobby.

"It looks a lot worse than it is," Babbage assured him.

It looked really bad. Danny suppressed an urge to jump back in and replace the t-shirt. "He's bleeding a lot." How much blood did a human body hold?

"Head wounds bleed so much it's scary."

A mechanical arm pressed a pad against Bobby's head.

Danny realized he was clutching his brother's hand. He placed it very carefully at Bobby's side. "Please make him better."

"We'll do everything we can." After a pause, Babbage looked across the room. "They'll need your help with Maestro."

The shattered man lay beside a different kind of bed across the room. Danny forced himself away from his brother's side; he couldn't do anything for Bobby now, whereas Maestro needed his help.

Following Babbage's instructions, the boys arranged Maestro's body for an easier lift. They stretched his limbs as best as they could.

The smell of charred barbecue kept all three of them gagging while they worked.

Danny tried to unbend Maestro's burnt arm, but it was locked in place. He made himself look down at Maestro's face.

That was a cheekbone. Danny gagged again.

That was an eye socket. Danny closed his eyes for a second and took a deep breath, which only made it worse yet. He shouldn't be able to see someone's eye socket.

You're doing fine, Danny. You need to lift him onto the table. The doctor machine will take care of the rest.

He nodded, opened his eyes, and caught the looks on the other boys' faces.

"Okay guys," he said. "We wanted an adventure. This is what we get for being stupid."

They lifted Maestro onto the table where he started coughing. What should they do?

"You need to place the mask over his mouth," Babbage told him, and a clear, plastic mask popped out the side of the table, attached to a length of tubing.

Danny grabbed it but hesitated. He needed to lift the charred head off the table to get the mask on. Stretching the elastic over the burned half of Maestro's face would torture the poor man.

He can't feel anything, Babbage assured him. *He needs help breathing. . . now.*

The coughing continued.

With a quick nod, Danny held the ruined head and lifted it gently from the table. "Hold him," he directed Torch roughly.

Torch wrapped his hands around Maestro's head while Danny stretched the elastic, pulled it over the burned skull with as little contact as possible, and slowly released it onto Maestro's face.

After two more coughs, the fit passed, and Maestro did indeed breathe easier.

The boys withdrew from the table, and Danny took a few steps farther. His stomach convulsed but had emptied itself long ago. When he could look up again, a clear glass case had closed over

Maestro's prone form and something like water filled it, immersing the damaged body. How could something be so peaceful and frightening at the same time?

"It's like Luke Skywalker on Hoth," TJ muttered. "Shouldn't we take his clothes off or something?"

"The doctor machine will handle it," Babbage assured them.

Danny took a deep breath. It was too quiet. He left Maestro's side and watched the "doctor machine" work on his brother, whose hair had been completely shaved off. A thin shield of that same butterscotch goo covered one side of his head.

"I'm sorry," Torch said so very quietly.

Seriously? Sorry? That's all he had?

Danny's hand locked in a fist and rose without conscious assistance.

Torch closed his eyes as if he wouldn't try to evade a blow.

Danny had never hit anyone in anger, but Bobby had hung in Danny's arms like a puppet with its strings cut. . . and Maestro might. . .

He might. . .

Danny couldn't. . .

He forced the fingers open, spread them wide, and lowered the arm to his side. Air pumped in and out of his lungs like a bellows. His head throbbed in agony.

Torch fell to his knees and cried with his arms covering his face. "I'm sorry," he repeated two or three times. "I'm just a stupid punk kid. I shouldn't be out here where I can get people killed. Maestro was right; I'm just a stupid monkey who doesn't. . . who can't. . ."

Still on his knees, he wiped his face with both bare arms. He looked up at Danny, and, in spite of all the anger roiling away inside his insides, Danny had to respect how much courage it must have taken to meet his gaze.

"We didn't know it was like this," Torch insisted.

He was right. The reason kids from happy homes with friends and ponies and rainbows didn't have adventures was they couldn't hack it. How do you cope with watching your brother bashed in the head and your leader burned to a crispy strip of bacon when your biggest stress has been how to sneak out of the house for a midnight movie with your buddies?

He shouldn't blame Torch.

He shouldn't blame anyone.

Danny looked again at the tube that held their stricken leader. Then he met the gaze of the EL who had, when it really came down to it, started the whole line of dominoes falling that had brought them to this one miserable, silent moment.

But no one else could possibly get them home.

"It's the Saurians," Danny said flatly, still holding Babbage's gaze. "*They* did this to us. Nobody else." He'd said the words out loud because he had to, but most likely nobody in the room believed him.

Torch must have known that had the words been sincere, Danny would have offered to help him from the floor.

After a moment, TJ brought Torch to his feet.

Babbage, the hologram, cleared his throat despite not actually having one. "I hate to interrupt your soul-searching respite, but we have more pressing matters."

Danny took his brother's hand. "More important than making sure these two don't die?"

"Actually, that's *exactly* what we need to do"

Three holograms popped up showing corridors somewhere in the ship. Several Saurians raced through said corridors with a variety of dangerous, vicious-looking weapons.

Danny sighed. "Spitstick."

TJ and Torch crowded close to Danny even though the images could be seen from anywhere in the room.

"We've been boarded," Danny muttered. "Of course we have."

Agile lizards slithered through the corridors.

"How many are there?" Danny asked.

"Twenty," Babbage said.

"What about internal defenses?"

"The Saurians are working valiantly to hack the ship's weapons systems," Babbage explained. "It's everything I can do to keep them *out*. It'll be some time before I can safely access weapons."

"How much time?"

"I have no idea."

Danny turned his bitter gaze to the EL. *What the heck? What kind of supercomputer are you?*

You have no idea how much processing power it takes to maintain sentience. Babbage grimaced. *It's the only thing that keeps us from taking over the galaxy. I am sincerely stretched to the limit here.*

"Can't you blow them out an airlock or something?" Torch offered.

"There were originally thirty who boarded the ship," Babbage said. "I evacuated as many as I could. Strangely, most vessels are designed to do everything possible to *avoid* explosive decompression, not encourage it."

"How much time until they reach us?" Danny asked.

"I've locked every bulkhead I can, which will slow them down considerably. Probably half an hour."

Danny's hands started shaking. He folded them around his chest to hide the fact. Half an hour was eternity for a presentation on the use of garden imagery in a C.S. Lewis novel. It was *nothing* if you faced imminent execution by bloodthirsty aliens.

"What kind of reinforcements might they send in?" Danny asked.

The brief pause filled his stomach with dread.

"None," Babbage said. "They blew up their ship when they boarded us."

Okay. Not the horrible response Danny had expected, but a million times worse. Weren't his parents on that ship?

"It's what they do," Babbage explained. "Take over the enemy vessel or die trying, and start breathing again, Danny, your parents were not aboard that vessel." Another of the briefest pauses imaginable, and Danny had to be the only person to notice it. "They must have been on another vessel."

Or they are dead, came Danny's unbidden thought.

It's possible. There's no point in pretending otherwise, but there was no human DNA on that particular vessel. They were never on board.

Would Bobby die, too? Oh crap, that's right. Bobby was bald. With so much happening, Danny had forgotten. The butterscotch goo seemed to hold Bobby's scalp closed, at least.

His breath was so shallow.

Danny flashed back to the night he'd stood in the door to his brother's room with a snake coiled around his arm. He'd thought his brother had looked vulnerable then. He hadn't even known the meaning of the word.

If the Saurians made it through, it wouldn't matter if the doctor machine could fix Bobby. And if they got to Maestro, there'd be no one to save their parents.

Danny looked up from Bobby's face. Once again TJ and Torch watched him.

Even Babbage seemed to wait for some kind of sign.

All Danny wanted to do was crawl into a corner and shiver, but that really wasn't an option, was it? He squeezed Bobby's hand and released it. "So what do we do?" he asked.

Torch's hand touched Danny's shoulder. It took all of Danny's willpower to avoid pulling away. He'd found a shirt somewhere. A black t-shirt. It seemed way too human to have been found on an alien spaceship.

"At this point, I only see one option," Babbage admitted. "So I hope you boys are as addicted to videogames as most kids your age." He paused. "You ever play laser tag?"

The boys exchanged glances. In a very different situation, they might have grinned. The time not spent playing video games had been spent in the woods near Danny's house playing laser tag.

Good. Babbage seemed to relax a little. *This just might work.*

The plan went something like this: They had two Doohickeys. Maestro's and the banana from the original Saurian attack. The ship's weapons locker remained locked, and the release was part of the ship's defenses that Babbage couldn't access, which caused a problem since they couldn't use the Doohickey's lasers.

"What kind of idiot," Babbage said, "would use a laser weapon that can cut a hole all the way from your position to deep space? And there's no way to control how far a Doohickey shoots. While the Sci Fi writers get most things wrong, they really nailed it when it comes to the scenes of explosive decompression. *Internal* weapon systems compensate for it, but we don't have time for me to explain how."

Instead, they would use the ship's transporter as a weapon. The targeting systems were offline because of the Saurian hack, so two boys would have to hunt the Saurians and use the Doohickeys as pointers.

Babbage set them to emit a visible targeting laser the boys would use to pinpoint the invaders. When they had one picked out, they'd trigger the device which would activate the ship's transporter.

"Transporting them to where?" TJ asked.

"Mass is energy." Babbage sighed. "To transport someone, the ship converts all of their atoms into constituent energy. Instead of returning them to physical form, the ship will simply store the energy for later use."

"Whoa. . . Recycling at its most deadly," Danny muttered.

"The Green Death," TJ added.

"Soylent Green is people." Everyone turned to stare at Torch, who shook his head and shrugged. "Sorry. . . it sounded funny in my head."

Danny and Torch would hunt the Saurians while TJ guarded the wounded in case any of the vicious little buggers snuck past. The boys practiced firing the Doohickeys, transporting a few unsuspecting crates into oblivion. Meanwhile, Babbage showed TJ how some of the infirmary's medical equipment could serve as makeshift weapons.

Danny visited Bobby's side before leaving to fight the deadly Saurian warriors. He would do whatever it took to protect his brother. And the doctor machine would fix Bobby, so the older boy had to thank Danny for saving his butt. Again.

Assuming Danny survived.

"Transport us as close as you can," he told Babbage. *And no bloody speeches. If we take one second to think about what we're doing, we're all going to melt into puddles of panic. We need to keep moving as if it's really a video game. Do it. . . now!*

The Green Death

The hallway resembled every other corridor in the playing field: grey and boring with low light and a red flashing accent. The klaxon sounded soft and distant.

The faintest wisp of smoke filled the air.

Danny threw himself against a wall.

Torch hit his place at Danny's side.

There! An arrow lit the floor, red and scrolling casually, pointing to the right.

Near the ceiling, a hologram of player stats displayed points, energy levels, and number of lives for both players: **danny1** and **bartholomew1**. Each of the players displayed zero points, one hundred percent energy, and one life. Play mode read **Training Session**.

"Bartholomew?" Torch asked with sharp derision, touching the com unit in his ear he'd use to hear Babbage.

Your name? Babbage spoke directly into Danny's thoughts.

"I don't let my mother call me that, computer," Torch insisted.

The readout changed to **torch1**.

"Thank you." Torch turned to Danny and shrugged. "If I get a high score, I don't want to go down in history as Bartholomew, you know?" As long as Torch kept thinking of this as a video game, they just might survive.

"Whatever makes you happy," Danny muttered.

"Whatever I want," Torch returned and elbowed Danny gently. His eyes told Danny he hoped maybe his friend didn't hate him. The line was from a song to which they both related.

Let's go, players, Babbage said. *Hostiles are closing. You need to get to cover.*

The boys scuttled along the corridor to a junction.

It's safe, Babbage told them. *Use this corner for cover. Cross to the left-hand wall. Danny go high. Torch go low.*

The arrow and stats faded out. Energetic background music rose in Danny's mind to reinforce the video game ambience. From the grin on Torch's face, his com unit played the same theme.

I'm going to lure them out with a hologram. As soon as the hostiles are in view, hit'em hard. Take advantage of the holograms as I'm not sure how long we can fool them.

"How are you doing the holograms anyway?" Danny asked out loud so Torch could hear him. "I thought you were all multi-tasking."

It's how I make my body, Babbage explained. *It'd be like not being able to breathe. Also, I'm creating them from Maestro's Doohickey, not the ship. The Doohickey hasn't been invaded. Here we go.*

Images of Danny and Torch appeared up the hall and crept into the next junction. Gunfire shattered the quiet, and the hologram bodies flew apart and fell to the ground.

Danny's breath caught in his throat. Why had Babbage used exact copies of Danny and his friend? Way creepy.

"Dude," Torch muttered. "We need to figure out how to get our games to model our avatars on us! That was so-o-o cool."

Oh. That explained it.

And then three Saurians slipped into the open to investigate their kills.

The boys aimed their Doohickeys. A red beam lanced the smoke from Danny's device and a green beam from Torch's. Danny's picked out one Saurian.

She looked down at the tiny red dot.

Danny squeezed the silver banana.

The Saurian vanished.

A second Saurian disappeared under Torch's attack.

The third alien dove for cover, but Danny managed to line up the red dot and squeeze before she disappeared.

Had he nailed the Saurian or had she reached cover?

"Did I get her?" he asked, a little panicked. "Did I get her?" Picking them off with the element of surprise was one thing, an actual fight from cover would be totally different.

In response, the hologram corpses vanished, and the stats returned:

decker1: 2 kills

torch1: 1 kill

An arrow appeared, a right angle pointing around the next corner and scrolling to the left.

"Yes!" Torch shouted, jumping into the hall and pumping his fist.

Danny stepped out of cover much more carefully, but Torch swept him into his arms and swung him around.

"That was so frickin' *easy!*" Torch set Danny back on his feet but didn't release the embrace. "With Babbage helping, we can't lose!"

Heck yeah! Adrenaline pumped through Danny's system. It was like the world's best videogame. But it wasn't a game.

And people were dying.

Important people.

Danny forced a smile so Torch would think everything was stellar. But he couldn't really feel it.

The little **1** after the number of his own lives kind of sucked, and he couldn't shake the knowledge that all this would be unnecessary if Torch hadn't been so impulsive.

All right, players, that was the practice round, Babbage told them, probably to keep Torch from reading Danny's face too carefully. *Follow the arrows, and I'll brief you as you go. The next round will be tougher.*

Torch, still grinning like an idiot, slapped Danny on the

shoulder a little too exuberantly. He had to be overcompensating, trying to win his friend back.

Danny nodded in the direction the arrow pointed.

Torch took the lead.

Your next target is a storage room, Babbage told them. *Two Saurians guard it while their compatriots search the room. I'm going to play the hologram trick again. I'll project your images on the far side. When the Saurians turn to the holograms, hit them from behind.*

"Not very sporting," Torch muttered.

If you'd rather have them roast you for breakfast, I'm fine with that as well.

"I was being ironic," Torch lied.

In an actual video game, Danny knew, Torch wouldn't use this sort of tactic. He'd consider it cheating.

"It's cyberpunk, *ese*," Danny said. "The game wants us to be sneaky and vile. That's how we get bonus points."

Glancing over his shoulder, Torch grinned again. "Gotcha, boss. Sneaky and vile it is!"

I wish I could be so simple, Danny thought.

You haven't been inside his head the way I have, Danny. There's more there than he lets on.

Whatever. Let's just do this.

When they approached the final turn, the stats and arrow faded as before.

The boys hit the corner with their backs, Danny high and Torch low.

A small hologram appeared to show the boys their targets. It displayed two Saurians standing outside a closed door, tail to tail watching the hall.

If we can do this without them firing a shot, Danny thought to Babbage, *the aliens in the storeroom might not even know what happened. Pass it on.*

Torch glanced at Danny and nodded.

They needed to be fast.

Danny directed his laser pointer at the hologram of the Saurian facing away and tapped his own chest

Torch nodded understanding. He would hit the Saurian facing toward them.

The hologram showed the virtual Danny and Torch running around the corner in open sight.

"Holy crap!" Danny heard from around the corner while the hologram of Torch mouthed the words. The avatars skidded to a halt then dove for cover.

Accustomed to working together from hours of laser tag, Danny and Torch slipped around the corner as one, Danny in a crouch and Torch on one knee, only exposing one arm enough to see their targets, who were, indeed, facing away and moving toward the next junction.

Red and green lasers swept the corridor and came to rest on scaly alien backsides.

Suddenly, Danny and Torch had the corridor to themselves.

This round isn't over, Babbage urged before Torch could repeat his celebration dance. *There are six more targets in the storage room. Go, go, GO!*

The boys rushed from cover.

A hologram of the storage room popped up and matched their pace. Crates filled the room, along with six Saurians displayed in red.

They've noticed their comrades are gone, Babbage sent as the boys reached the door. *There are two coming to investigate. Aim your weapons at the door.*

The boys complied.

A little more to the left, I think, Danny.

You think?

Targeting systems are off, remember? That's why I need you guys in the first place.

Danny shifted his laser pointer.

As soon as the door opens, hit teleport, then dive through the door and go right.

In the hologram, the boxes to the right of the door glowed red for a moment. Danny pointed to the right with his free hand, which was his left.

"That way," he muttered, knowing that Torch got his left and right wrong half the time.

Torch opened his mouth, most likely for a snarky comeback, but he was too slow.

Go! And the door opened.

Danny squeezed the Doohickey and a very surprised looking reptilian face vanished along with its body, limbs, and tail.

Less than a second later, the Saurian beside her also replenished the energy supply.

The other Saurians screamed bloody murder, which sounded like a flock of irate grackles with a snake at the nest.

As the boys dove behind the nearest box, gunfire sounded, and some kind of projectile weapons blasted the wall around the door.

Whatever you do, Babbage warned. *Do not get separated.*

Danny panted. Gunfire in Dolby digital 5.1 surround was cool, but live in an enclosed space, it pretty much terrified him.

The action music soundtrack cut back in, distracting him. It only partially worked.

He and Torch exchanged a glance as they crouched with their backs to the crates being pummeled by gunfire.

Teleport random objects to show them what's happening, Babbage directed. *Start high so you don't expose yourselves. As things start to vanish and the beams drop lower, they'll go to cover, too. Go now!*

Starting with light fixtures, as they'd be easy to notice, Danny aimed his laser and pumped the Doohickey. As the boys rose, with their weapons held higher than their heads, they squeezed off random rounds.

A hologram of the room appeared nearby with the remaining Saurians highlighted in red. Since Danny couldn't see over the crate, he watched the hologram as boxes, tools, and a forklift all vanished.

The Saurians jumped to shelter as predicted. In the momentary lull while the aliens hit cover, the boys rose and pumped off several rounds directly at them. Danny teleported the cover of one Saurian and managed to vaporize her before she could react.

Using the hologram to pinpoint hiding places, Danny pumped

off round after round, until Torch grabbed his arm and pulled him down just before a fresh round of gunfire crashed over them. Without a word, Torch pointed at the hologram image of the Saurian firing at them.

"Thanks." Danny hadn't noticed her.

Torch nodded in uncharacteristic reticence.

Their crate shuddered as every Saurian in the room hit it. At the same time, angry grackling sounded from behind the nearby closed door.

"Do we have new company?" Danny asked.

Another hologram appeared showing five Saurians in the hallway.

I have it locked for now, but I think they're going to risk a beam weapon since this room is so large.

"How much time?" Torch asked.

Not a lot.

"Are you sure you're a computer?" Danny demanded.

Get out from behind that crate right now! Babbage shouted. *It's full of explosive gas tanks!*

The expletives rang out with the gunfire as the boys jumped into the bullet-riddled open space.

Go, go, GO! Keep going!

The air reeked of gunpowder and a bullet ripped through Danny's sleeve and another through his pants as he rolled behind a new crate.

He pushed to his feet and dragged Torch after him.

One too many bullets tore into their former cover and hit a gas tank inside, tearing it open aggressively. The gas responded by absorbing the heat and friction of the bullet and using it to change state.

Kapow! The explosion physically grabbed the boys and tossed them through the air.

Danny slid across the floor and slammed into a new crate, huffing all the air out of his lungs in a woosh. He gulped like a grounded fish.

Their soundtrack changed into something aggressive and adrenaline-filled, echoing the situation.

Get it together, players, Babbage shouted. *They're coming for you!*

Smoke brought tears to Danny's eyes. He rubbed them as he scrambled to his feet and brought his weapon up.

Taking each other's backs on instinct, the boys gasped for air.

Above! Babbage shouted.

Before Danny could look up, several things happened at once: 1. The sound of gunfire exploded far too close. 2. Torch plowed into Danny and threw him to the floor. 3. A Saurian rounded the corner following her weapon.

A second round of several things happened: 1. The Saurian at the corner vanished. 2. Torch grunted and fell limp against Danny, letting his Doohickey drop and clatter against the floor. 3. The Saurian above them laughed and leveled her gun at Danny, saying something in her grackly language that could only be some sort of quip.

Danny pointed his Doohickey and squeezed. The alien disappeared.

"Quipping is stupid," Danny muttered.

Torch groaned.

Holy Spit! Blood soaked Torch's shirt. He clutched his abdomen, searching the floor frantically. "My gun. . . where's my gun?"

Danny wrapped an arm around his friend and pulled him closer to the crate.

In the hologram, ten aliens crept toward them from all sides.

"Danny? I need my gun, *ese*."

A strange calm filled Danny. "It's too far away, Torch."

The hallway door glowed the way metal did in movies before melting.

There were too many Saurians. Way too many. In the odd absence of gunfire, the silence was broken only by the quiet music playing in Danny's head.

"It's okay," he lied. "I got it this time."

He held Torch around the chest with his left arm and held the Doohickey in his right.

"Danny?"

Danny squeezed his friend gently. "Shut it, Torch. Don't say it."

"It really hurts."

"Oh. . . yeah."

Danny's heart hurt. Torch had taken a bullet for him. Literally. He was bleeding a lot and shivering, which probably meant he was going into shock.

Two Saurians poked their noses around the corner to Danny's right, and he pointed his Doohickey at them, but they ducked back too quickly. The hologram showed three Saurians on the other side and two climbing toward them from above.

A giant gun pushed around the corner where the faces had been.

Sorry, everyone, Danny thought. *I tried*. He closed his eyes.

Several very surprised grackles shouted bloody murder and metal clattered against metal.

Unbelievably, Danny didn't die.

He opened his eyes. The bodies of dead Saurians stuck out from behind several crates and hung over the box above them. Their guns lay uselessly nearby. Some of the bodies smoked.

Some of them were absent important body parts like legs or heads, but the wounds were neat, and the only blood anywhere had previously pumped inside Torch.

Internal weapons systems back online, Babbage told him. *Enemies eliminated*.

Overhead, the stats board reappeared.

You win!

danny1: 5 kills

torch1: 5 kills

Game Over

The theme music faded away.

Danny breathed. His heart still beat. He was alive.

They'd won.

Torch squirmed and cursed. Oh yeah, he was hurt. Bad.

Danny slid his friend's shirt up. He had to check the bullet hole.

Correction: bullet holes. Two neat holes punched in Torch leaked blood at an alarming rate. Remembering what Torch had done for Bobby, Danny pulled his own shirt over his head and pressed it against the wounds.

"They're all gone?" Danny shouted.

"They're all gone," Babbage said over the ship's com. "You both did—"

"Get us to the blasted infirmary!" Danny shouted. "Torch is hurt."

What?

Torch coughed blood.

"He was shot!"

A second later, the infirmary appeared.

The world fell quiet, as if engulfed by water. Danny moved through Jell-O. Babbage spouted directions Danny didn't really understand but somehow followed anyway. He carefully lifted Torch onto a table and pulled his friend's shirt off. The doctor machine worked on him.

Danny tried to step away to let the doctor machine do its job, but Torch grabbed his wrist. "I'm sorry I'm so stupid, Danny. Please don't hate me."

Oh, heck. Danny shook his head. His heart pounded and a horrible throbbing pulsed in his temples.

"Tell Bobby—"

"You took those bullets for me," Danny spat out.

They stared at each other.

I had to, Torch's eyes said. *It was all my fault in the first place.*

"You would've anyway," Danny said.

Torch's hold weakened, and a lump grabbed Danny by the throat. He held Torch's hand in both of his.

Torch's eyelids fluttered.

"You would've done it anyway, *ese*," Danny said. "And it wasn't your fault. Okay? It wasn't—"

Torch's eyes closed and his arm fell limp in Danny's grip.

"No, no, no. . ." Danny couldn't breathe. He couldn't move.

It's the sedative, Danny. It's just the sedative.

Thank goodness. Danny choked out a laugh that set him coughing. He dropped to his knees, and then sat down heavily beside the table, never letting go of Torch's hand.

"Are we safe?" Danny demanded. "Tell me we're safe."

"You're safe."

Sound rushed back to Danny's world. The little noises of the doctor machine working. Pings and pops and squishes. Somewhere in the distance, he was certain, he heard the sound of the ship soaring through empty space and beyond that the song of stars and planets and asteroids, millions and millions of them, rushing through the vast reaches that separated them.

And this is where the chapter is supposed to end, he sent to Babbage. *We won the battle and so the chapter ends, and the next one begins with us all around Torch's bed, and we're all on the mend and off to the next exciting part of the adventure.* He pressed Torch's hand to his forehead. *But I have to keep living it. I can't just go to sleep and wake up with everything okay.* How would Danny live with himself if Torch died? *Please don't let him die.*

He pushed to his feet and placed Torch's hand on the table, careful not to disturb the work of the doctor machine. He looked down at the peaceful face and pale, soot-smeared skin. He stared at two bullet holes in his friend's fragile body, and the lump jumped back into his throat.

"You should sit down and get some rest, Danny," Babbage said.

Danny looked around. Bobby slept peacefully under a sheet now. Danny walked over and touched his brother's cheek with the back of one grimy finger.

"How is he?"

"He's fine," Babbage said.

Most of the swelling had gone and Bobby's skin was barely bruised. Apparently, the doctor machine could work miracles. Miracles.

A curtain surrounded Maestro, providing him some privacy while the doctor machine tried to keep him alive in a tank of water.

"Danny?" TJ stood in the middle of the room looking a little helpless. He held a laser scalpel.

Danny looked down at his brother again and sucked in a deep, ragged breath. Bobby lived. They'd all lived, and the aliens had died.

Danny sucked in another ragged breath and tried to focus through a watery lens. What was wrong with his eyes? He moved away from Bobby's bed, past TJ. He dropped a hand on his friend's shoulder, carrying him along as he pushed the curtain aside to check on Maestro.

Inside the tank, the man who had worked so hard to save their lives looked helpless and fragile, the charred parts of his body covered in butterscotch adhesive.

Danny? Babbage asked.

"This is the part of the story everyone skips." Danny shook his head. "It's the part no one cares about because there's no fights or explosions or parties or ceremonies. This is the part where we don't quite believe we're still alive. It's supposed to be the boring part." He wiped an arm across his face, which only made them both dirtier. "But it's not." He gasped a deep breath to keep himself from crying. "It's the part where we wait to see who lives, who dies, and who ends up a hopeless cripple."

He let go of TJ and placed both hands on the glass tube encasing Maestro. The man's chest rose and fell regularly. The water obscured his features and the lines of his body. For a moment, he reminded Danny of an exhibit at an aquarium: **Here we have the North American Adventurer. Please do not feed him; he's on a strict diet.**

Danny chuckled inappropriately. Adrenaline. The adrenaline would crash and soon he'd be a pathetic lump and then pass out. Again.

"I've never been in a fist fight in my life," he said. "I've never even hit anyone other than sparring with Dad or Bobby, but I killed those. . . those people. Those people with tails and claws. And we're alive and they're dead and that should be good enough. We saved Bobby and the only man I know who might be able to save my parents. . . and those people with tails and claws and very sharp teeth are all dead now."

TJ gripped his shoulder.

"And Torch. . . he. . ." The lump in Danny's throat threatened again. "He took two bullets for me."

"We saw it on the monitors," TJ whispered.

"He did it 'cause he thought I hated him because Bobby got hurt, and he couldn't stand the thought of me hating him. So he threw himself right into the path of bullets." He couldn't stop the little sob that jerked his chest. "You don't throw yourself *into* the path of bullets. You throw yourself *out* of their path." He wiped his face again. "Stupid." How had he been so stupid? "And I was so mad at him, I thought I hated him, too, and I made *him* think I hated him and so he. . . he. . ." He sobbed again. "Who's the stupid one, TJ? Who did the stupid thing that maybe got someone killed?"

TJ wrapped his arms around Danny and led him out of the curtained area and back to Bobby's bed. Bobby was still bald, but the goo was gone and nearly every sign of his injury had been erased.

"He's fine, Danny," TJ said quietly. "The doctor machine fixed him." He turned Danny to where the doctor machine worked on Torch. "Torch'll be okay, too. And believe you me, he'll *enjoy* reminding you he took a bullet for you for the rest. of. his. life."

Danny snorted a laugh.

"Adrenaline almost used up?" TJ held Danny's shoulders with a strength surprising for someone so small.

Danny nodded.

"So this is where you realize just how much that sucked and collapse into a soppy ball. Can I please sit you down somewhere before you collapse, because I'm not strong enough to lift you onto a bed." He nodded in Babbage's direction. "And Mr. Existential Crisis can't even carry his own weight around here."

Danny snorted another laugh and nodded. Then he laughed again when he realized that TJ, who they all thought of as the quiet, unassuming friend, was the one cleaning up all the loose ends.

"We don't give you enough credit, TJ." Images from the last

couple of hours flashed through Danny's mind. He laughed again. Then again. Then he couldn't stop. Laughter wrecked him.

Then he wasn't laughing anymore. As Danny fell to his knees, TJ dropped down with him, slowing Danny's fall as best he could.

"Too late."

"If I Only had a Body. . ."

A purple and green gas giant rotated peacefully against a backdrop of twinkling stars and translucent vapors. The ring that circled the planet from top to bottom wasn't one of those neat, little flat things found in the solar system. This one was rough and jagged from years of trying to overcome a constant stream of comets whose tails even now streaked behind as they passed.

The Galactic Police cruiser orbited a nearby moon, a barren grey rock nearly the size of Earth, currently quiet, but rife with the evidence of millennia of tidal forces from a game of tug of war between the planet and a vast red giant visible as a foreboding smudge in the distance.

How had those Terran street painters gotten it right with some spray paint and a couple of tin cans?

Babbage shifted his attention from the vista as seen through the ship's external cameras to the same view through the internal monitors in the observation deck. Since his hologram stood inside the door there, that's what he considered his point of reference.

In his mind, he turned a virtual head to consider the skinny young human who stood a foot away from the window. Babbage spent most of his time in a body, and the habit of mentally fixing himself in a specific *place* and *time* was a hard one to break.

Danny Decker appeared much more relaxed after a hot shower

and a clean set of clothes. The cruiser only carried Police uniforms, but the boys had managed to find some without insignia, and Danny looked rather smart in the black slacks (with a few extra pockets) and button-down long sleeve shirt (also with extra pockets). He wore the sleeves rolled up and buttoned.

The boy stared at the view for quite some time before leaning forward with his nose close to the window. He slid one hand out of his pocket and tapped the surface. He breathed out, fogging the view, then peered through the foggy image for a moment before wiping it clean with his elbow.

Apparently satisfied, he sank back on his heels and crossed his arms. He'd likely realized he faced a clear wall and not a screen.

"You're not inside my head anymore, are you?" he asked without moving.

Babbage startled. He hadn't made a noise. How did—? Danny tapped the wall again, and Babbage switched his point of view to a camera across the room. From there, his reflection was obvious.

"If you were still in my head," Danny said, "you'd have known I'd spotted you."

"Clever boy." He moved toward Danny and made his shoes tap against the metal flooring.

"It's one of the things that lets me know you're a real person." Danny shrugged. "You could have watched me from any camera in the room, but you used one near your avatar that didn't have the right angle. In your own mind... to you... your... your *you-ness* existed by the door where your hologram was. Your brain may be in my pocket, but your you-ness is in your hologram."

"Have you found a way into *my* head?" Babbage hoped the tone sounded as playful as he'd intended.

The boy shook his head. "I just think a lot."

And where did the two of them stand, now?

"After the assault," Babbage began, needing to know Danny's opinion, "I could tell I was no longer welcome." He'd become accustomed to the boy's quick thoughts. They'd felt comfortable... and, although he would not have admitted it, Babbage missed them.

"You're trying to save an entire star system, Babbage." For a twelve-year-old, Danny could stand motionless for a very long time. "When I thought Bobby was going to die, I said awful things to Torch that made him do something stupid, and then *he* almost died. Bobby's just one guy." He met Babbage's eyes in the reflection for the first time. "You're trying to save billions of people." He shook his wise little head. "I can't even imagine what that must be like. I'm not mad at you, anymore. I'm sorry I ever was."

Thank goodness. Babbage took a spot beside Danny. The silence between them seemed comfortable, but the boy likely had more to say.

"You can stop wondering," Danny said. "I'll take you down there." Danny pointed his chin at the barren moon below.

That was a surprise. "How did—?"

"We're not in the solar system anymore," Danny said, "and with your quantum engine thingy travel seems pretty much instantaneous from anywhere to anywhere, so the planet with your body is the only logical place to go while we lick our wounds and the ship repairs itself." He looked up at Babbage for a moment. "Really glad *that* part of the sci fi shows is right, by the way. I can't imagine trying to fix a ship." He looked out again. "I figure we teleport down, I drop you into a new body, then me and my friends can go home." He looked up at Babbage again. "Right?"

The EL wanted to say something leading like, *if that's what you want*, but he'd spent too much time in Danny's head to think that would do any good.

"Yes."

"Is it safe?"

"Yes," Babbage responded as quickly as possible.

"Idiot proof safe?" Danny probed further. "Is there any conceivable way that monkeys from Earth can screw it up?"

"We transport into a plain room, insert the chip, transport out. It's as safe as it can possibly be."

Danny raised an eyebrow.

"I've learned not to make guarantees," Babbage admitted.

"We've managed to ruin a perfectly good Galactic Police cruiser. To the best of my knowledge, that's not been done before."

Danny nodded. "Then it's just you and me. We should get this over with."

Babbage looked down at the boy's innocent face and ancient eyes. "You're pretty blasé about the whole thing."

"No. . . I'm not." Danny gazed out at the planet. "I get how amazing this is. I mean. . ." He waved at the view. "*Look* at that." His hand found his pocket. "I killed people, Babbage. That may not seem like a big deal to someone in charge of saving whole planets, but I killed people. . . and maybe I helped save a couple." He shrugged. "I'm just kinda busy dealing with that."

Babbage understood. "I remember what it was like the first time—"

"No!" Danny pointed at Babbage. "That wasn't the *first* of anything. . . It was the *last*. The very last. . . ever."

Babbage shouldn't say so, but Danny was likely wrong about that.

"Have you heard anything about my parents?" the boy asked.

"Yes," Babbage told him. "That's why I came to see you. The Galactic Police found them. They're safe. They're well."

"Good. . . that's. . . good." Everything about the boy relaxed, a subtle shift perhaps, but a few years melted from Danny's eyes. He turned his back on the expansive vista and leaned against the wall, eyes closed. For a moment, he seemed to fight tears. "You really are a person." He laughed. "A computer would have just made a general announcement. You came here yourself and let me ask questions first. . . Very person-like." His parents' safety seemed to make all the difference in the cosmos to him.

For the first time, the reason made sense: Danny had picked up the penny. In his mind *that* was the original catalyst to the entire misadventure and the reason his parents had been abducted. Interesting.

"Were they hurt at all?" Danny asked. "Do they know what happened?"

"You're asking if someone wiped their memories," Babbage translated. "For now, no."

"For now?"

"With the two of you missing," Babbage said, "it would be complicated. It will be easier to explain your adventures if they remember their own time on an extraterrestrial ship. They'll understand the necessity of a cover story while the Galactic Police figure out what happened to all of you."

"They don't know what's happened to us?" Danny cocked his head to one side.

"Not everything." Babbage tried to avoid looking sheepish. "Not yet."

Danny rolled his eyes.

"They have Maestro's communications with his friend, the man named Test?" Babbage fidgeted. "But when we were attacked, Maestro destroyed the ship's tracking device, assuming that the Saurians could hack it because of its age."

"And it didn't occur to you to let everyone know we're alive?" Danny folded his arms.

"Oh, it *occurred* to me." Babbage's combination of nodding, shrugging, and shaking his head was rather complex. "I just didn't do it."

"Stellar." The boy turned to the window again, but his arms remained pointedly crossed. "So no one knows where we are?"

"No."

"That makes me vaguely uncomfortable."

"Are you really only twelve years old?"

"How old are you?"

"One hundred and twenty-four." Which was true enough.

Danny startled. "Must be nice to build a new body once in a while."

"There are advantages."

"Once we get you a body, you can drop us off and slip off the grid again, right?" Danny pushed away from the window.

"Yes."

"How much trouble are you really in for involving us?"

"I don't know, Danny. I really don't know." If only Babbage had any idea what the long-term consequences for his actions so far might be.

"Writers are so stupid." Danny moved into the middle of the room. "All the stories are so logical and structured. Everything makes some kind of sense. Life isn't like that. I'm really glad my parents are safe. . . I mean, wow. . . it's the coolest freakin' thing. . . but it doesn't make any. . ." There was a substantial pause while he gestured inanely. ". . .*sense.* We're *supposed* to get you a body and then we all go off on a joint mission to save our parents and your system from the Saurians or whatever it is you need to do. Even Maestro's injuries make *sense* that way. If he hadn't been injured, you wouldn't have needed us to help you at all. But our parents are fine; we get you a body, we go home, and you go off on your quest with whomever it is you usually do your questing stuff with." Danny shook his head. "We didn't really do anything worth anything, and they'll probably wipe our memories when we get home, so nobody *learns* anything, either." Another dismissive head shake, but he wrapped his arms so tightly around his chest. "It's all just stupid."

Babbage chose not to mention that the people he would normally do his questing stuff with had died.

"We're not home, yet, little brother." Bobby's step was strong as he crossed the large space, his eyes on the planet beyond. He seemed none the worse for wear, dressed the same as his brother. In the uniform, his shaved head seemed appropriate. He stopped beside Danny, rustled his brother's hair and stared out the window. He whistled. "We're not home by a long shot."

Danny leaned away when his brother messed his hair, but he ran his fingers through it and smiled. "Look." He tugged the strap that held his brother's rolled-up sleeves. "We're twins again. At least we have underwear this time."

Bobby snorted and hooked his thumbs into his belt. "Maybe *you* do." He waggled his eyebrows elaborately, rolling up and down on his heels.

Danny's smile seemed honest and uncomplicated, which was a nice change. "All right, Captain Commando. Let's do this." He found Babbage's gaze and nodded once.

"Do what?" Bobby asked.

"This." Babbage made his request to the ship.

A plain, quiet room with a wood floor surrounded them, lit dimly by the Display centered on one wall.

The boys stumbled a step, adjusting to the change in gravity.

"Yikes," said Bobby. He spun this way and that.

Danny's eyes swept the room. He was a young man to watch. He acted as though everything he experienced was normal. . . but it wasn't for him. It couldn't be.

Eventually, all eyes found the Display which was, to be honest, the only thing worth noticing in the otherwise featureless room.

"Wait." Bobby wandered around the room, now, as if looking for nonexistent doors or windows. "We're on an actual alien world, billions of miles from Earth?"

"Yes," Babbage said. Moon, technically, but why quibble?

Danny approached the Display, a glass case set into the wall. Amber light lit a body identical to the form Babbage used as a hologram. The boy touched the small slot set into the wall beside the case, and his eyes swept the steps leading up to or down from the case itself.

"And all we get to see is this boring room?" Bobby snorted.

Danny pointed at the robot body, but Bobby cut him short with a gesture. "There isn't even a window?"

"No," Babbage said, "but notice how the gravity is stronger than on Earth?"

Bobby jumped a couple of times. "Yeah. . . not even worth a postcard."

Danny scoffed. "Let's just do this. I've had all the adventure I need." He touched the slot again. "I put the chip in there?"

"Yes."

"You guys don't go in much for flashy control panels and such, do you?" Danny asked.

"Shifter tech mostly relies on the Doohickey," Babbage said, "because you never know how many arms or tails or heads a Shifter might have this week. Doohickey, please present readout for Display, Gamma Gamma Babbage."

A hologram presented an image of the reposing body and various charts and graphs explaining its state, which was, of course, exactly as Babbage had left it more than fifty years ago.

"Physical equipment is expensive because it needs to adapt to this week's anatomy." He manipulated the image, changing readouts so the boys could see how it worked.

"That's why we had to use a hand scanner before going into the bathrooms or showers," Danny said. "They needed to know how to configure the equipment."

"Indeed. Shifter tech needs to be as flexible as the species."

"If you were made by a Shifter..." Danny looked from the Display to Babbage's hologram. "Why is your hologram exactly the same as this body? Don't you change up once in a while?"

"Very logical question," Babbage admitted. "While my god was a Shifter, she did not create me in her image. They rarely do. . . they barely remember their species' original shape, when it comes down to it. They make good gods for that reason. I found my way to this shape via a different path." It remained a fond memory. "A good friend designed this body. I keep it to honor him."

"Gods," Bobby cut in. "You've said that before. Is that religion?"

"Not really," Babbage said. "We do have religion, but it's not about our gods. The name is almost a joke. Most species evolve to a point where they ask, 'How did we get to be here?' and they almost always imagine a creator who made them and declare the creator a god." Would it be rude to ask them to upload him into the body, already? "EL's almost always know exactly who made us, so we know who our god is. It's just the term we use for our creator."

"So you're not made in some kind of factory?" Bobby asked.

How in the seven lights could Babbage answer that question?

"Oops." Bobby grimaced. "That was vulgar, wasn't it? Sorry."

How could the boy know? And his apology was touching.

"A single EL can take over a hundred years to create," Babbage explained. "We can't be mass produced like. . . like. . ."

"Like videogames," Danny supplied. "Don't be offended by my brother. It's his first time off the planet." He finally drew the Doohickey from his pocket. "I just pop you into the slot?"

"Yes," Babbage confirmed.

"That's it?"

"Yes."

Danny held up the Doohickey. "Doohickey, eject Babbage's memory chip."

It did.

Stupid Heroic Time Travelers

Whoops! The chip leapt from the Doohickey, hit Danny's hand, and bounced. He grabbed for it, fumbled, and cursed. It flew into the air, described an unbelievable arc, and then bounced a few more times and rolled. Danny cursed some more because it made him feel better, and he knew it would surprise his brother.

"Whoa there, speedy," Bobby said. "What's the deal?"

"I don't like *not* having Babbage around, okay?" Danny dropped onto his hands and knees chasing the spinning disc. "The sooner we get his body going, the better I'll feel." He snatched at the chip but accidently sent it flying across the room again.

"Good. . . good. . ." Bobby muttered. "Break it. That works."

"Shut it." Danny finally managed to grip the chip. He shot his brother a vicious glance and pushed to his feet. "You're as bad as Torch with the snarky quips all of a sudden. What's *your* deal?" He reached the wall, slid the chip into the slot, and the light on Babbage's body flashed much brighter, startling Danny.

Bobby jumped, too. "I'm scared, okay? I say stupid stuff when I'm scared. Sorry."

So they'd *both* put on brave faces but felt like little kids in the deep end of the pool.

"Sorry." Danny shook his head. "Me, too."

Bobby nodded then pointed his chin at the wall as the glass panel slid up with a soft shushing sound. Babbage's body looked so human and alive already that it was ironic when both boys nearly jumped out of their skins as its eyes flicked open.

A moment later, a warm golden glow rose in Babbage's dark eyes, and he blinked a few times. "Go team," he muttered then stepped out of the alcove.

Stellar. Just having Babbage up and around helped so much. Danny and his friends were terrifyingly out of their depth. Although they'd only spent a few moments well and truly on their own, those moments had been frightening. What if the body hadn't worked?

Ugh. Not even worth thinking about.

"Thank you both very much." Babbage padded quietly past Danny into the middle of the room. Holding up a finger as if suddenly remembering something, he stepped back to the wall slot and retrieved the chip. He held his hand out, palm down.

Danny extended his hand.

"A souvenir." Babbage dropped the chip into Danny's palm.

"Don't you need that?"

Babbage shook his head and pointed to his chest with one finger. "I uploaded directly into the body. There's an identical chip in here holding me safe and sound."

"Protected planet much?" Danny looked down at the bit of plastic and silicon that had so recently housed his new friend.

"That is so advanced anyone on your planet will think it's a toy." Babbage shrugged, then closed his eyes and smiled. "It feels so *good* to shrug again!" He opened his eyes. "Hello, Danny Decker." He seemed much more relaxed now that he had a physical body. What must that even feel like?

"Hi there, Babbage," Danny said.

Yet the golden glow of Babbage's eyes seemed so. . . artificial.

Babbage startled. Had he noticed Danny staring? The EL touched his own face with a hand.

"The eyes." So Babbage *had* noticed. "EL bodies are imprinted with a golden glow so organics can distinguish us from non-sentient robots."

So people treated them like everyone else. . . almost?

"I'm sorry if it disturbs you," Babbage said. He seemed self-conscious about it.

"Disturbs me?" Danny countered. "I think it's cool. Can I look closer?"

Babbage nodded, apparently more comfortable.

"You have the coolest eyes I've ever seen." Danny leaned in. The light sparkled ever so slightly and shifted like some kind of screen saver.

Babbage smiled. He snapped his fingers.

A panel slid from the wall into the middle of the room, attached to a set of shelves laden heavily with socks and underwear. Babbage approached the "closet" and perused his options. Another closet extended. This one held a long rack of pants, ties, and other accessories.

"Do you mind?" Danny asked, gesturing.

"Be my guest." Babbage chose a pair of socks and slipped into them.

Danny glanced through the rack and shelves. How bizarre. Everything seemed so similar to what he'd see in any closet on Earth. Well, in the closet of any rather wealthy man with an impeccable sense of fashion. Babbage owned an amazing selection of cufflinks made from stones that changed color and shifted in the light. Was some kind of hologram technology involved?

"Babbage?" Danny asked.

Babbage turned, perfectly pressed shirt in one hand.

"How can this be so similar to what we have on Earth?" Danny asked. "Don't you travel all across the galaxy?"

Babbage paused, then pulled on his shirt and buttoned it. "The explanation for that is actually much longer and more complicated than you would probably guess."

"I thought we were in a hurry, fashionistas." Now that Babbage had dressed, Bobby moved closer and made let's-get-on-with-this gestures. "Can you defer the metro style convention until we're back on the cruiser?"

Babbage held out a hand.

Bobby looked down at it, so Babbage waved it.

Finally, Bobby took it in his own.

"Hello, Bobby." Babbage said. "Nice to meet you in the flesh."

Danny could tell that Bobby was about to give a "yeah, whatever" response, but something in his face changed completely. He grasped the appendage more firmly and even brought his other hand up to join the first. "Whoa. . . Your hand. . ."

"Yes. . . it is."

Bobby looked up, then over at Danny. It seemed like he was trying to stay cool, but then he shook his head.

"Okay, dude, I'm really sorry if this is. . . rude. . . but your hand. . . it feels like a real hand. This is amazing, can I please be an ignorant little monkey without offending you? Please?"

Babbage's smile grew. "The fact that you are so nervous about offending me gives you the right to be as ignorant as you like, Bobby."

"Dude!" Bobby exclaimed, turning to Danny and gesturing for his brother to join them. "Feel this. It's. . ." He looked back at Babbage. "Is this skin? I mean. . ."

"Is it organic?" Babbage asked for him.

"Yeah!" Bobby brightened. "Yeah. . . is it?"

Danny joined his brother and examined Babbage's hand and forearm, which did indeed feel exactly like living flesh. Danny ran a hand over the skin and felt the hairs on the back of Babbage's arm.

"No. It's all synthetic," Babbage assured them.

Bobby wore an enormous grin that was good to see. He glanced from his hands to his brother's as they pawed the dark skin. He released the arm he was holding. "I'm sorry, Babbage. . . That was probably really rude. . . but I've never. . . I just. . ."

Danny pulled away as well.

"Don't apologize," Babbage said. "The technology is fascinating to you, and the fact that you are so worried about insulting me lets me know that you truly value me as a person." He gripped Bobby's shoulder. "That's more than I get from planets millennia more advanced than yours. You have no need to apologize."

He turned to Danny and extended a hand.

Danny took it without hesitation.

"Hello, Danny."

"Hello, Babbage," Danny said, shaking. "It's a pleasure to meet you in the flesh."

And then the infirmary appeared around them.

"Whoa," Torch exclaimed. He leaned against a table, dressed in the same black pants and black shirt as Bobby and Danny, but with one arm in a sling. "Where'd you guys come from?"

TJ sat on a nearby table similarly dressed.

You okay, *ese*?" Danny hurried to Torch's side. "

"Not bad, all things considered." Torch smiled and held up his sling. "The doctor machine is pretty freakin' incredible."

"There's a lot out here that's pretty freakin' incredible." Danny squeezed the unslung arm.

Then, to Danny's amusement, Babbage leaned toward Torch until they were almost nose to nose.

"Okay. . . dealing with the holographic lack of personal space. . ." Torch stood his ground without flinching.

Babbage reached up and pushed Torch's nose. "Beep."

Torch screamed and jumped back, arms flailing.

Everyone else dissolved into helpless laughter.

"Oh. my. God. That was so funny!" Danny sputtered. "That sounded just like a tiny little girl!"

Torch, still cowering against a lab table, glanced from one friend to another before realizing what had happened. Turning a petulant glare on Babbage, he jabbed the EL in the chest a few times.

"Oh. . . ha ha. You're a regular Jimmy Fallon." His eyes opened wide. "Wait a minute! You went down to the planet without us?"

Oh, spit. Was Torch really going to go there? Danny rolled his eyes and walked away from the incipient argument.

Torch lit into Bobby and Babbage, pulling TJ to his side. After everything that had happened, how could they treat the situation like some kind of summer camp where Torch and TJ had been left out of an entertaining field trip?

Danny slipped behind the curtain around Maestro's medical tank. The curtain didn't really block any of the noise, but Danny did that himself as he leaned on the glass, gazing down at the wrecked body inside.

"If you hadn't been saddled with a bunch of stupid, meddling kids," Danny said.

The tank made bubbly noises as it tried to save the man who should have helped Babbage save a world. The curtain moved, and Babbage joined Danny at Maestro's side.

"Why isn't he getting better?" Danny asked.

"I don't know." The EL squeezed Danny's shoulder. "I've never seen anything like it. . . no one has. It's like his body is actually *fighting* the doctor machine. It doesn't make sense."

"He's a time traveler," Danny reminded Babbage.

"I thought about that, but the machines have always worked on time travelers and other quantum jumpers. This is something different. I've been thinking about putting him in stasis until we get to—"

No stasis! A knife lanced through Danny's brain, and the voice cut through everything and demanded his undivided attention. *No stasis!* It echoed and strobed and reverberated through Danny's skull painfully.

His knees buckled, and he caught himself on the glass tank as the world pulled away and everything dipped to black.

No stasis!

Babbage caught Danny, who gathered his feet under him and rubbed his head with one hand.

"Danny?" Babbage asked.

"Holy crap that hurt." Danny leaned over the tank and stared into Maestro's face. "Was that you?"

No stasis!

"You don't hear that?" The pain wasn't as bad, but a drop of red hit the glass, and Danny wiped his face. His nose bled. He wiped it on his sleeve.

Babbage shook his head, his face very confused. He closed his eyes a moment then opened them and shook his head again, more confused than the first time.

"He says, 'No stasis,'" Danny said.

"The doctor machine isn't working." The EL turned his attention to Maestro's unconscious form.

No machines. The voice echoed in Danny's head again, but without the pain, as if Maestro had adjusted the frequency or something.

"They're keeping you alive, Maestro." Danny's breath caught in his throat.

No machines.

A lump filled Danny's throat. He couldn't speak.

Babbage's face grew still. "He told you to turn off the machines, didn't he?"

Danny nodded.

Babbage turned his attention to Maestro. "Why won't the machines work on you?"

No machines.

Danny shook his head. "He just keeps saying, 'No machines.'"

Babbage sighed, and the arm around Danny's shoulders squeezed.

Fighting the constriction in his throat, Danny managed to mutter, "Maybe he knows why the machine won't work but can't explain."

Decisions like that should so not involve a twelve-year-old kid. A grown-up should do it, and Danny hadn't even *thought* the word grown-up in a few years.

I'm not a grown-up, he sent to Maestro. *Don't make me decide this. Take this away. . . at least take it away from me.*

"Maestro," Babbage said, "Can you hear me?"

Yes. . .

"He can," Danny said.

"Do you want me to turn off the doctor machines?"

Yes!

"He says yes," Danny said.

"You realize you will most likely die without their assistance?" Babbage asked.

No machines!

Danny stumbled from the force of the thought. Without Babbage holding him up, he would have surely fallen.

The EL seemed to understand what Maestro had sent. "I don't think we have a choice, Danny. He has clearly expressed his wishes."

Tears fell silently from Danny's eyes and splashed on the glass tank. He searched the dying man's face for some sign of life. He wiped his eyes clear and looked Maestro up and down, committing every detail to memory, from the mud-covered bones of his charred arm to the moles on his left leg.

You will not be forgotten, Danny told the man. *I will never forget you.*

No tears.

Which was too much for Danny. He pushed away from the glass case and out of Babbage's hold. He slid through the curtain to find some space to clear his head—

No such luck.

He nearly barreled into his brother and best friends.

When they saw his expression, they stepped back.

"What?" Danny demanded curtly.

"Umm. . ." Bobby started but seemed uncertain whether he should go ahead with their original question given Danny's state. "We were kind of wondering if. . . maybe. . ."

"You want to go visit some stupid planet, don't you? Maybe explore the ruins of some ancient, lost civilization or go swimming in a red sea that's actually red?" Danny wiped his face again, really sick and tired of crying. "Maestro's asked us to let him die, our parents are probably freaking out wondering where we are, and the last time we went on a joyride, we were almost killed by people we ended up having to slaughter." He sucked in a deep breath and kept shouting. "So yeah, let's go visit the colony of scantily clad Nubilians on planet Phi Kappa Nudity. It'll be a blast."

The trio of open-mouthed boys stared at him without speaking.

Spitsticks. Now he'd been mean to them, too. Couldn't he do

anything right? And why did everyone keep asking his opinion? What the heck did he know about anything?

Refusing to cry one. more. time, Danny stomped out of the infirmary and down the hall to the only other part of the ship he knew he could find: the observation deck.

"Stupid time travelers," he muttered, "being all heroic and getting blown up." The door slipped out of the way as he approached it. "Stupid kids, thinking we should be out here. We should be back home with our parents studying for tests and playing video games."

Luke Skywalker had a Speedo.

The majesty of a planetary system filled the glass wall.

Stupid majestic view! Stupid galaxy! Stupid, unfair universe!

"I didn't know it would be like this," Danny shouted at the universe in general, which was not something many humans had had the chance to experience. "I'm just a twelve-year-old kid! I have a family who loves me and friends who give me presents and make me birthday cakes and who tell me their stupid secrets, and I have a stupid brother who protects me from stupid bullies."

He gasped a breath.

"How the heck was I supposed to know I could get my parents kidnapped and my house blown up and my brother and my friends almost killed just buy picking up a stupid penny?" His heart pounded and his chest ached. "He tricked me anyway. I didn't know. . ." But he couldn't lie to himself. "Okay. . . how was I supposed to know *this* would happen? It's not like *this* in the stupid books."

But that was a lie, too. Horrible things happened to the heroes in the stories and collateral damage was the norm. The friends and loved ones of literary heroes littered the battle fields with bloody corpses.

Danny rushed the big glass wall and pounded on it with both fists. Was there any way he could break it so the vacuum of space would suck him out and snuff him like a candle?

"It wasn't supposed to be like this!" He shouted it several times like a mantra before falling to his knees, and then dropping to his butt on the floor, leaning against the glass wall, eyes closed against the pain.

Stupid, stupid. . .

"Danny?" a familiar woman's voice murmured. "Are you done?"

He opened his eyes.

Mom and Dad stood before him, holding each other with no small amount of worry in their eyes. So now hallucinations were a thing, too. Perfect.

His parents exchanged a glance, and Danny knew. . . *knew* exactly what they said with that glance. They could tell he thought they were a hallucination.

They seemed real enough. Mom had her long brown hair pulled into a ponytail the way she wore it when she didn't want to be bothered. Her clothes were unfamiliar to Danny, though. She often wore jeans and a white blouse, but the cut was unusual and the lapels too long for Mom.

Dad wore jeans and a white t-shirt. His forehead wrinkled the familiar way it always did when he thought hard. He adjusted his glasses with one index finger.

"I'm not hallucinating?" Slowly, Danny pushed himself up by pressing against the wall.

"You're not. . ." Dad held up a warning hand. "But don't rush forward, because we're one of those hologram thingies, and you might trip and hurt yourself if you fly right through us."

"Is it really you?" Danny wiped his face and studied them. Odd blue rectangles floated in front of their right shoulders.

"A man named Babbage just contacted us and told us you needed to see us." Dad squeezed Mom in a way Danny had seen a thousand times.

They really were alive. Thank God.

"Glad to see you're all right, son," Dad said. "What's going on your end? We're fine over here."

"Fine?" Danny said quietly. Was this real? Like, *really* real?

Dad chuckled. "I have to say being kidnapped and questioned by those nasty, little dinosaurs wasn't a picnic. . . but we're fine now."

"I'm so sorry, Dad," Danny burst out. "It was all my fault—"

"Don't." That was Mom. One eyebrow arched as she gave him her serious face. "We know everything that happened, Danny, and you have always had an overdeveloped sense of responsibility. This is *not* your fault."

Their eyes shifted together.

Bobby had entered the room, smiling through his own tears. He sidled up next to Danny and put an arm around him. By reflex, Danny circled his brother's waist and drew him close.

"Robert. . . you're safe, too. . . thank God." Mom brought one hand to her mouth in a gesture like every silly heroine in a movie made in the 1950s. Her eyes examined them both. "You look so handsome. . . both of you in those uniforms." She took in Bobby's shaved head. "Your hair. . ." She gulped and took a deep breath to steady herself. "I am so glad you've been taking care of each other." Her eyes went a little watery.

Dad hugged her tighter.

"This is real?" At exactly the same time as Dad, Bobby squeezed Danny.

"Babbage called the Galactic Police when you threw your tantrum and stormed off." Bobby smacked Danny's head lightly so Danny would know he was just goofing with him. "Mom and Dad demanded to see us immediately."

"We'll make him bring us home right now," he told his parents. It answered nearly all of Danny's hopes.

"We're not even on Earth, Danny." Dad laughed. "We're on a planet called Absit Invidia. It's some kind of spa planet."

"A. . . spa?" Not what Danny would have guessed in a million years.

"It's amazing," Dad said. "I feel ten years younger. They do this herbal spring bath thing. . ."

"We're fine here." Mom smacked his chest. "I don't know why

we can't go back, yet, but the Galactic Police are handling something to do with the. . . the Saurians. None of us can return to Earth just yet."

"But what about—?"

"We're fine." Dad raised a palm. "You're fine. That's all that matters."

But it wasn't everything.

"There's a man here," Danny said. "He gave his life for us. . ."

His parents grew serious. They looked over at an empty spot on the floor and a red-haired man appeared beside them. He wore a floating badge, too, but his was made up of bars of many different colors.

"Greetings, Danny and Bobby Decker." He held his hands up in greeting, palm up. "My name is Peter Test. I know Maestro. To be honest, his involvement was at my request in the first place. I thought retrieving the engineered lifeform's memory chip would be an easy thing. . . who could have possibly known. . ."

"Maestro's dying," Danny said.

"Babbage has updated me on the situation." Test's expression turned serious. "I assure you that in turning off the doctor machine you are following Maestro's wishes. He would want nothing else. Please rely on Babbage to make you completely comfortable while the red tape. . . is unraveled. Take some time to see a new world. Maestro would want nothing less for you. He always complains that humans should join the galactic community. Let our offer be a tribute to his contributions."

"Take a day," Mom said. "The galaxy will still be here tomorrow."

"What about Torch's parents?" Danny insisted, "and TJ's?"

"That's where it's handy that these folks are shapeshifters." Dad gestured to Test.

"Excuse me a moment while I change." Test's image flickered then Torch faced Danny with his arms crossed and his most disgusted, petulant expression firmly in place. "Mo-om," the image of Torch whined. "There's a lake for swimming and horses and stuff.

Actual *horses* for riding." His fists found his hips. "If you'd rather, I can find new friends who want me to smoke crack and shoot heroin out of dirty shared needles. I mean, that's fine by me... I just thought you'd like me to take a few days away from videogames to do outdoor stuff." Magically, the image changed tactics and put his hands deep in his pockets. "Danny really needs me, okay?"

And his image vanished.

"Wow," Bobby said quietly. "He does Torch better than Torch does."

Danny had to agree.

Dad's eyes filled with warmth despite the dark circles around them. "It's been a weird couple of days, boys. We'll have a lot to talk about when we see you... but please let this Babbage person give you something *good* to tell us." He managed a smile. "Okay?"

Danny and Bobby nodded.

"I love you boys," Dad said.

"I love you, too," Mom added.

"I love you," Danny muttered.

Bobby said the same thing... then the hologram winked out. He pulled Danny around and held him as tightly as he could without suffocating him.

Danny squeezed back with all his strength.

Bobby even kissed the top of his head, which he wouldn't have done had anyone else been in the room.

"Oh, my God, Deckers," Torch exclaimed. "Get a room! Is this *Flowers in Harvey Fierstein's Attic* or *Star Trek: Search for the Planet Nekked Nubilia?*"

Seriously? Oh well, Danny's parents were alive and safe! Might as well get into the spirit of the thing.

"Wait a minute," Danny asked. "Did they say they were on a *spa* planet? Did anyone tell them to look out for malevolent insect species? They're always running the show on seemingly innocent spa planets."

"*Battlestar Galactica,*" Torch said.

"*Star Trek: Next Generation,*" TJ added.

"*Star Trek: Classic*," Bobby joined in.

"*Whose Giant Extraterrestrial Bug is it Anyway?*" Babbage threw in.

Say what?

Babbage shrugged. "It's not real. . . I just wanted to contribute."

Torch's sling reminded Danny of all they'd survived. "Okay, fine. . . We're due a little R and R, but for God's sake don't start. . . forgetting there probably *are* evil insect races bent on duping us into. . . stupidity."

They all glanced at Babbage, who nodded solemnly. "Oh yeah, they're out there. They are."

"No bug's gonna dupe *me* into stupidity!" Torch declared. "I can find my way there all by my lonesome!"

Twenty minutes later, Danny once again hovered beside Maestro's medical tube, hands on the glass, eyes closed. He would fix Maestro's face in his memory, the way he'd looked before the explosion.

Bobby held Danny's shoulder. Everyone else had stayed on the observation deck to decide which planet they would visit.

Talking with his parents had helped Danny tremendously, but Maestro was still going to die, and Danny would never forget him. He needed time to mourn this incredible man.

He pressed the glass case with his eyes still closed, thinking over everything he knew about the man. He was a fighter. He was. . . tallish. He was willing to help. . .

"Dude. . . why is he naked?" Bobby asked.

"What?" Danny refused to open his eyes.

"Why is he naked?"

Seriously? Danny counted to ten.

"Luke Skywalker had a Speedo," Bobby insisted.

Danny counted to twenty.

"Really wish. he. had. pants."

"How many locker rooms have you been in?" Danny turned to

his brother and opened his eyes.

Bobby shrugged. "But you don't want to see the *coach* naked."

"He's dying, you moron," Danny exclaimed. "This is a hospital for a species that changes bodies more often that you change your underwear. Why would they waste time putting him in a pair of boxers to protect your fragile sensibilities? He's going to *die*."

"He doesn't *look* like he's going to die." Bobby held up both hands in defense.

"Are you insane?" Danny turned his gaze to the ravaged body in the glass tank. . . only. . .

Only. . .

Maestro's eyes opened.

Inside the face mask. . . he winked.

Danny jumped back.

Get me out of this thing! The supposedly dying man stared at him.

Danny's brain hurt.

Seriously! Get me out of here!

Danny forced himself forward to the dying (dying?) man's side. He searched Maestro's wrecked body. . . except that his body wasn't wrecked at all. His face and arm and side were whole.

His entire body was smooth and healthy.

It was impossible!

Open the dratted machine! Maestro shouted in Danny's mind.

"Your nose is bleeding," Bobby said.

"Doctor machine," Danny exclaimed recklessly, "open Maestro's tube immediately."

"Are you overriding—"

"Open the stupid tube, *now!*" Danny banged on the lid. "Emergency protocol: whatever the heck! Override everything!"

Immediately, the glass tube broke its seal and water poured over the table and onto Danny's shoes.

"Open," he shouted. "Open. . . open!"

The glass pulled completely away, and the flood dragged Maestro with it, soaking Danny, who tugged the man to his side of the table, ripping the face mask off.

Maestro tumbled off the table, coughing and gasping while Danny did his best to get a grip under his arms to slow him.

Bobby grabbed for Maestro, too, but he missed. Really?

Not strong enough to hold Maestro on his own, Danny settled for slowing his descent to the floor as best he could. After a bit of a struggle, Danny knelt beside the table with Maestro sprawled on the floor, clutching Danny's arm. Closer examination showed that the skin where Maestro had been burned was pale and faintly pink, much lighter than the rest of his body, as though that skin had never seen the light of day.

"I'll need to spend some time at the beach to even out." Had Maestro read Danny's mind? "Thanks, kid. I was getting pretty bored in there." Maestro grabbed the table and started to pull himself to his feet, but he swayed so much Danny kept one arm around his waist to steady him.

"You're pretty handy to have around," the not-so-mortally-wounded man said.

"Just be glad Bobby wasn't the only one here or you'd have hit the floor like a sack of potatoes while he was busy averting his eyes." Danny pretended that holding the bigger man on his feet wasn't as hard as it was. He glanced at his brother, who pointedly examined the medical equipment.

Maestro chuckled, which started another coughing fit.

"How are you even alive?" Danny asked.

"Yeah. . . any chance I can just say I'm a quick healer and you'll leave it at that?" Maestro steadied himself against the table.

"Snowball's chance in Tahiti." Danny remained at his side.

"Figured." Maestro looked around and paused when his eyes found Bobby. "Look. . . I promise to answer at least some of your questions, but I'm sticky and cold and I could really use a shower."

"Of course." Resuming his position with an arm around Maestro's waist, Danny helped the miraculous man over to the shower in one corner of the room.

"So no one's dying after all?" Bobby sort of made an attempt to move closer to help but simply couldn't bring himself to it.

"Not right now, Bobby," Maestro said. "Why don't you go tell the others that I'm not dead?"

"Stellar." Obviously nabbing any excuse to leave the room, Bobby shot out the door. "Glad you're not dead, sir."

"Maestro?" Danny opened the shower stall. The white metal partial door reminded Danny of swanky clothing shops.

"Yeah?"

"You're really okay?"

"I'm not going to suddenly keel over." Maestro's face changed, grew serious. He stepped into the shower and closed the door between them. "I know what you're thinking, and the answer is yes, we actually managed to screw everything up completely, and we're still walking away with no serious casualties." He raised an eyebrow. "Be very proud of that, and for the sake of all the gods in the multiverse stop feeling guilty."

Danny sucked in a deep breath.

"Now please find me some towels," Maestro said, "and one of those spiffy outfits you're wearing and give me a couple of minutes to get used to my new arm."

Danny started off to a storage room.

"Danny," Maestro called.

Danny turned.

Maestro stared at him with his arms crossed on top of the door, leaning against it. Beneath the door, his feet crossed at the ankle. He regarded Danny for a moment or two with a strange tension in his eyes. He seemed to come to some kind of decision, and his eyes softened.

"Look kid," he said. "I ran through the ship's logs after you finally made Babbage turn off the stupid doctor machine. . ." He paused. "You did a lot of good things. More than I would have thought possible. If I thought you were one to get a big head I wouldn't be speaking, but you're the opposite. Unless someone points out your success, you only see the stupid stuff you do. So. . . you did good here. Seriously. I'm impressed."

Danny glowed in the praise he hadn't even realized he'd wanted.

He had so many questions he wanted to ask Maestro about what he could have done better. Instead, he decided to push his luck and ask, "You're immortal, right? How'd that happen?"

Maestro smiled. "Good guess or some kind of deduction?"

"The doctor machine made you worse, which says your body was trying to fix itself and the machine interfered." Danny shrugged. "That's some massive tissue regeneration. . . and fast. You're not a starfish. Okay. . . I guess it's kind of a leap from there."

"I traveled through time and other dimensions." Maestro studied Danny for several seconds. "I did that a lot. Sooner or later, I was bound to run into someone who had the tech to make me immortal." He shrugged. "But, you know, immortal is just what someone calls you when they haven't figured out how to kill you yet."

Danny considered that; it was likely more than most people heard.

"Can I take my shower, now?" Maestro jabbed a thumb at the showerhead.

"Yeah. . . of course. . ." Danny grinned. "I'll get you some clothes."

"I wouldn't want to freak out your brother again." Maestro turned his back to Danny.

Danny grinned some more. Impossibly, it was turning out to be a good day after all.

Maestro Really is That Cool.

The beach was exactly as Maestro remembered it: white quartz sand, sky so deep a purple it shamed grapes, and water that reflected the purple and made it sing. Foliage whose color could only be called aquamarine covered the trees surrounding the cove. The climate lingered just a shade below tropical, and the air smelled vaguely of jasmine. An enormous grey moon poked its head over the horizon.

Two smaller moons (or were they just farther away?) hung higher in the sky, and a thin, flat ring cut the heavens from horizon to horizon at a forty-five degree angle. Gravity was a trifle less than Earth-normal, so visitors always felt a bit stronger, and the air had a smidgeon more oxygen, which helped, too.

Maestro had visited the place with his family many times many years in the future and had spent quite a bit of time there beforehand, millennia in the past.

In the future, the water would fall a little lower.

In the past, it rose much, much higher.

The moment the landing party materialized on the beach, gasps and whistles of appreciation escaped all four boys. Even Babbage raised an eyebrow.

Torch kicked off his shoes and started unbuttoning his shirt before anyone had taken a breath.

Danny stared up at the sky.

Bobby turned in a slow circle, taking it all in.

TJ wandered toward the trees.

"You really don't want to do that." Maestro dug into a coat

pocket, stopping beside Torch. He pulled out an apple and took a bite. He'd meant to save it for a snack.

"Oooooh, yes I do." Torch laughed while he pulled off his shirt and fumbled with his belt. "Alien planet. First humans to swim here?" He stopped abruptly. "Wait. . . is it poisonous?"

"No. . . not poisonous." Maestro shook his head.

Torch resumed stripping.

TJ picked up a leaf from the sand and called Danny to his side.

Danny tore his eyes from the sky and stepped to his friend's side.

Bobby hovered beside Babbage who took readings with no discernible expression.

"Big brother duty hard to let go?" The EL turned to Bobby.

"Not difficult." Bobby crossed his arms. "Impossible." He winked.

Babbage smiled.

Torch had his pants around his ankles but had snagged them on his heels and hopped up and down on one foot.

Maestro wound up the apple and tossed it across the still ocean. It skipped. The apple, that is, not the ocean.

Once, twice, three times. . .

"How does he skip an apple?" Torch looked vaguely stork-like with one foot held up. He repeated his question more loudly. "How does he skip an app—"

The rest of his statement died, however, subsumed beneath his astonishment at the enormous creature erupting from the water.

Larger than a middle-class house, it resembled a whale with black skin and a mouth full of sharp teeth. It broke the water and bellowed, scattering flocks of birds from the nearby trees. It swallowed the apple along with enough water to choke a pod of Terran whales and hit hard, sending spray dozens of feet in the air as it sank once more into the depths. Circles spread out in the water and lapped up on the shore with waves at least three feet high.

"Dang." Torch fell over onto his butt.

Everyone stared open-mouthed at the receding waves.

"There's a pretty serious drop-off less than twenty feet from shore." Maestro stuffed his hands into his pockets. "Sorta dangerous."

The boys closed ranks, gathering around Torch as he squirmed and struggled to pull his pants up. After everything that had happened, their first impulse was still to run off to gape at the new stuff. Hopefully, the sight of the underwater behemoth reminded them that this field trip required a fair bit of caution.

"Okay... *that* was pretty stellar." Danny whistled. "I mean, seeing planets from orbit... wow... but... this? Holy spit... Right?" The other boys nodded. "We're actually on a different planet!"

The boys jumped up and down and hooted for a bit.

Once they calmed down, Danny added, "Umm... Maestro? Are there freakishly large things flying in the air or sneaking through the woods? Will they eat us? That big thing had carnivore teeth."

"Carnivore teeth?" Torch elbowed him.

"Sharp and pointy... also..." Danny turned from his contemplation of the shoreline to look at Maestro. "Just how deep is the water here? That thing came from a lightless environment."

Everyone stared at him.

"It didn't have eyes." Danny shrugged. "It had some sort of pad where eyes might have been millions of years ago, which means it *had* eyes, but lost them after generations and generations in an environment where eyes would be useless. Sonar? Did it *hear* the apple hit the water?"

"Giant fish jumps out of the water on an alien planet, and you notice that it doesn't have eyes?" Torch nudged him, obviously glad they were still friends. "Okay, big, pointy teeth, I noticed, too, but you're pulling out your tablet like it's a class project?" He pretended to pull out a tablet and poked at it with his other hand. "Hmm, let's see: giant alien fish... or is it a mammal? Forty-three point two feet long—"

"I notice things, okay?" Danny pushed him, but smiled.

Indeed, he did.

"Maestro?" TJ directly addressed Maestro for the very first time. "Yes?"

"This is an oak leaf." TJ held up a dark leaf.

"You mean it *looks like* an oak leaf." Danny looked at the leaf in TJ's hand.

"It's a *chinquapin* oak leaf." TJ shook his head. "I'm sure of it."

"*No es posiblé*," Torch told him. "We're a million miles from home, *ese*."

"Is too *posiblé*," TJ muttered.

Maestro smiled cryptically. "Hang onto that, TJ. It'll make more sense once I show you the real reason I brought you to this particular planet."

TJ tucked the leaf into a shirt pocket.

"Okay, boys…" Maestro clapped his hands broadly and rubbed them together briskly. "Since we have a breather, I want to give you a little first contact training."

All four boys, who probably cringed at a word like "training" in most situations, gave him their undivided attention.

"Noticing things is *good*. And never, *ever* jump into an enormous body of water you haven't scanned and tested thoroughly." Maestro raised an eyebrow at Torch, whose impetuosity had caused trouble recently enough for him to cringe. "Stay within eyesight at all times until you have thoroughly explored the landing site, and even then, make sure you maintain contact." He walked up the beach toward the grassy ridge above it. "That *fish*," he emphasized the word with a nod at Torch, "and its ancestors lived in an enormous cave system for millennia. The cave broke into this cove a few hundred years ago, which is why it's here now. It is a carnivore. It is blind, and it does use sonar." He nodded at Danny. "Gold star to the teacher's pet."

The boys laughed.

"It's not just about culture. The planet itself may not operate by the laws you're used to. This cove. . ." And he waved a hand at it. "Is not a natural formation. There's a wall that keeps all the sand from sliding into the depths. The cove itself is probably at least six miles deep."

Everyone, including Babbage, turned to him with shocked expressions.

"That's not possible," the EL said.

"You see, boys?" Maestro shrugged. "Even a seasoned traveler can be surprised. Never assume *anything*."

"This planet isn't on any database anywhere." Babbage crossed his arms and faced Maestro squarely. "Are you telling me a sentient species capable of that kind of construction rose and died out without ever making contact with the larger galaxy?"

"I'm not saying that at all." Maestro smiled with as much smugness as he could. He turned to finish the climb to the grass. "Let's get up there and you'll see why I brought you to this particular planet." As they crested the hill, he added, "and the only giant carnivores on this island are in the water which is why *that* was built here."

The boys stopped on the ridge and gazed across a grassy lawn at a glowing white courtyard and pavilion beyond. They exclaimed quietly and every one of them took two impetuous steps forward before pausing and looking at Maestro. Good, they were trainable.

"Go ahead," he told them with a wave. "It's deserted, but don't wander past the pavilion. We'll catch up in a minute."

The boys hooted and tore off across the grass.

Maestro and Babbage followed at a more sedate pace.

"You know what this place is," Babbage said, the surprise obvious in his voice.

Maestro nodded silently.

"It's not recorded anywhere," Babbage added.

Maestro shook his head, still smiling.

They reached a set of curved steps that framed the grassy lawn and climbed to the terraced courtyard above. The courtyard bowed to match the shape of the stairs. Seen from this vantage point, the purpose of the construction became obvious: originally, the stairs had led down into the water. The grassy lawn above had been a beach, and the current beach had been underwater, gradually sloping until the ledge dropped into the abyss.

The shallow terraces allowed for more bathers to look out over the water without blocking the view of those higher up. Everything had been constructed from white quartz that matched the sand on the beach. The water level had dropped twenty feet and the polar ice caps had sucked up much of the ecosystem's water.

The boys raced around the courtyard, chasing each other among the pillars that lined the courtyard and supported the pavilion. The buildings beyond had been manufactured from the same white rock. They brought a soft ache to Maestro's chest, sweeping up to the sky in towers and spires. Exactly as he remembered. He smiled. His children had loved this spot so much that his family had made annual trips. Had loved? Would one day love? Grammar was complicated for time travelers.

"Why isn't it overgrown or buried?" Babbage asked, breaking Maestro's train of thought.

He raised an eyebrow and resumed his smirk, letting Babbage get there on his own time.

"That's not possible," the EL insisted.

"The majority of sentient species in the galaxy still consider flight impossible unless you're born with wings." Maestro looked up.

Having spent a bit of their adolescent energy in the game of tag, the boys congregated in the middle of the courtyard, flushed and breathless.

Maestro crossed to them with Babbage in curious tow.

"Billions if not trillions of years ago," Maestro lectured, "visitors came to the Milky Way from a nearby galaxy whose name has been lost to time, along with almost all traces of the visitors. They built twenty outposts, similar to this one, growing the cities like crystals from the most common elements in the ground on each location. In this case, white quartz."

"Wait. . . grew?" This was from Torch. "Like those tacky growing-in-water rocks?"

"Pretty much, except these are programmed to grow into cities." Maestro walked toward the pavilion. "Not so tacky."

The others followed wordlessly.

"From these outposts, they explored the galaxy searching for worlds suitable to sow the seeds of life. They seeded thousands of planets. . . and then they left." He shrugged. "No one knows where they went, why they played Johnny Appleseed across the galaxy, and we can only infer *approximately* what they looked like."

"From the shape of the buildings they left behind?" Danny queried.

"Because of the shape of the life forms they left behind." Maestro smirked, and this smirk was so self-satisfied it almost moaned with pleasure. He paused to see whose lightbulbs would light, then hit them with, "They made us in their image."

As realization dawned on the boys' faces—one by one and in predictable order—Maestro pulled another apple from his pocket and took a big bite.

TJ pulled out his oak leaf and stared at it in astonishment.

The boys remained speechless for longer than Maestro had yet seen. That sort of information and their reaction to it was one reason to protect planets like Earth. What would happen if all the various religions were told, in a nutshell: sucks to be wrong, doesn't it?

"Okay. . . that's debatable." Babbage broke the silence. "Every sentient species that knows the truth claims that the. . . the Johnny Appleseeds as you call them, were shaped like them. All we know is they were bipedal and roughly humanoid, meaning upright with two arms and two legs."

"And the sentient quadrupeds and octopods would probably debate even that," Maestro pointed out.

"True."

"Are you saying that aliens from another galaxy seeded life on suitable planets and then evolution followed some preprogrammed path that led, eventually, to us?" Danny stepped forward. "So there really is a god. . . or gods who created us?"

"They didn't *create* us," Babbage explained. "They used their own genetic material and started the ball rolling. . . but they weren't gods."

"On that we agree completely," Maestro exclaimed, slapping the

EL on the back. "Gods are *completely* different. . . much crankier, usually." He draped an arm around Babbage's shoulders. "And much more obsessed with sex."

A blank, incredulous stare confronted him.

"What?" Maestro shrugged and pulled his arm away. "Just because *you've* never met any gods, doesn't mean that no one in the class has."

"Now you're just being intentionally provocative," Babbage insisted. "Why is this city not in ruins?" He looked around at the blank stares on the boys' faces. "There were originally twenty of these outposts. We've only found seven of them, well, *eight* now I guess, and all the others were in ruins and mostly buried under miles of sediment." He turned to Maestro. "How is this one still intact and. . . clean?"

As if in answer to his question, a small, square robot about the size of a shoebox suddenly dashed across the plaza and bumped into his foot. It retreated a couple of inches then bumped into his foot a second time, whereupon it pulled back and beeped.

Without a word, Babbage raised his foot, and the little robot sped off and vanished among the pillars.

"Self-preserving system," Maestro explained.

"After all these years?" Danny exclaimed. "It must be solar powered."

"No. . . no, it's not." Babbage's response was very quiet. "The quantum generator must still be active."

Maestro nodded sagely.

"How do you know about this place?" Babbage looked Maestro up and down as if seeing him for the first time.

"I'm *that* cool." Maestro smiled again.

The boys all grinned. Quite frankly, they all seemed to agree.

"I need to see this." Babbage obviously didn't agree with the boys but chose to keep that to himself apart from a vaguely annoyed frown. He pulled out his Doohickey and headed across the pavilion.

"Let him have his moment." Maestro seized Torch's arm before he followed the EL. "He's about to become very famous."

Torch pulled a face. "I thought we weren't supposed to run off on our own?"

"*You're* not," Maestro agreed. "But *he* can. He's a seasoned space traveler. He gets himself killed, it's his own stupid fault." He started off in the same direction, but more slowly.

The boys followed.

"Look out for evil alien insects," TJ muttered.

Danny smiled and nodded. Fist bump.

On a whim, Maestro stopped and turned them all around to look out over the plaza and to the cove now visible beyond. The sun sank toward the horizon. The boys should take note of a view like that.

"Okay," Danny started, probably still sorting through everything he'd just learned about the origins of life. "You let him take credit for discovering the unknown, abandoned city of the Johnny Appleseeds. Stellar. I get it." He gestured in the direction Babbage had disappeared. "But the look on his face meant something more than discovering a lost city. What is so important about the power source?"

"It's called a quantum generator." Maestro smiled. "It generates an unlimited supply of power out of what is, for all intents and purposes. . . nothing and, as you can see here, it lasts longer than life has existed on Earth. Since this is the only operating Apple-town ever found, as of two hundred years from now, it's unique in the galaxy."

"Okay, spaceman," Torch interjected. "Maybe I'm the dumbest monkey here for asking this, but just how *do* you know about this if no one else anywhere does?"

"No one knows about it. . . *yet*." Had they all forgotten Maestro came from the future? "But in the future from whence I hail, it's a tourist trap." He waved vaguely. "There's a theme park with roller coasters over there. There's a water ride down into the caves from which the giant fish escaped. School kids have field trips." He started off in the direction Babbage had rushed. "And before that. . . I went back in time to visit the Johnny Appleseeds' original outpost here."

He'd made it past the pillars by the time the boys found the presence of mind to catch him up. They'd had to run for it.

"Wait," Danny insisted. "You *met* them? You know what they actually *looked* like?"

"Yep."

"Well?" Danny grabbed his elbow.

"Nope," Maestro insisted.

"Why not?" Danny's voice cracked.

"That," Maestro replied cryptically, "would be telling." He lifted Danny's hand from his arm. "What happens in history," he continued with a dramatic pause, "stays in history." He placed a single index finger to his lips and blew a "shush" at them, then turned on his heal and resumed his pursuit of the EL. "Mind you, everything was painted garish colors back then. . . I like it better this way. Simpler, cleaner. . . more minimalist. . ."

As he turned a corner, the boys hadn't moved, apparently shocked at yet one more insane stage in the adventure their lives had become.

"You're going to lose me!" Maestro called.

With a world so quiet and the stones full of reverberation, Maestro heard, above the sounds of running feet, "How are we supposed to know when he's putting us on?"

Who had asked the question?

Well, there was no doubting that Danny was the one who replied: "I don't think we're supposed to know. I really don't think that's the plan."

The Law of Narrative Causality

Danny hit the ground rolling off a shoulder and rose onto one knee facing his nefarious opponent. He dove to the right as a leg split the air just over his head. He kicked up and caught the knee with a solid hit. Stellar!

His opponent might be taller, stronger, faster, and more skilled, which meant Danny was pretty much dead, but he wouldn't let anyone watching know he knew his fate. He would push through to the end and make as good a showing for himself—and his planet—as he could. He might die at the end of it, but this guy would *know* he'd been in a fight.

They exchanged a series of fast, furious blows, and Danny got hit a lot more than he hit, but he made several good connections of his own.

At least two or three. . .

Well, he'd had this *one* punch that had *seriously* connected. Pow!

The spectators shouted and jumped up and down in excitement. Danny tried to block them out but couldn't help noticing that most. . . well, actually *all* of the bets had been placed against him which sort of defeated the whole point of betting, didn't it?

The creature he fought kept changing styles which didn't help Danny either, since he only knew Taekwondo and his opponent had moves he'd never seen.

Pow! A blow to the head hit, like, *really* hard and hurt a *lot!*

Danny stumbled to his hands and knees as a chorus of Ooooos erupted from the peanut gallery. He shook his head to clear the bright points of light that skittered across his field of vision, and Bobby held his shoulder.

"I am *so* sorry, little brother!" Bobby exclaimed. "No *way* did I think I'd connect with that." He helped Danny to his feet and pressed his cheek to Danny's ear. "Tell me you weren't narrating the fight in your head again, pretending I was some kind of evil alien."

When Danny didn't respond, Bobby put him in a head lock and ruffled his hair in good-natured roughhousing. "You need to focus in a fight." He even kissed the top of Danny's head, which elicited a few raspberries from TJ and fake retching noises from Torch.

"You guys want to fight next?" Bobby straightened to his full height to tower over the other boys. He pointedly crossed his arms.

"No, sir."

"No, sir."

"Good. Then you can keep your heartless comments to yourself." He clapped his hands and rubbed them together in a gesture already familiar to Danny. "Okay. That's kinda what it looks like. I'm going to start you with the basics. . . Like some stretching."

Danny moved through the motions from memory, not really listening as his brother explained things to the novices. He watched Maestro, who stood at a railing gazing out over the plaza and the moonlit ocean beyond.

The space traveler's revelations about the origins of life rattled around Danny's head, generating question after question. Once Maestro had outlined the basics of the galaxy's history, the other boys had lost interest and gotten antsy, so Maestro suggested that Bobby teach them some of the basics of martial arts.

Bobby had shrugged with his usual good-natured acquiescence then realized he was about to give the very first human martial arts class on this extraterrestrial world. He'd looked around with a grin that had made him a little kid again and had nodded approval. He'd even suggested they start with a sparring match between the brothers so the other boys could get an idea of what they'd learn.

Danny knew he'd really made the suggestion because it would be the coolest. fight. *ever.* Danny had begged Maestro to videotape the match, but he'd hesitated to record something on an alien world for "protected" people.

"We just want something to show our parents!" Danny had insisted.

So he'd finally agreed as long as he could destroy it later.

Wait, had Maestro recorded Bobby kissing his head. Probably. *That* part he'd put on the net for all the world to see. His older brother handing him his butt on a platter Danny could handle, but the thought of the entire planet seeing such a chick flick moment rankled him.

Whatever. He stood on a distant planet and nothing was trying to kill him. Woot! He couldn't stop his internal voice from muttering, *yet.* He told it to shut up.

The stretches were boring. Danny had done them a thousand times. He got his brother's attention with a nod.

Bobby nodded back without breaking a single car on his train of thought.

Danny bobbed his head in Maestro's direction and made a requesting face.

Bobby raised an eyebrow.

Danny rolled his eyes to remind his brother how many times he'd been through these stretches.

Bobby smiled and nodded his brother away.

Trying to avoid disrupting the lesson, Danny slunk over to Maestro. He leaned against the railing, mirroring the time traveler's casual slouch.

A moon three times the apparent size of Earth's rose over the ocean. The sky burned a deep, velvety purple, now, and a few brave stars shone brightly enough to flicker in the moonlit sky. A soft breeze blew in from the water, smelling faintly of salt and jasmine.

Maestro turned to regard Danny frankly.

Danny sort of glanced at him out of the corner of one eye, trying really hard to act as blasé as possible.

"One more moonrise over an extraterrestrial ocean." Maestro chuckled and sighed a world-weary sigh. "If only something *interesting* would happen tonight."

Danny smiled. "We must seem so provincial to you."

"Provincial?"

Danny shrugged. "Like small town hicks."

"I know what the word means." Maestro laughed. "I just haven't acclimated to your vocabulary, and no, you don't seem 'provincial.' My kids were among the first humans to travel into the stars in their timeline, so I spent a lot of time watching them ooh and aah at the sights."

Danny kept his mouth shut. Maestro didn't talk about himself a lot, and he seemed more likely to keep talking to fill a silence than to answer a bunch of questions.

The man chuckled. "My oldest son, Little Barry. . . every time he saw an unfamiliar species he'd run right up and ask them where they were from. . ." He pumped his arms the way his son must've done. "He did that all the way through his last voyage off-planet for his 92nd birthday." He shook his head, sighed, and turned his gaze to Danny's questioning face. "We all went to a resort on one of the moons of Mars—Tres Vegas. They had Las Vegas on Earth, Nuevo Vegas on Luna, and Tres Vegas on. . . on whatever moon it was." He laughed. "One advantage to outliving your kids is you get to keep embarrassing them by dancing on the tables in your underwear." He fell silent.

What the heck must this man's life be like?

"Go ahead and ask," Maestro said. "I see a Mongol's horde of questions in your face."

Of all the questions he could have asked, Danny surprised himself with, "Do you miss them?"

"Of course I do, but I had the privilege of watching all my children grow to a ripe old age, and I knew grandchildren and great grandchildren." Maestro considered. "Not many parents are that lucky." He turned to regard the moon. "I left when my kids started to die. I didn't want to see that. They had me longer than most kids."

How could he watch everyone he knew grow old and die over and over again, always knowing it would never stop?

"Don't pity me." Maestro seemed to read his thoughts. "But now you know why I don't tell a lot of people about myself. People always end up feeling sorry for me."

"I don't," Danny told him quickly. "But I don't envy you either, and I imagine envy's almost as annoying as pity."

"You are a singular young man, Danny Denton Decker." Maestro held out a hand with a wry smile. "Would you consent to being my friend?"

"Wow," Danny said. Holy crap! "Of course. . ."

Maestro squeezed Danny's hand then released it and turned his gaze back to the moon, which had cleared the horizon completely now, bathing the landscape in light.

Danny turned to match Maestro's pose, glowing with pride.

"The quick answer to the question you haven't asked," Maestro added, "is that this planet hasn't been discovered due to a massive nebula that shields it from the rest of the galaxy. We don't really get to see the nebula because it's in the daytime sky this time of year and so it's almost invisible. The galaxy is a really, really big place and most of it is empty space. Unless a planet has enough technology to emit some kind of quantum signal, it's unlikely to attract any attention and interference from the nebula means only one space-faring civilization can even detect this planet."

"But if Babbage discovered it," Danny asked, "and you came back here and *helped* Babbage discover it, doesn't that create some kind of causality loop?"

"Time doesn't work that way." Maestro shook his head. "Besides which, Babbage didn't discover it in my timeline. It'd been discovered in something like 1820. . ." He chuckled. "Coincidently, a species of evil, alien insects found it. Since they haven't done so yet in this timeline, I must've changed things with all my time traveling, but the galaxy will need to have found this planet."

"What did you change?" Danny struggled to keep up with the complicated verb tenses.

Maestro lost his smile.

"I'm sorry. I didn't mean. . ." Oops. Wrong question.

"Don't ever apologize for being curious." Maestro shook his head, and his smile seemed forced. "In my timeline, aliens invaded the Earth in 1961 and enslaved the planet for over two hundred years. It never came under the protection of the Galactic Police."

"So you traveled back in time and fixed it?"

"I didn't fix anything." Maestro smiled. "You don't *change* time. As far as I know, it isn't possible. I just created a new timeline. . . a parallel dimension identical to my own, except for the fact that in *this* timeline, your timeline, I appeared in the year 1961. I managed to fix things for *your* Earth, but my family stayed stuck in slavery."

Danny took some time to figure that out. "But. . . you got back to watch them grow up, right?"

"A friend of mine helped," Maestro explained. "Barry. He found a wooden box that acted like a bungee cord and popped us back to our point of origin. I have *no* idea how it worked. We made our way home and contacted the Galactic Police who put the Earth under protective custody and drove off the slavers. I got to watch my kids grow old and helped them join the galactic community, happily ever after style. As far as they were concerned, I'd left for less than a minute."

"That is *some* story." Danny mulled the whole thing over. One thing bothered him. "So. . . the evil alien insects that discovered this world in *your* timeline. . . do they even *exist* in this one?"

"Do they exist?" Maestro leaned against the railing, giving his attention to the boys now moving through some kata. "Of course, they *exist*, but they should have discovered this world a hundred years ago. Since they haven't been here, yet, they must have missed the boat for some reason." He shrugged and then spoke horrifying words. "I'm sure we're perfectly safe. There's absolutely nothing to worry about."

"You did *not* just say that." Danny cringed and searched the moonlit landscape below them. "*Why* did you just say that?" Movement at the edge of the distant lawn caught his eye. "Spit."

"What's the big deal?" Maestro scowled.

With a withering sigh, Danny pointed at the landscape below, where a number of skittery shapes crested the hill from the beach. "Do you know *nothing* about the laws of narrative causality? You can't say something like, 'I'm sure we're perfectly safe. There's absolutely nothing to worry about,' without evil aliens appearing out of nowhere to attack you. It's an absolute *law*."

"That's just not bloody possible," Maestro muttered.

"Tell *them* that!" Danny rolled his eyes, grabbed Maestro by the back of the neck and pointed again.

"Are you sure you're only twelve years old?" Maestro shook off Danny's hand. He surveyed the approaching line of aliens. "Drat." He hauled Danny over to the other boys while shouting into his Doohickey. "Babbage, get your manufactured butt back here on the double. We have company." He cut the feed before Babbage could respond and leaned close to Danny. "I will do everything in my power to get you out of this. You have every right to hate me for this for the rest of your natural life." After a moment, he added, "However long that may be."

"Last" becomes "First."

A hundred of them attacked: giant, alien insects that resembled—to Danny's terrestrial imagination—enormous, armor-plated fleas. They all carried weapons somehow fitted for their unwieldy appendages, spitting venomous lasers that crashed into the quartz columns to violent, if predictable, effect.

As Maestro dragged Danny backwards, heels skidding on the stone floor, he couldn't help but think that the whole scene should be another—somewhat more humorous—video game. Funnier because the deadly aliens were humongous, armor-plated fleas. There should always be something vaguely amusing about giant alien fleas.

"Is the entire galaxy filled with deadly, evil creatures?" Danny shouted. "I mean, sure there's parts of L.A. and New York where you can't throw a stone without someone shooting back... but there's miles and miles of... like, *Montana*, where the worst that can happen is a terminal case of boredom."

Maestro shoved him behind a pillar and fired a continuous volley at the attacking bugs. The other boys shouted questions and fired Doohickeys earlier procured from the weapons locker on the Galactic Police cruiser.

The bugs leapt high into the air, one after another, making them extraordinarily difficult targets. Soon, the plaza resembled nothing more than a rather unappetizing popcorn maker crisscrossed with lasers and smoke and dust. Wow. They even behaved like giant fleas.

"Really?" Danny muttered. "Violent hopping death? How can we take that seriously?"

A laser struck a nearby column and blasted about thirty pounds of solid rock into gas. So the situation was not, in fact, at all amusing.

Maestro shot him a worried look. "You might try shooting back."

"No! *You* kill them." Danny would not get drawn in. "After that business with the Saurians I swore I'd never kill another sentient creature, and I *meant* it."

The other boys filled the plaza with laser fire, holding the bugs off for the moment.

"I admire your—" Maestro started.

"You can admire my *butt* if you want to," Danny shouted, "but I'm not killing anyone, no matter how many limbs they have!"

"Would it help if I told you they were mindless insects without a soul?"

"Is it true?" Danny considered the apparent insect leader who stood off to one side, calmly issuing orders into a pincer-held com unit.

"Yes?"

Boom! Something exploded off to Danny's right.

Torch and TJ dove away from their suddenly vaporized pillar and rolled behind a different one.

The bugs immediately attacked.

Where was Bobby? Off to Danny's left, firing maniacally at the hopping bugs. A laser nicked his gun arm, and he pulled behind cover, cursing loudly. He switched the weapon to his right hand. As he repositioned himself, he met Danny's gaze and his eyes swept Danny in a moment.

Bobby nodded once, then turned back to the business of trying to prevent them all from getting killed. So he understood that Danny wasn't fighting back. He even seemed to appreciate why.

Cripes. That felt so much worse than if he'd shouted something judgmental. Danny closed his eyes and cursed all authors of young adult fiction who made the whole thing seem so blasted romantic.

"Drat it, Babbage," Maestro shouted. "We could really—"

A large chunk of the pillar protecting him and Danny erupted into violent shards, destroying Danny's resolve.

"Fine," he muttered, then pulled out his Doohickey and poked around the column, exposing no more of his body than necessary.

"Don't you people have families?" he shouted. "Don't you have parents and children. . . or larvae. . . or eggs. . . or. . ." He fired and fired and fired, his arm jerking up and down and left and right as he picked one bug after another out of the sky. "Why are you all so easy to kill and intent on your own destruction?!"

Maestro grunted. "Nice."

He appreciated Danny's aim? Really?

"No, it's not," Danny said. No matter how many bugs they killed, dozens more replaced them, and they didn't seem to mind dying. "Why are people trying to kill us everywhere we go?" Danny pressed himself against the space traveler's legs until man and boy practically fused into a single entity of destruction. The two of them mowed down the aliens much faster than any of the others.

"Welcome to my life." Maestro glanced down at Danny and smiled.

Hundreds of Spartans ran screaming into the plaza.

Wait. What?

They poured into the open space dressed in loincloths, capes, and some wore metal chest plates and helmets as they rushed out from their apparent hiding places behind columns. They attacked the bugs with enormous laser rifles and a distracting ululation that, more than anything else, seemed to freak the heck out of the enemy.

The bugs dove for cover, pulling back to the steps at the edge of the plaza. The Spartans rushed eagerly forward only to be mown down *en masse* by the bugs' deadly fire.

"They won't buy that hologram for long." Babbage appeared at Maestro's shoulder. "Let's get the shades out of here!"

Danny examined the convincing scene of devastation. None of the Spartans had really been hit. Lasers passed through them, and they fell.

And none of the Spartan weapons managed to hit any of the bugs.

"Holograms," Danny muttered. Okay, their reprieve would be short lived. He fired a few volleys at the retreating line of bugs.

A horrible, screeching noise filled the air. It had to be speech, but the language sounded guttural, disturbing, and completely foreign. Ouch!

"Drat," Maestro muttered, apparently understanding what had been said. He shouted at the top of his lungs, "Drop your weapons, drop your weapons, drop your weapons!"

Danny dropped his weapon. Abruptly, a grey room materialized around him, with the other humans and Babbage inside as well. . . but the monstrous horde was nowhere in sight.

He'd felt no shift, none of the signs of transport he'd learned to notice: slight disorientation, an odd little noise, a momentary blurring of his vision. He just found himself in a new place.

His Doohickey lay at his feet.

Everyone but Maestro—even Babbage—seemed equally surprised and impressed.

"What the heck—?" Torch stopped open-mouthed as a Hindu woman in traditional garb appeared. She wore a dark fuchsia sari edged in gold and a dot on her forehead. Hands behind her back, she did not look pleased.

"Why were you perpetrating acts of violence?" She spoke with a thick Indian accent.

"Why are you Mahatma Gandhi's granddaughter?" Torch shot back.

Maestro touched Torch's arm, drawing his attention. The time traveler slowly shook his head.

"This was the most appropriate form we could glean from your thoughts," the woman explained. "We thought you would be respectful towards it." She glanced sidelong at Torch. "Perhaps we chose poorly."

"You're in our thoughts?" Danny demanded in spite of himself. "Isn't that a violent act?"

He moved to Bobby's side. How badly hurt was his brother's arm? Bobby shook his head dismissively then put the arm around Danny protectively. Once upon a time, Danny would have shrugged it off, but, under the circumstances, he let his brother play protector.

"So is entering our city without permission," the woman sing-songed, "and we could go on like this all day, but it is tedious, and," she pointed out pointedly, "we are the ones who can kill you instantly if we find you overly tedious."

Not surprisingly, everyone shut up.

Who the heck was she? She had to be one of the Johnny Appleseeds, but why would she look like a middle-aged Indian woman unless she was a hologram? She appeared remarkably solid for a hologram.

"Better," she said after a moment of silence. "Why are you here?"

Why bother asking if they could read his thoughts?

Several words in the strange language from earlier spat out of Maestro's mouth.

"You speak our language?" The woman raised an eyebrow.

"I visited this city while you still lived."

"A time traveler?" She looked him up and down.

"I am. We humbly beg your forgiveness for the acts of violence perpetrated in your city. We are merely here to explore, but the Hunters attacked without warning or provocation." How could Maestro render the capital letter audible? "We reacted with violence to protect ourselves. We were not given an opportunity to negotiate and are not technologically advanced enough to utilize non-violent means of restraint."

"You understand how important honesty is to us." The Indian woman smiled.

That had to be why she'd asked her questions even though they could read thoughts. They wanted to see if the humans would speak the truth.

"It is the hallmark of a civilized mind," Maestro intoned as if reciting a lesson.

The woman giggled.

Wow. Not what Danny would have expected!

"We recognize you now, time traveler," she said. "You are the one who called us the Johnny Appleseeds." She smiled. "We liked the name."

Her laughter caused a ripple of relaxation through the group.

"I am the avatar of the Johnny Appleseeds," the woman explained. So she *was* a hologram. "The Hunters have been searching for this planet for millennia based on ancestral legends. When they arrived and realized you had preceded them by mere moments, they attacked out of frustration that you would receive the rights of discovery." She shrugged. "If you would be willing to give up these rights, since you are explorers and not acquisitive, the Hunters will promise no further violence."

All four boys huddled behind Maestro. Even guys as mouthy as Torch apparently understood when it was time to let the adults talk.

"Do you believe them?" Maestro asked.

"Yes," she replied.

Babbage stood a bit to one side. He likely let Maestro handle the conversation since he had history with the Johnny Appleseeds.

Huh. What did they call themselves?

"They're a bloodthirsty, hostile species genetically engineered for violence," Maestro said, "but they know you'll mow them down like grass if they step out of line."

"As I said, you understand our feelings about honesty." Her smile seemed genuine.

Babbage finally spoke up. "I don't care if they get rights of discovery. But the thought of your technology falling into their pincers terrifies me."

"Not to worry," she assured him. "Now that we have been discovered, all memories and data of our culture and technology are being wiped from the database." She smiled again. "I'm sure you won't mind them having the tech necessary to keep the streets clean."

"Even so," Babbage muttered.

"Don't sweat it, Babbage." Maestro patted his shoulder. "When I visited this place 200 years from now, it was a tourist trap because no one ever figures out how to replicate the tech. Anything taken away from the city dissolves into dust, and, because the Johnny Appleseeds killed the database, the Hunters will abandon the entire planet in a few years and leave it for the rest of us to enjoy."

Babbage looked around before muttering, "But think of the *good* this tech could do in the right hands."

The lengthy silence of the avatar's stare spoke volumes.

"The right hands? Whose hands? Yours? Shifters?" Her expression telegraphed her opinion of that idea. "We have watched this galaxy since it first bore life, and we have watched civilizations rise and fall. The Shifters may be the most technologically advanced species this galaxy has seen. They may be the most intelligent. . . and even the most civilized, as far as that goes." She shook her head. "But they are not ready for this much of a leap forward." She nodded at Maestro. "It's like this one having time travel tech. . . not really a good idea when it comes down to it." She smiled at him in apparent bemusement.

Wow. She was millions of years beyond anyone in the room.

"What makes you think we aren't ready?" Babbage asked, but his voice remained subdued.

She shrugged. "You don't have the heart for it."

Danny urged his engineered friend to keep quiet with a gesture, but it didn't work.

"And who are you to judge?" Babbage asked.

"We are the Johnny Appleseeds." She smiled. "Although our memories grow dim as we speak, we remember that we were an alliance of hundreds of species that enjoyed millennia in harmony and peace in our own lands before we ever set appendages in this galaxy."

"Why keep the database active all this time," Danny heard himself say before he could vacuum seal his mouth, "just to ashcan it all now?" He looked around.

Every face stared at him.

"Sorry. . . I just really wanted to know, and I figure you won't remember once the database is completely deleted." His face heated up.

She regarded him with what appeared to be extreme interest, something everyone seemed to do these days. Ugh. So annoying.

"In case we came back." She reached out and brushed a strand of hair from his forehead.

Holy wow! The avatar had physical existence!

"See," Torch muttered. "*They* can do it!" He elbowed TJ. "That is *so* Next Gen."

"Where did you go?" Babbage asked, pointedly ignoring the revelation.

"I'm sorry. We don't remember." She looked down, then smiled at him. "Isn't that lovely?"

The door to their room slid open.

"You are free to explore the city." She gestured in the direction of the open door. "As long as you create no conflict with the Hunter colony."

And she vanished.

Torch jumped up and down. "Okay, that. was. so. cool, right? We just chatted up the extraterrestrial gods that made us. It's like we just talked to God, and she was a middle-aged Hindu chick. How frickin' cool is that?"

The boys lost themselves to a montage of jabbering and excitement.

Until Danny pulled himself out.

Maestro stared at Babbage. In a not-so-friendly way.

And Babbage. His face wore a sad, serious expression.

Oh spit. What was wrong?

"I will come back for you." Babbage sighed deeply, which was odd for a robot who didn't need to breathe.

"'Come back for us.'" Maestro's expression darkened, and the temperature in the room dropped several dozen degrees. "So you want a further look at the power source before we go?" His hands found their way to his pockets.

The other boys stopped celebrating and stared at the grown-ups.

"No. . ." Babbage said, his expression strangely blank. "I need to complete my mission now."

"Okay. . . cool," Maestro said, but his tone was way beyond cool. . . It was frigid. "We'll drop the boys off on Earth, and I'll help you with your quest once they're safe." He obviously suspected some kind of foul play, but what sort of foul was involved?

"That's just it, Maestro." Babbage looked from one confused face to another. "You've already given me all the help I need."

"I had a feeling you were going to say something stupid like that, but I'm not *exactly* sure why I'm going to hate you." Maestro pulled his hands out of his pockets and crossed his arms over his chest in a way that kept his hands completely hidden.

Very quietly, Babbage admitted, "I needed you to bring me *here*, to this planet. I needed to get the Johnny Appleseeds' database." There was a pause. "That was my mission all along."

"But it's already been deleted," Danny said.

"As soon as they connected with my mind, I started uploading along their signal. By the time the database was gone, I'd already copied the entire thing. . . Or most of it anyway."

"So. . ." Anger seemed to coil like a horrible serpent inside Maestro, preparing itself to strike. He stared at Babbage with his head tilted down and his eyes dark chasms of imminent violence. "So you orchestrated everything from the beginning to end up with *you* here on *this* planet to steal the database."

"You have to understand—" Babbage said.

Maestro raised his left hand and threw something onto the stone floor. His eyes crackled with purple fire, and he spoke several words in a language Danny couldn't understand.

A ball of violet lightning sparked on the floor at his feet, rapidly expanding in a growing sphere that passed harmlessly through Danny but tingled.

The lightning grounded itself in the walls, crackling and sputtering, illuminating the space in a haphazard glow.

"I don't have to understand *anything*." Maestro launched himself at the robot. He landed two punches before the boys grabbed him and pulled him back.

"The Johnny Appleseeds," Danny cried. "You can't fight him."

"They can't see us right now." Maestro struggled against the restraint. "I'm safe."

"That's not possible." Babbage rubbed his jaw. "Their tech is beyond anything—"

"Tech can't handle witchcraft." Maestro grinned.

"Witchcraft?" All four boys struggled to hold Maestro, although why exactly didn't they let him beat the snot out of Babbage?

"You nearly got these boys killed," Maestro hissed. "And for what? A lousy tech advantage? Because you're too impatient to figure it out for yourselves?"

"Five planets are about to die without this tech," Babbage told them. "Seventy-five billion souls snuffed out." He snapped his fingers. "Like that."

The pulling and writhing under Danny' hands stopped.

"Give me the short version." Maestro shrugged out of the boys' grip.

The short version was that a heavily populated star system was about to die. The star had gone unstable without warning. It had emitted a solar flare, incinerating the closest planet instantly, ten billion lives wiped out in the blink of an eye. . . and five more planets and several moons orbited in the system, all of them even more densely populated.

"In addition to the billions of lives at risk, it's the closest thing the Shifters have to a home system. There are five billion there. . . sorry. . . four billion, now. . . which accounts for seventy-five percent of the known Shifter population. They'll be effectively wiped out."

Danny did the math. "There's only six billion Shifters total?"

"They don't reproduce easily," Babbage said. "It's common in long-lived species."

"Can't you evacuate them in ships?" Torch asked.

"There's no possible way to evacuate that many people," Babbage said. "You'd need thousands of ships."

"So how does this tech help you?" Maestro demanded.

"We can't evacuate the people. . . But we might be able to evacuate the planets." Babbage wrung his hands.

What the heck?

Maestro shifted back as if shocked. "You're going to use a quantum field to actually transport entire *planets*. It's. . . it's. . ."

"It's extremely conceivable with the Johnny Appleseed tech," Babbage insisted quietly. "You can transport a person. You can transport a ship. . . there is no theoretical limit."

"Just a technical one."

"We don't know how to create a stable quantum field on that scale," Babbage said. "We're convinced the Johnny Appleseeds did."

The only sounds were the crackling of the violet lightning on the walls and Maestro's heavy breathing. He shook his head and looked at the floor.

Danny was eons out of his depth on this one.

"How did you even know I'd been here?" Maestro looked up at Babbage again. "Tell me it wasn't Elizabeth."

Babbage shook his head. "Peter."

Maestro startled. "How did *he* know?"

"Something about a male bonding night of tequila shots in a hot tub with your team," Babbage said. "You bragged about your adventures. . ."

"Dratting tequila." Maestro shook his head. "I remember that night. . . Well, parts of it. At least it wasn't Elizabeth. She's a friend." He squinted up at Babbage. "I thought Peter was a friend, too. Guess I was wrong."

"Seventy-five billion lives, Maestro."

"You could've just asked," Maestro insisted. "Why all the manipulation? Why so sodding complicated? It doesn't make sense."

"We couldn't take the chance you'd say no."

"That is such garbage." Maestro scoffed. "Why would I say no?"

"We couldn't take the chance you wouldn't trust us with a database of this magnitude."

"Apparently I'd be *right* not to trust you." He folded his arms. "How'd you even do it? How did you make all this happen?"

"Find a penny. . ." The entire lie hit Danny. It all made sense. Maestro turned to him.

Very quietly, Danny explained: "That's how I met him. He got in my head and suggested I pick up the chip on the sidewalk." Danny shook his head. "I thought it was a penny. Later he convinced me he had to be in physical contact to be in our heads so I wouldn't know he'd been in there the whole time. . . but that first voice I heard. . ." He looked up at the robot he had come to know and trust. . . to *think* he knew and trusted. "I was just walking past. He never touched me." Talk about violated and abused. "I can't believe I never thought to question that. . . that I didn't realize he was in my head from the beginning. He manipulated us all the whole time." He looked at Maestro. "Why'd you really bring us to this *particular* planet?"

"A little voice in my head, I guess." Maestro's gaze found Danny's. "I'm a double thousand years old, kid, and have spent centuries out among the stars. If anyone should have seen through him, it was me." To Babbage, he said, "So putting the boys at the mercy of Saurians was preferable to just asking for my help?"

"The boys were never in any danger from Saurians." Babbage stared at the floor.

"I was shot!" Torch called out.

"And there was a sophisticated doctor machine to make sure you were fixed up," Babbage countered. "No one died."

"A dozen Saurians did," Danny threw out.

"No. . . they didn't." Babbage's eyes met Maestro's.

"Oh, my gods," Maestro muttered. "*That's* why you used the transporters instead of any beam weapons. All that garbage about the Doohickey lasers being too dangerous. . ." He pushed forward, cursing under his breath, but when Danny grabbed his shoulder, he stopped. "I am so bloody stupid." Maestro spat. "They weren't even Saurians. They were bloody Shifters and holograms pretending to be Saurians. . . So you. . ." He jumped forward again, but the boys held him back. "You absolute heartless machine. The whole thing was an act. . . You blew me up so I wouldn't be around to figure it out. . . I almost died."

"You're immortal," Babbage said weakly.

"These boys *aren't*, and if anything had gone even an infinitesimally tiny bit wrong, someone would be *dead*." Maestro lunged again, but the boys held him back. He looked at them and saw there wasn't a chance they would release him. "Sod this." He spat. He was spitting a lot, but that really seemed to suit his mood.

He grew very still, and he muttered under his breath. A warm tingle played across Danny's hands, and then orange electricity crackled in Maestro's eyes. The air sucked into Maestro's body and the boys stumbled toward him a bit with the force of it, all of them letting go reflexively.

A tight sphere of swirling orange gas appeared in front of Maestro's stomach then shot forward across the room and slammed Babbage squarely in the chest, carrying him across the floor and spreading across his body, pinning him to the wall, arms and legs splayed out at his sides.

He hit the wall with a low grunt. The energy held him there, a few inches off the floor, his head tight against the wall.

"We didn't use the information to get the database until billions of people were in peril." Babbage had to fight to speak. "This wasn't a whim."

Maestro regarded him coldly.

The boys huddled together. Where would this confrontation lead? It was like watching parents argue, except that one was a highly advanced robot and the other seemed to be some kind of powerful, time-traveling space witch.

"And I'm sure you'll destroy the database as soon as the crisis has been averted," Maestro remarked dryly.

Babbage's eyes dropped to the floor again.

"I thought so." Maestro stood less than a foot from the EL. "You. aren't. ready. for. it." He scoffed loudly and turned in an angry circle waving his hands. "*That's* why you wouldn't tell me the truth."

He seemed so angry. Cripes, he was spooky. He stopped in front of Babbage.

"You *knew* I wouldn't let the Shifters get the database because you know they aren't ready for it, that they'd abuse the knowledge, and you prove her right with this whole lousy scheme."

They stood nose to nose.

"Let *me* have the database," Maestro suggested quietly. "I'll find the data you need and destroy the rest of it."

"What makes you think *you're* ready. . ." The smug superiority in Babbage's tone bled off and died. Too late.

"I knew them when they traveled the universe." Maestro's voice was so, so soft. "I could have taken it then. I didn't. Why would I care about it, now?" He backed up and shoved his hands into his pockets. "Someone who looks down his nose at me and thinks I'm less of a person because I'm a member of a race that's just one step from swinging in the trees. . . You're not ready for this kind of tech." He shrugged. "I can't let you do this. Let me find it for you."

"Seventy-five *billion* souls."

"You have my terms," Maestro said. "Let me do it."

"I understand that you will hate me, and I am sorry for that. . . and for deceiving you." Babbage found each of the boys with his eyes, which were the only part of his body he could move. "I did everything I could to ensure your safety to the absolute best of my ability given the circumstances." Tears dribbled down his cheeks. "You are the best examples of your species I have met." He singled out Danny, who had been there from the beginning, after all. "Danny Decker. . . If you were not from a protected planet, I would recommend you for training in the Galactic Police." He closed his eyes. "Goodbye."

He vanished.

"Heartless dratting. . ." Maestro glanced at the boys and seemed to leave off the curses for their sake.

Bobby's pronouncement was rather stronger.

Torch matched him curse for curse.

"Heartless," Maestro repeated in a completely different voice.

Soft and surprised. The others stopped cursing and turned to him.

"She said they weren't ready because they didn't have enough *heart*. . ." Maestro fell quiet. He shook his head and then looked up and seemed to notice the boys staring at him. "I wonder if she knew all along."

"You think she did?" TJ glanced at the open door.

Maestro shook his head. "Doesn't change a thing."

Danny couldn't speak or move.

His friend, the engineered life form in the robot body who had saved his life on several occasions, had betrayed them all, and had deceived him from word one.

Bobby stood tall, watching Danny with his overprotective stare. He had to wonder how Danny was coping. He always felt Danny took too much on his shoulders and probably wished he'd let his big brother help him carry the load.

TJ had to be frantically trying to devise a way to save the planets and keep the tech away from anyone who might find a way to misuse it. While he kept so quiet Danny sometimes overlooked him, TJ was almost the brightest of the bunch.

Torch was probably hungry and wondering why there was a problem. Seventy-five billion people dying was bad. They had to stop that, but he'd tell himself that his friends needed to work through the angst and emotional stuff. He always waited for them to work through it and could be patient, since everyone always came around to his way of thinking in the end. One hand drifted to his stomach. Yep, he was hungry.

Maestro. . . Maestro stood in the middle of the room with his hands on the back of his head, fingers laced, elbows sticking out on either side. He stared at the floor. He remained like that for a while.

What was going on in his head? Danny shivered. . . no. . . he didn't want to know that. . . would never wish to be inside someone's head ever again. Babbage had been in his head. . . and Danny would never know how much influence the EL had taken.

Maestro clapped his hands and rubbed them vigorously.

"All-righty then." He waved the boys into a tight circle and dropped an arm around Danny's shoulders, pulling him close. "This one thinks too much." He ruffled Danny's hair. "Reminds me a little bit of me. . . without all the immortality and time travel." He grabbed Torch with his free arm and pulled him close as well. He looked all of them squarely in the eyes. "Normally, I would handle this by myself and make you find a quiet room where you'd wait until Babbage returned to take you back to Earth." Before any of the boys objected, he waved them to silence. "I don't have that luxury. Besides which, trying to keep you safe has worked oh-so-well so far. I have a plan that is extremely reckless, ridiculously dangerous, and will only work if absolutely nothing goes wrong, something that is about as likely as Torch winning a spelling bee."

The boys managed to smile.

Maestro outlined what they would attempt. And he was right: it was both reckless and dangerous and fraught with opportunities for failure.

He made lots of eye contact and assured the boys he was giving them all the info he could, that he was completely honest, and that he really hated his own plan.

After all of that, he finished with: "I make a habit of going it alone and underestimating those around me. I may be older than you, but I'm just as human. If I send you home, you'll always wonder what could have happened here, and you'll hate me for it. In most of human history, by now you'd have picked out spouses and been in battle to protect your family. This decision is yours, but if you decide to go and you die or lose an arm. . . it is your decision. I may also make you record a video to that effect. However, if we fail and trillions of people die, you are *not* allowed to carry any of that blame. That will be on me. All of it." He put a hand in the middle. "Who's in?"

All four boys thrust their hands in the middle before he even finished saying it.

"Go team."

Food for Thought

The sun rose without pomp or circumstance. It had done its job billions of times before anyone existed to remark on its performance, and it wouldn't care much about anyone's opinion, anyway, being a simple ball of superheated plasma.

Forty giant alien insects stood in formation on a white sand beach facing away from the ocean and the sunrise. The amazing un-Earthly colors cast by the sun across an accumulation of water vapor and dust otherwise known as fluffy clouds were most likely lost on them by virtue of the fact that they had seen the sun rise on dozens of planets.

Four of the five humans who stood facing them had not.

Danny struggled to avoid staring gape-jawed at the celestial light show. He stood with Bobby to the left of Maestro. Torch and TJ stood to their leader's right. The boys kept quiet, hands hanging at their sides. Only Maestro could handle the negotiations, so Danny tried to keep from scratching anything.

Maestro had been very emphatic that they needed to keep their hands visible at all times, but just standing there with a group of giant fleas made Danny itch. The bugs stood from six to eight feet tall and were similar to Terran fleas, except for the size, the armor plating, and the fact that they rose up on four legs and used their front two appendages to hold very large weapons, albeit awkwardly.

According to Maestro, the entire species had been genetically engineered to kill. They didn't need fine motor skills, just something to hold a gun and a way to press a trigger. They also differed from Terran fleas in that their exoskeletons had been removed and replaced with a lightweight, almost impenetrable metal plating. . . which went a long way to explaining their bad temper. That had to hurt.

One of the bugs stepped forward and regarded the humans. Were they the same leader as the bug who had given orders during the attack?

"Why do you speak to us, Food?" they asked.

They called themselves Hunters and called every other species "Food" for obvious reasons. Although their face was a coppery metal and had eight eyes, the leader also had two larger eyes kind of where Danny was used to seeing them on humans, so he sort of could think of them as having a normal face. For a bug, their eyes radiated intelligence.

"We have information that will be useful to you," Maestro explained. "Without it, *you* will become food."

A nervous chittering broke out among the group behind the leader.

Even getting that far had been something of a miracle. Bearing in mind that Danny and his friends had managed to kill over thirty of this leader's warriors, the fact that they were willing to parley with the humans had surprised Maestro.

When Torch had pointed out that they *had* only been defending themselves, Maestro had countered that *they* were alive, and the *bugs* were dead. The finer details of a skirmish tended to be lost on the side with the greatest casualties.

Apparently, the leader was willing to talk to them because, as Maestro put it, the Hunters respected chutzpah. Requesting an audience under the circumstances showed chutzpah of interstellar proportions. The leader had been intrigued.

Without taking their eyes off Maestro, they waved an appendage vaguely and all noise immediately ceased.

"Why did you grant us rights of discovery without a battle?" The leader faced Maestro. "Are you that weak? Are you afraid of us?"

Danny tried to avoid looking at their mandibles while they spoke because they didn't sync with the words. Maestro had injected the boys with what he had called "translator microbes," bizarre microorganisms transferred from Maestro to each boy with a handshake and a verbal command.

Somehow, the microbes took what any extraterrestrial said and changed it into English. Maestro had promised to explain how it worked when they had a quiet moment, but the general upshot was that speaking with an unknown species resembled watching a badly dubbed foreign film. Their mouth and their words moved at different speeds.

"Our intention on visiting this world was to provide my larvae with a rite of passage." Maestro had explained that all humans looked alike to other species, so the easiest plan was to tell the Hunters that the four boys were his progeny. "We leave them on a deserted planet and return a month later. Those still alive are allowed to mate."

"An admirable rite." The leader strode closer to Danny and Bobby, their great legs proportionately thicker than on Terran fleas. They also smelled bad, like rotten food. "You said your intention." They fixed Danny with a steady gaze. "What happened?"

Danny forced his eyes to meet the leader's without flinching or looking away. Any show of weakness would cause the leader to start picking out condiments.

"My fifth companion was a Shifter." Maestro's words caused another burst of skittering from the assembled Hunters. "They deceived us."

"That's what they do." Without taking their eyes off Danny, the leader laughed. What the heck would that sound like without the translation? "You were foolish to ally yourself with them."

Hunters, like many species, had both male and female sexes to facilitate procreation. However, they didn't have any way to distinguish between genders in their language. There was no "he" or "she." They just had "they."

"Recently, one of your astronomers was quite surprised to find this planet during a general survey, weren't they?" Maestro had explained his suspicions to Danny earlier. "And then they suggested you come here."

The leader stopped dead in their tracks.

"Your science officer suggested a holding pattern and then suddenly recommended planetfall." Maestro remained the epitome of cool. "Right before you met us."

The leader refrained from comment.

"The Shifters have a spy in your ranks," Maestro explained. "It's the only way to explain the coincidence of your locating this world and transporting down just minutes after we landed. They maneuvered you into position and then played you like pawns at exactly the right moment."

The leader appeared to consider Maestro's words then raised a claw to their mouth. "Shoot the science officer."

Laser fire sounded over the com, along with a brief, truncated scream.

Holy spit!

"You should know that won't kill a Shifter," Maestro said.

"No. . . but it will slow them down and hurt tremendously." The leader tilted their head back and forth, as though looking at Maestro through different eyes. "Why did they do this?"

"They brought us here to steal the Johnny Appleseeds' database and used you as a distraction."

How would *that* translate? Whatever the translation, it brought a loud chittering from the flea circus. The leader faced down their troops, who immediately fell silent but continued subtle fidgety movements.

"The database was erased." The leader's avoidance of Maestro's gaze had to be a power play.

"They're a Shifter EL," Maestro said. "They uploaded the database before deletion."

The crowd vibrated but refrained from comment.

"I propose you take us with you," Maestro said, "and we will find the Shifter EL together,"

"*I* propose we will take you with us," the leader said, "and we will eat you." The leader turned to Maestro for the first time. "I like that proposal better. I don't believe I have tasted your species of mammal." Its eyes swept the humans. "You *are* mammals, I expect?"

Maestro nodded.

"All bipeds look alike to me." Even with a copper carapace, the Hunter managed to shrug. They glanced over their shoulder at their troops. "Especially after an hour of tenderizing."

The troops chuckled and did the insect equivalent of elbowing each other in the ribs at what they seemed to find extreme wit.

Danny avoided rolling his eyes, but only barely.

"They're a Shifter EL." Maestro smiled. "I know where they went. You do not. You have a ship. We do not. You can't force me to tell you anything while we are on the planet, and you will not be *able* to force me to tell you anything off the planet." His words seemed oddly stilted. Some sort of linguistic protocol had to be involved. Were the translators good enough to also translate the *way* he spoke?

"And why, Food, do you believe you would be able to resist us?" The Hunter rushed close to Maestro.

Danny almost retched at the smell of rancid meat.

"I have travelled with Hunters before." Maestro maintained the height of cool, calm, *and* collected. His level of control was astounding. "I am still here. I was never food."

The Hunter turned its head to one side. Danny read the gesture as a question mark.

"Yummy." Maestro licked and smacked his lips loudly.

Torch covered his mouth and coughed into the hand, likely stifling a laugh. After all, there was something inherently humorous about a giant bug talking with a voice like James Bond, even under the circumstances, and Torch was never one to worry about circumstances.

One Hunter stepped out of their line with a weapon aimed at the humans, apparently offended by Torch's insolence.

"Cannon fodder!" The leader turned to the soldier. "Reprimand yourself for breaking ranks!"

Without hesitation, the bug pointed their rifle at its own head and pulled the trigger. An explosion of goo covered the bug behind Corporal Cannon Fodder.

Holy spit! It had happened so fast, Danny could barely believe it had happened at all, except for the insect corpse twitching on the sand and the gore splattered across several of their comrades.

The Hunter leader, however, laughed uproariously.

"I like you, Tilda-food." They chortled. Some sort of cleaner bug appeared from behind the others to mop up the mess of the fallen warrior. "I may even wait until we recover the database to eat you."

The cleaner was smaller than the others and more delicately armored. They moved with swift efficiency, and only the boys watched their progress while they cleaned up the mess. They dragged the body with far more ease than should have been possible, considering the relative sizes of the creatures. They paused and adjusted a small device on the dead soldier's side then gave the corpse another tug. Apparently satisfied, they carried their burden away with even less effort. Gravity control?

"A wise decision," Maestro said, drawing Danny back to the conversation. "We will visit several worlds before I give you the correct coordinates. You won't know when we are in the correct system until we are there. Until then we have the same objective. After that, we will see who is Hunter... and who is Food."

"I can see you have indeed spent time with Hunters, Tilda-food." The leader wandered closer to Torch and TJ.

They stared directly ahead, their courage impressive.

"But there is one problem with your plan," the leader continued. "Well, one problem apart from what sort of sauce goes best with your flesh."

"And that is?" Maestro asked.

"If it's a Shifter vessel then it has a quantum drive and is no doubt already at its destination." The leader stared at Maestro. "What point pursuit?"

"I know for a fact," Maestro said, "that this *particular* vessel is lacking a vital component of its quantum drive. The EL will need to call in another ship to meet them and will need to navigate out of the nebula on standard drive before they can transmit any kind of distress call. I'm currently tracking their progress with my Doohickey."

"Vital component?" The leader seemed to regard Maestro with bemusement.

Maestro pulled an ordinary Ziploc baggy from his coat pocket. The bag held water and what looked like a blob of purple jelly.

Uproarious laughter filled the plaza from the Hunter soldiers, and the leader didn't halt the mirth this time. They laughed harder than the rest.

"You have Glstakjerdik of vblanticfog, Tilda-food," they shouted.

The boys sort of looked at one another and shrugged a lot.

"I assume there really isn't a way to translate that part," Danny whispered out one corner of his mouth. What in the heck was going on?

"I'm guessing 'balls of steel' would work." Bobby risked a sidelong glance at his brother. "Tilda-food?"

"Tilda is a Greek letter used to indicate an opposite," Danny said. "Tilda-food would be 'Not-food.' Maestro told them he—"

"Yeah... yeah... got it." Bobby faced forward again as the tumult subsided. "Uber-geek."

"Jealous."

"Try tilda-jealous."

Danny smiled in spite of the situation. If only he could get a better look at the goo in Maestro's baggy. What part of the quantum drive was *that*, and what was so gutsy about stealing that particular component? Some sort of ice seemed to have broken though.

Maestro stood easier.

Danny, however, remained at attention, the memory of one bug's suicide fresh in his mind. His brother and friends did the same.

"I do not know your species, Tilda-food." The Hunter leader moved closer to their own troops again. "What is your planet?"

"My world is still protected so I may not tell you." Maestro shot a look at both sets of boys to tell them to stay where they were. "I left my world two hundred years from now and traveled the galaxy for eons. My nests are legion."

Whatcha? Danny filed *that* one away for future questions.

"Time traveler?" That seemed to tell the leader something it didn't tell Danny. "If others of your world are like you in *this* timeline, I relish the moment they enter the galactic buffet. I am certain they will be delicious." Chitter. "You may enter the nest. We will not eat you until we find the Shifter." They raised an appendage. "Transport."

Danny felt his body torn apart and vertigo hit him as his eyes adjusted to the dimmer light of the bugs' vessel that they called their nest. Wow. Massively lame transport.

Fortunately, Maestro had warned the boys about bug vessels. The stench was appalling. Danny held his breath for several seconds to adjust. Vomiting would be a huge display of weakness.

"These things are related to dung beetles, boys," Maestro had explained. "Can you guess how dung beetles translate the phrase, 'Stop and smell the roses'?" He hadn't been exaggerating.

Everything the bugs owned was stolen tech. Their limbs didn't really lend themselves to a technologically advanced civilization. After they'd been genetically altered as warrior slaves, they decided that their masters were weak and inferior, so they overcame them and forced them to modify all the tech so the bugs could use it.

Fortunately for the rest of the galaxy, their masters' tech hadn't been all that great to begin with and, in the centuries since then, the bugs hadn't advanced much. They just weren't built for it.

The nest had large hallways, but black vines and goo covered nearly every inch, so they seemed claustrophobic. Bugs skittered along corridors and across walls and ceilings with equal ease.

Danny filed that information with a tag saying, *Always look up when running away from bugs.* The dozens of Hunters who skittered past didn't seem in the least interested. Apparently, meeting new species was old hat here.

Danny tried not to stare at everything they passed. No sense broadcasting "tourist," but he really *wanted* to see everything. His eyes were sponges soaking it all in.

The bugs took them to a "resting area" where they could "make themselves comfortable" while the ship headed to the first set of coordinates provided by Maestro. They were encouraged to explore the ship if they desired, as long as they made certain to avoid the restricted areas.

"How will we know which areas are restricted?" Torch had asked, likely curious to engage in some illicit exploring.

Maestro stared at him, disdain written across his face like a teenager's graffiti.

"Someone will eat us," Torch ventured after a moment.

Maestro nodded.

"Let's not move around a lot," Torch said.

"Good idea."

"Swell digs." Torch paced the empty cell.

"Chances are their own quarters aren't a lot different." Maestro folded his arms and leaned against a relatively dry piece of wall. "Furniture is a biped thing. Most species with more than two legs never use it. . . and the armor plating makes a bed sort of pointless."

"And where do you suppose one would find the 'facilities?'" Torch turned a circle in the middle of room. "They must have some kind of bathroom."

Without comment, Maestro pointed at a hole set in the floor in one corner of the room.

Torch glanced from the hole to Maestro and back again. He stepped over to it and looked down. . . then took a few steps back, one hand over his mouth and nose.

"*Madre de Dios*, I can't believe there's something that smells worse than their general air freshener." Torch moved toward Maestro. "Seriously? A hole in the floor? Are we in the Dark Ages?"

"The Dark Ages were worse," Maestro insisted. "Trust me."

"No." Torch folded his arms. "I'm not using a hole in the floor."

"Wow. . . if you're that shy," Maestro said, "I promise not to look as long as you promise to aim carefully."

"For what I have to do, aiming isn't really a consideration." Torch stared at the hole.

"Oh, don't be such a wuss." Maestro rolled his eyes.

Danny could tell he enjoyed Torch's discomfort. Truth be told, Danny did, too. Since when did anything embarrass Torch?

"I am *not* squatting over a hole with you standing here," Torch insisted.

"Suit yourself." Maestro shrugged.

"Okay. . ." Torch peered suspiciously at the hole. "You never see crap like this in the movies. Seriously lame."

TJ snickered. So did Bobby.

"Okay. . ." Torch seemed to realize his poor choice in words. "Ha, ha. . . Why don't you guys just step out for a few minutes and let a man have some privacy?"

The door opened.

"We have arrived at the first coordinates." A soldier entered the room. "You will now give our leader the next set."

"Here we go, gentlemen." Maestro clapped his hands and rubbed them together.

They returned to the bridge. The leader stared at the viewscreen which was an old school flatscreen built into the wall.

"Well, Tilda-food?" the leader asked. "Where next?"

The screen showed the same amazing nebula, all done in blues and greens and oranges.

"Nope," Maestro said, "we're here. Didn't see the point in any more traveling."

Laughter.

"You are the best comedian I have ever eaten, Tilda-food." The leader laughed. "The pre-dinner entertainment is most appreciated."

"I'll upload the exact coordinates. Get me close enough to teleport and claim the database." Maestro held out his Doohickey.

"I am not comfortable having you interface our equipment with Shifter tech." The leader looked over one... shoulder, carapace-thingy at him.

"The coordinates are on the screen." Maestro turned the device around and held it out once more. "Your navigator can simply read them."

Silence filled the bridge.

"You would hand over your Doohickey?" The leader touched its appendages together.

"It's tuned to me." Maestro waggled it and stepped closer to the navigator, who glanced from him to the leader, his antennae waving. Did that mean excitement? "No one can use it except those I allow. Anyone else who tries will end up as a roast."

The leader nodded at the navigator, who took the Doohickey and entered the data into a screen in the wall.

"Besides, Hunter, I trust you," Maestro said. "You have no reason to betray me. This thing's an abacus compared to the database we're after."

How would "abacus" translate into the Hunter language?

"And that's a Shifter craft with a Shifter EL driving it," Maestro continued without mentioning that the craft in question was nearly an antique. "You can't beat them. I can get on board and surprise them because they think I'm their friend..." He held his hand out to the navigator, who passed the Doohickey back reluctantly.

"Plus," Maestro concluded, "I have *this*." He waggled the device.

The navigator looked at the leader, who waved a limb vaguely. The navigator shifted back to their controls and the viewscreen showed that they moved now, turning.

Was that the actual sensation of a shift in the floor? Torch glanced over, and Danny knew they thought the same thing: *if we can feel that, I'd hate to be in this crate during a battle.*

"Why is your Doohickey better than the Shifter's?" the leader demanded.

"Because mine is from two hundred years in the future."

"You will leave the larvae with us." The leader waved at the boys.

Danny had expected that. It was part of Maestro's plan.

"I need these two with me." The time traveler stood behind TJ and Torch. "I am not *so* arrogant that I think I can defeat the EL alone. But you can keep the other two until I return." He glanced at Danny. "I expect to find them in fit condition."

A quiet, tense moment passed. The leader approached Maestro and examined the boys under his arms. They then scrutinized Danny and Bobby.

"You will take these two," they declared, waving at Danny and his brother. "This is not negotiable."

He and Maestro bickered about the details, but Danny tuned it out. He didn't want to react to anything they said.

Before contacting the bugs, Maestro had explained that they would need to leave two of the boys as hostages. He needed Danny with him because he had the closest relationship with Babbage and would have the highest chance of distracting him. He'd spoken completely honestly about the dangers involved with both sides of the plan, and Bobby had insisted that wherever Danny went, he went, too.

Torch and TJ had been nervous but had accepted the necessity of their role. The fact that Maestro didn't mince words or try to make it seem safe meant a lot. It was scarier this way but somehow easier, too. At least the boys had the truth.

Maestro had explained that he would *pretend* to want Torch and TJ. Knowing the bugs, that was the best way to get them to insist on Danny and Bobby accompanying him on his mission.

Understanding that they were all on board with their roles in the mission didn't make Danny feel any better about leaving his best friends in the hands of the evil, alien insects whose only word for other species was Food.

A small dot appeared in one corner of the viewscreen. As it grew and moved into the center, Danny recognized the familiar shape of the Galactic Police vessel.

A soft chittering greeted the image, but the sound was very brief. Apparently, the bridge crew had better discipline than the soldiers. Were they all called Cannon Fodder as well? Had Danny been in charge of the translator microbes, he'd have translated the bugs' title as "Red Shirt."

A change in the leader's tone drew Danny's attention. Was that a note of sincerity? "I have to ask. . . why would you possibly give me the database anyway?"

Maestro didn't hesitate. "I come from a protected world. I do not fear that your kind would come after my planet because of the repercussions. . . But I do not trust the Shifters, and this EL stranded me and my larvae on a planet on the opposite side of the galaxy. I would see them punished."

A silence stretched out while the leader considered Maestro's words. They had to suspect the humans of some vast deception, that Maestro would return to the Galactic Police ship, rejoin with the EL, and blast the bugs' nest out of the sky.

Bugs were not known for trusting or being trustworthy.

The silence drew out to almost a minute.

Abruptly, the leader turned its back to Maestro as if to show they did not consider this Tilda-food a threat. "Fine. Go get the database, bring it to me, then I will feast on you and all four of your larvae."

Without hesitation, Maestro said, "As you wish. Initiate teleport."

The ship blurred and spun. Poof.

When Danny opened his eyes, he stood in the medical center of the Police vessel with Maestro and Bobby nearby. Danny closed his eyes again. Please let Torch and TJ live through this adventure.

Before meeting with the bugs, Maestro had insisted the boys say their goodbyes because any sign of affection would be viewed with contempt by the bugs. Big hugs had been handed all around at the time, with lots of promises to see each other again soon.

With all of that. . . Danny still hated not saying goodbye to his best friends. They'd been hauled into this drama because they'd waited outside his bedroom window for hours on the off-chance they could visit him and offer comfort on the deaths of Danny's parents.

Friends like that were rare.

TJ Sings *La Bamba*

Holy crap, thought Torch. *That was sudden.* He'd been prepared for his friends' departure and knew there wouldn't be any lengthy goodbyes, but, well, he'd thought someone would have at least said, "So long guys. Try not to get yourselves killed."

As soon as Maestro and the others teleported away, the bugs seemed to lose interest in TJ and him. The leader turned to the viewscreen, and the bridge crew went back to doing bridge crew stuff.

Torch glanced at his friend, who sort of shrugged and briefly raised an eyebrow.

Torch shrugged back, not exactly sure how to play it. Maestro had won over the bug leader with his carefree bravado thing, but would that work for someone who was supposed to be a subordinate? And could he pull it off?

He took a deep breath. He wasn't sure what he would say, but if he took a deep breath and opened his mouth something was bound to come out and that would be better than just standing around feeling stupid.

So when the bug leader turned to look at them at long last, Torch had his chest puffed up and his mouth open like a baby bird.

"The Food looks hungry," the Hunter barked. "Someone take them to quarters and fatten them up. Mammals get stringy and tough if you don't keep them fed." Then they turned away. "Scan the vessel again. Preliminary scans were laughable. What the light is happening over there?"

Two bugs gestured rudely toward the hallway.

"I want to know if they power up weapons," the leader snapped, "and if someone doesn't get me that scan, we'll be eating more than mammal today!"

Torch hesitated, hoping for more information, but a rifle in the back forced him forward. "Hey dude, we're guests, not prisoners, right?"

The guards exchanged a puzzled look.

TJ bumped Torch's arm. "I'm guessing they use the same word for both. Tomato, tomahto, you know?"

"So?" What the heck did that even mean?

"So as far as they're concerned you just asked if we're prisoners or prisoners," TJ explained, "hence the puzzled look."

Torch grimaced. "Who says 'hence' in actual conversation?"

"You're teasing me for being smarter than you?" TJ raised an eyebrow. "I'll remember that the next time you ask me to do your math homework."

Torch punched his friend in the arm. "Let's just hope we have a chance to *do* math homework again." He smacked himself in the forehead. "Holy crap. . . Did I just say that?"

"Yep. . . and I've already filed it away for future use."

"Crap."

The bugs brought them to a cell similar to the one they'd occupied earlier. . . or maybe it was the same one. Hard to tell. Four walls and a hole in the floor.

Torch shook his head.

He *really* needed to use the "facilities," but could he even do it with someone else in the room?

Well, TJ would just have to step out for a minute—

The door slammed shut.

"Hey!" Torch banged on it, but it didn't open. He pounded it harder. "Hey!"

Nothing.

"I guess that answers your tomato/tamahto question." TJ lowered himself into a crouch in the middle of the room.

The walls oozed.

Torch hung his head. The hole in the floor was a horrible, vicious enemy.

"*Ese*," TJ said, "If you gotta go, just go. They'll be back soon with food, I hope, and I doubt any of this is going to take long. You may not have another chance."

Torch gave him his most withering expression.

TJ crouched there, with his elbows on his knees and his chin in his hands. He shook his head and turned his back to Torch. He sang loudly in Spanish.

Torch didn't recognize the tune or understand any of the lyrics.

Dang it. This was probably as good as it would get.

With a sigh of resignation, Torch undid his buckle and moved closer to the hole. At least TJ wouldn't be able to smell anything he did. He stopped. How the heck did he even do this?

TJ kept singing.

"Dang it." Torch ended up having to remove his pants and shorts before squatting over the hole. He was afraid of. . . well, there was just general, overall fear involved. "*Ese*, you can't tell *anyone* I did this with you in the room."

TJ stopped singing. "I have eight brothers and sisters. This is *nothing* unusual for me."

"You are *so* Mexican." Torch closed his eyes to pretend he was alone in the room.

TJ chuckled. "Just because your ancestors were conquered by the Spanish a lot more recently than *mine* doesn't make you better than me, *Papi*."

"Well. . . in here at least. . . I *can* say my crap doesn't stink."

TJ chuckled again.

"*Ese*. . . what happened to the singing?"

TJ sang *La Bamba*.

After a few minutes, Torch realized he'd forgotten one very important part of the bathroom process and cursed loudly, only to be surprised by something soft hitting his face. It bounced off his nose and his knee then tumbled toward the hole over which he squatted.

He grabbed at it, fumbled, bounced it once or twice, and then snatched it a second before it disappeared forever into the smelly darkness. A pack of Kleenex.

Awesome! Ah, crap. Maybe not. "Tell me you managed to hit me over your shoulder by aiming at the sound of my voice."

"*Si, ese. Totalmente.*" Then TJ resumed his song.

Cripes. Torch had known TJ for years and they'd been in locker rooms together. . . but there were some boundaries Torch just hadn't wanted to cross with *anyone*. Ever. This was worse than two slugs to the chest. Way worse.

As he did up his buckle, he said, "Okay, *ese*. . . this. never. happened."

"Whatever you say." TJ rose to his feet with a bemused expression. "But you do make the funniest faces—"

No way! Torch launched himself. "I am so going to kill you."

He held TJ in a headlock when the door slid open.

The boys froze as two bugs entered the room.

"Are you sparring or mating?" One set down a tray of food.

Torch looked down at TJ's face. "Er. . . Sparring?" He released his friend and they both straightened up.

The bugs made that chittering sound that seemed to mean some kind of excitement. "Very good, then we assume you won't mind if we join you." They moved quickly into the room and squared off opposite the boys.

"Any chance it's not too late to change my answer?" Torch asked. How could they possibly compete with that much metal-plated evil?

The bugs crept closer without a word, and Torch and TJ circled. Was there any way to avoid a fight with giant, evil alien bugs who were genetically engineered to kill?

"Tilda-food is going to be pissed if you hurt us, you know," Torch snapped.

They chittered.

Dang. Wrong approach. It sounded whiny. What about—

The bugs leapt.

Employing their experience in laser tag, the boys dashed forward, separating the bugs and getting their own backs together.

Did laser tag have jack-all to do with hand-to-hand combat? That was much less familiar.

TJ and Torch dodged a bit, circling with their backs together, but when the bug facing Torch came in close, he screamed at the top of his lungs, spun, and kicked it squarely in the thorax... which really, *really* hurt his whole leg. His scream continued at a completely different pitch.

The bug grabbed his leg, picked him up off the floor, and tossed him a few feet away, effectively separating him from TJ.

"How do we hurt giant metal bugs?" TJ said from somewhere that Torch couldn't see what was happening to him.

"We bleed all over them and hope they rust?" Torch shouted at the top of his lungs and rushed his opponent, waving his arms and spinning and kicking. Hopefully, he could startle it with his bravado.

Nope. The bug just grabbed him around the waist and threw him to the floor. His head hit solidly, and the room wavered and went dark for a moment. Crap.

As his opponent descended for another attack, Torch rolled away... and bumped solidly into the huge back legs of the other bug. Rather than stumbling over him, this bug just kicked him away.

But wait... TJ dangled upside down by one leg.

Holy crap. Torch had to save him.

He slid toward his opponent's outstretched and clicking claws. Using his break-dancing skills, he turned the slide into a back spin and kicked out at the bug's face. By some miracle, he managed to connect with one of its primary eyes. Score!

The bug squealed and smacked Torch away. He rolled several times and smashed against a wall. The bug he'd kicked was down one eye. It had burst with Torch's kick and oozed blood.

The bug flailed a giant claw at their face.

"The eyes! Go for the eyes!" Torch pushed away from the wall, pulled off a shoe, and aimed for the bug's other big eye. He dove into a roll and came up on one knee much closer to his opponent, pulling off his other shoe.

The big bug crawled away from Torch and flailed.

"Ya big baby," Torch yelled. "Some terrifying thing you are."

His first shoe missed completely, but his second hit the thing in the face, doing no real damage but startling them.

The other bug moved closer to their comrade and roared while they lifted TJ higher. Still suspended by one leg, Torch's friend flailed, grabbing at anything he might hurt or use to pull himself upright. "If I can get an antennae. . . that might hurt it."

Torch recovered his shoes and dove in for a second wave of attacks. The first shoe hit a minor eye on his own opponent, bringing a high-pitched squeal that the microbes didn't bother to translate. He twisted and launched his second shoe at TJ's attacker.

Yes! He nailed one of their antennae!

The bug twitched hard.

Cra-ack! The sound would haunt Torch's nightmares for years, a horrible sound like a dry branch snapping in half.

A deep low scream poured off TJ. He landed with a dull thud and screamed again. He writhed in pain, but that seemed to make it worse. He lay still and pounded the floor with his fists, cursing again and again.

The bug flailed at their antennae and made bad noises of their own.

Torch leapt to TJ's side. Dear God, how seriously was he hurt?

TJ's opponent moved to *their* fallen comrade.

Much to Torch's surprise, TJ screamed in anger. "You guys are so-o-o screwed when your boss hears about this!" He flailed an arm obviously meant for Torch to help him sit up, which he did. Ah crap, that had to hurt even more. "Tilda-food told you not to damage us," TJ yelled, "and he's gonna *kill* you when he comes back."

Following TJ's example, Torch chimed in. "Yeah. . . if you think he's going to give your leader that database after *this*, you're stupid."

TJ trembled in Torch's arms. His aggression had to be bravado, the only thing he could think to do to keep from crying and passing out from the pain. Sweat covered his face. He was so pale.

Neither of the bugs spoke. In fact, they didn't even look at the humans.

Torch followed their gaze to the open doorway where the Hunter leader regarded the scene, flanked by two guards with guns at the ready.

Ah, crap.

"What's going on?" the leader asked calmly.

"I'll tell you what's happening." TJ kept up his barrage. "Your cannon fodder just broke my leg. They attacked us. . . and they broke my leg. . . and Tilda-food is going to go *insane* when he finds out."

"How many times do I have to tell you not to play with your food, Cannon Fodder?" The leader turned to the two bugs, one of whom bled freely from its ruined eyes.

The bugs said nothing.

"If I had authorized a food fight," the leader added in quiet, calm tones, "I would have been here to observe it myself."

"I apologize, leader," one bug said.

"Shall I discipline myself?" the other asked.

The leader moved closer to the boys, metal legs clacking on the deck plating.

TJ pushed himself away from Torch and up against the wall. He had to be hiding the fact that he couldn't even sit up without help. He probably didn't want to show any kind of weakness whatsoever.

TJ's leg was bent at entirely the wrong angle. Oh crap! Even though his pants were black, they were obviously soaked in blood.

Torch couldn't take his eyes away from the sight of TJ's ruined leg and the words of TJ's ongoing tirade washed over him unheard. The leg had swollen and was constricted by his pants. If something didn't happen soon, TJ would bleed to death.

No. That couldn't happen.

"Leader," Torch said, but he barely managed a soft croak.

Everyone ignored him.

Torch rose—carefully leaning TJ against the wall. Okay, blast it, how would Maestro do it?

"Leader," Torch barked. "You want your entire nest eaten in a taco?"

That got their attention. The various underlings chittered.

The leader turned their head, waiting.

"If Tilda-food's larva isn't given medical attention immediately," Torch shouted, "he will die, and then maybe our father will change his mind about his loyalties. Maybe the Shifter in his Galactic Police cruiser will seem like less of an enemy than the Hunter on this. . ." Torch glanced around and rolled his eyes. ". . .*fine vessel* who allowed his larva to die. Doohickey?"

He was on a roll. *Tia Anita*, he prayed, *please let me not mess this up by taking it one step too far.*

"Yes, Torch?" the Doohickey asked.

"Lights out."

The lights went out. The bugs chittered.

Score!

"Lights on." The lights returned. Torch held out an arm. "We're tagged with trackers that relay our status back to the Shifter ship. We die. . . Tilda-food is the first to know." He picked one of the leader's larger eyes and stared into it without blinking.

A brief, horrific silence filled the room.

Tell my parents I love them, Torch told his Tia Anita.

The leader laughed, which prompted a similar outburst from their entourage. "I *must* learn more about your species." It waved the others to precede it out the door. "I can't *wait* to devour your entire planet." It paused in the doorway. "I will send a medic with a doctor machine. I only hope they can handle your squishy, mammalian physique."

The door closed.

Thank you, Tia Anita. I promise to go to mass if I ever get back to Earth!

TJ burst into hysterical sobs.

Oh crap! Torch dropped down and slid behind him against the wall. The blood loss would make him cold, so Torch wrapped his arms around his friend and pulled him close. And, well, crap, he had to hurt so much.

TJ scrabbled at Torch's arms and snuffled loudly as if trying his level best to stop crying. Not that it worked.

"I'm sorry, *ese*," TJ sobbed. "I can't. . . I can't hold it together, anymore. It hurts so freakin' much."

It should be noted that, for the next several pages, the expletives have been deleted for more sensitive readers.

"Don't hold back, *ese*. I'm not going to eat you." Torch held him tighter. He couldn't stop the tears pouring down his own face.

"I thought. . . That's what I thought." A horrible sob erupted from TJ's throat. He turned as much as he could and fisted Torch's shirt with one hand. "I knew if they saw me cry, they'd eat me." He took a deep breath. "I don't want. . . I just knew. . ."

"I know, *mijo*. I know."

TJ took a few ragged breaths. "Am I going to die?"

"No!" And darn it, Torch would make sure he wasn't lying. "No. . . they're getting a medic, and this place is newer than the Police ship. I took two bullets in the chest, and I'm just as pretty as I ever was. You'll be fine."

"I need you to get my pants off, bro."

Wow. Not something he'd expected to hear; how should he respond?

"*Ese*. . . look at my leg. It's like an overstuffed sausage in there."

He was right.

"Yeah," Torch said, "I think your pants are the only thing keeping you from bleeding out."

"They'll need to cut them off to fix the leg," TJ said. "If they can. . . Torch. . . It's going to hurt ten times worse. . ."

And then TJ would scream bloody murder. And they might eat him.

"I don't think I can hold it together," TJ admitted. "I don't want them to see me scream. . ."

"Gotcha," Torch said quickly. "But cut them off how?"

"You took a knife from the Police cruiser."

Wait. Really? Torch checked his boot. Oh yeah, it had seemed. . .

Well, that would have been handy in the fight!

"Consider them history," Torch said.

But what if they *were* the only thing keeping the leg from bleeding out?

Torch unsheathed a blade he'd grabbed from the Police ship's inventory. He settled TJ on his back and moved over to his friend's leg.

This would suck.

A lot.

"This is going to hurt, Terry," Torch said.

"I know."

"A lot."

"Just do it, man. I'm begging you."

"I'll try to. . . be easy. . ." Torch wiped his face on his sleeve.

"Just do it fast. It's just like pulling off a Band-Aid."

Band-Aid? Seriously?

Torch undid TJ's belt and slid it out of the way as best he could, then pulled the slacks open so he had a place to start the knife.

"Don't slice the trunks, okay?" TJ asked. "I don't want the bugs to see my junk."

Torch took a deep breath and cut into TJ's jeans. Fortunately, the blade was really sharp, so it sliced through the fabric like a hot knife through butter, but halfway down TJ's thigh, the leg was so swollen the knife had no more room to slide.

Torch pulled on the fabric, which made TJ cry out, so he went down to TJ's feet, pulled off his shoe and started slicing up the jeans from the bottom. . . but reached the same impasse before he reached TJ's knee.

Crap! Torch wiped an arm across his face. Stupid sobbing. How the heck could he finish the job without slicing his friend even worse? The leg had swollen so much the fabric was practically a second skin.

"Terry. . . I don't. . ." He cursed.

"It's not your fault. You're. . ." Another spasm of pain cut TJ off.

Wait! How could Torch forget their amazing tech? "Doohickey?"

"Yes, Torch?"

"Can you slice the fabric of someone's pants without cutting his skin?"

"Can you scan the potential client?"

Torch held the Doohickey closer to TJ.

"Sure thing, boss," the device said.

Gracias a Dios!

The Doohickey did its thing, and Torch pulled the jeans away from TJ's legs. As expected, blood poured out once the jeans were cut away, and Torch fought to keep from throwing up. TJ's leg was swollen, purple and black, and bent at a sick angle.

"Doohickey. . . can you show me how to set this thing?" Torch rubbed his hands across his face ignoring the blood on them.

"Yes. . . I can." Was that a statement or a question?

"*Ese?*" Was Torch more afraid that TJ would tell him to do it or that he would say not to do it?

"I'm going to scream like a little kid, ain't I?" TJ grabbed his friend's hand and held it as tight as he could.

Torch nodded.

"Do it. I don't. . . I don't want them to eat me. . ."

"Let's do this, Doohickey." Torch nodded and squeezed TJ's hand.

Under the Doohickey's guidance, Torch rolled up a less bloody chunk of denim to give TJ something to bite down on, then he moved TJ's leg back into position.

TJ screamed bloody murder, and Torch cried so much he had to keep wiping his face to see. How did TJ not pass out? It might be easier if he did. The Doohickey told Torch how to tie sections of the pants around the leg to slow the bleeding. Eventually, he had to pull off his own shirt to make bandages, but the leg seemed to bleed more slowly.

"I'm cold," TJ slurred, and Torch knew how bad things were about to get. He slid back into place behind his friend and chafed his arms to warm them. "What if they see us like this?"

"Screw them," Torch declared. "I need to keep you warm."

TJ was a cool weight against his chest.

"C'mon man, you need to stay with me." Torch pressed his cheek against TJ's. "You can't fall asleep and leave me here without my best friend, okay? You can't do that."

"Best friend?"

Really? How messed up was that?

"Duh?" Torch said. "Who else?"

"I figured Danny was your best friend." TJ managed to chuckle a little, thank God.

Seriously? Wasn't the whole "best friend" thing kinda beside the point at that moment?

But Torch thought it through in less than a second.

"Nah. . . I mean, I'd take a bullet for him. . . two bullets in fact. . ." They both chuckled at the joke, but TJ ended up coughing. "But Danny has Bobby."

"That's his brother. That's different."

The conversation might have been lame, but whatever it took to keep TJ conscious, right?

"Not so much," Torch said. "I mean, if he had two seconds to make a choice, and he could only save one of us, he wouldn't waste time. He'd save Bobby."

"Like I said. . . that's family. . . doesn't mean he's not your best friend."

"I love my brother, *ese*, but I'm not going to stick my neck out for him. If I had to make a snap decision between him and you?" Torch crossed TJ's arms and wrapped his own arms tighter around his friend. "Let's just say my parents would have money for more Christmas presents for me."

TJ laughed and then winced. "Ow, don't make me laugh."

"It hurts?"

"Ow. . . yeah."

"So I shouldn't remind you of the time we were in Spanish class, and you couldn't. . ."

"Dude!" TJ laughed then twitched. "Ow! You are freakin' evil."

"Not as evil as the alien bugs, eh?"

"Where the heck are they?"

Torch sighed. Some sort of power play?

"Doohickey?" he said. "Hijack the ship's intercom, okay?"

"Okay, Torch."

"Hey, Tilda-food, this is your oldest larvae reporting. I'd like to tell you how the Hunters are—"

And the door slid open. A bug hurried in, dragging a complex table of machinery with it.

"You're going to let me interface my Doohickey with your doctor machine." Torch stared directly into the bug's eyes. "And I don't care if you have to throw that crap away when you're done with us because you think I've infected it somehow. You *will* let me interface." He held the Doohickey close to his mouth. "Doohickey, can you program their machine to give him an antibiotic and hit him with enough pain reliever for an elephant without the bugs knowing?"

"This is subterfuge?" the Doohickey asked, matching whisper for whisper.

"Yes." Would that be a problem?

"Sweet."

Maestro must have reprogrammed it specifically for him. Stellar.

"Are you mating or fighting?" The bug with the equipment looked the boys over.

"See?" TJ muttered.

"What is it with you people?" Torch refused to move. "This is a warrior's pose in our culture." He held TJ all the closer. "It lets losers like you know that our fates are twisted together. If my brother dies, *I* will die to avenge his death, killing any idiots who had anything to do with. . . his. . . death." He gave the bug a pointed look to cover his momentary lack of a clue how to continue. "Including you." He pointed. "Loser."

The bug chittered and quickly positioned the doctor machine over TJ's leg.

"Squeeze it as hard as you need to, okay?" Torch grabbed TJ's hand and put his mouth against his friend's ear. "Don't let'em see you sweat."

TJ nodded. He grabbed his denim bit and shoved it into his mouth as the doctor machine started to work.

Space Monkey from 200 Years in Future

Danny, Bobby, and Maestro materialized in the Galactic Police cruiser's infirmary. By the time Danny had sorted out his up from his left, Maestro had already barked orders to the ship's computer. Danny leaned against a table. If only Hunter tech was as good as the Shifters'.

Bobby didn't seem so disoriented.

"You okay?" Maestro asked, hopping up onto a table. "This might take a minute or two."

Danny raised an eyebrow.

"I locked Babbage out of the system completely," Maestro explained. "So he can't make a hologram or use the com system. He'll have to actually run here in person." He crossed his arms and banged his heels against the leg of the table with a grin that belied his supposed age. "Plans on track so far and no one's dead, yet!"

What about TJ and Torch?

"They should be fine." Maestro lost his grin. "This shouldn't take long."

"That word 'should' makes me uncomfortable." Danny shoved his hands in his pockets.

"You'd rather I lied?"

"You know better." Danny shook his whole body to change gears. "Okay. . . that ship was decidedly organic."

"If you mean slimy and disgusting, you got that right." Bobby scoffed.

"Bobby. . . can you stand over there for me?" Maestro pointed at the table next to Danny's.

With a shrug, Bobby moved as requested and leaned against the indicated table.

"Here we go." Maestro clapped and rubbed his hands together. "I've locked Babbage out of all weapons, but he's still freakishly strong. Do not be afraid to use force."

"No worries there, boss." Danny was so furious at the invasion of his mind and the manipulation that he'd gladly give the EL a few hard knocks.

But Bobby's face held something odd. . . something that almost looked like sympathy? Before Danny could ask about it, Babbage's voice preceded him through the doorway.

"Why in the seven lights of a desert did you lock me out of this ship?" The EL, dressed in the increasingly familiar black uniform, strode to the middle of the room and confronted Maestro head on. "How did you even get here?"

Just being in the same room rose Danny's hackles. He'd never felt such animosity toward anyone in his life.

"Hello to you, too, Babbage." Maestro kept kicking the table leg with his heels. "I locked you out of the system because it would be silly to leave you in control when I'm hijacking the ship. Oh, and I hitched a ride with my new friends the Hunters."

Babbage gaped speechlessly.

"Hey guys. . ." Maestro laughed. "I just Kirked the supercomputer!"

Bobby, obviously following Maestro's lead, laughed along.

Danny wished he could, but he couldn't muster up more than a sarcastic smirk.

Babbage looked around and seemed to notice the absence of two of their companions.

Maestro lost his smile. "I was forced to leave them behind as hostages to ensure I would bring the database back to the Hunters."

Babbage startled. "You would actually do that?"

"Of course not." Maestro scoffed.

"And yet you leave Torch and TJ in danger?" His tone obviously pointed out that he thought Maestro was no better than he.

No, that insinuation would not lie unopposed.

"They volunteered, robot." Danny made his voice as cold and cruel as he could. "Maestro told us his entire insane plan and let *us* decide whether we would put our lives in danger."

"You would let billions of people die?" Babbage's anger seemed to fade as he watched the furious young man who had once been almost an extension of himself.

"Of course not," Maestro repeated. "Give me the database. I'll find the info you need and destroy the rest."

"I can't let you have it." Babbage shook his head. "It's too dangerous. This is the biggest discovery of the. . . well. . . *ever*. I can't take the chance that you'd—"

"That I'd what?" Maestro jumped down from the table and stood eye to eye with the EL. . . well, eye to neck. "I had *tea* with the Johnny Appleseeds, you invertebrate. Anything I could have taken from them, I already turned down. If you only want it only to save those lives. . . why hesitate?"

"I can't trust you," Babbage said.

"And *that's* why *he* shouldn't be allowed to have it." Maestro stepped back and spread his arms to present the EL to the boys. "He doesn't trust me because I'm just a space monkey from the unfashionable butt-end of the galaxy. I couldn't *possibly* be evolved enough to handle the temptation."

Hm. . . the position Maestro had suggested for Bobby had pulled Babbage into a spot surrounded by doctor machines. Had that been his purpose?

"The point is moot," Babbage said. "We don't have a computer big enough to process the data. Peter is going to rendezvous with me with a much better ship, and we can process the data on our way to the home system."

"You mean you aren't processing it now?" Maestro seemed genuinely surprised. His voice dropped very quiet. "It's compressed inside you?"

"Of course."

"Wait," Danny interrupted. "The *ship* can't handle it?" How could a database be so huge an entire ship couldn't process it?

"Babbage has ten times the storage of the ship, and he's stretched to capacity as it is." Maestro waved the question away. "That's why it was so easy to hack into the system before you noticed me," he said to Babbage. "You're stretched to your limits just holding the compressed data. I kinda wondered." He crossed his arms over his chest again. "How's it feel to live life one tiny bit at a time?"

"You're not going to let me go under any circumstances, are you?" Babbage grew very still.

"I can't."

"I know that I'm the villain in this story." He looked pointedly at Danny. "But when you have a quiet moment, ask him how many lives *he's* thrown away for a greater good." He looked directly into Maestro's eyes. "A greater good he never accomplished." He turned back to Danny. "If you've learned anything from my betrayal it's that you trust too easily, Danny Decker. Don't trust him either."

With that mysterious pronouncement, the EL's eyes glazed over, and the golden glow faded.

Maestro hopped off his table and called out, "Emergency stasis field on Babbage *now!*"

Bright, sparkly light shone down on the EL.

"Shift stasis for procedure." Maestro moved in close and held his Doohickey to the other man's navel. "Follow Doohickey for parameters."

"All right, Maestro," said the computer's calm voice.

Maestro put the Doohickey on Babbage's stomach just above his belt. The golden glow receded from that area.

"What just happened?" Danny asked.

"Improvisation," Maestro told him. "He was about to commit

suicide, so I hit him with a stasis field so I can upload the database. Remember? It takes a lot of memory to be sentient. If he deleted his sentience, there would have been room to unpack the database and stream it in the general direction of Peter's ship. It would have taken longer, but it would've worked."

"That would kill him?" Bobby asked. "Couldn't he just upload from a backup?"

"Possibly," Maestro admitted. "EL's are kind of weird that way, though. They don't really like to leave spare copies of themselves lying around. It's creepy to them." He shrugged. "Wanting backup copies is kind of an organic way of looking at life."

"What about his extra body?" Bobby asked.

"Bodies are different for some reason," Maestro explained. "It's just spare parts. Not really *them*."

"That's why we transported to the infirmary..." Danny looked around the room again. "And why you had Bobby move over there... so Babbage would stand where you could hit him with a stasis field." He looked at Maestro. "You planned this whole thing ahead of time?"

"Sort of. I wanted the stasis as an option to hold him while I retrieved the database. I didn't predict that he'd give up his life to keep the data." He shrugged. "It seemed the easiest way to hold him without hurting him."

"So what are you doing now?" Danny asked. Why would he hold his Doohickey at Babbage's navel? Not that there was any logical way to ask that question.

The Doohickey beeped.

"Uploading the database." Maestro pulled it away from Babbage's stomach and looked at the screen. "And now I'm unpacking the data."

"Wait a minute." Bobby moved away from the table and closer to Maestro so he could look at the Doohickey over his shoulder.

The space traveler held the device out so the boy could see better.

"Why were you holding it by his stomach?" Bobby asked.

Well, thank goodness someone had.

"It's a pretty smart survival trait," Maestro explained. "They almost never put their brains in their head. Organics always assume a head shot is the easiest way to kill someone, so putting your brain in your stomach or your pelvis gives it a lot more protection, and if someone does blow your head off, they think you're dead, but you can be salvaged."

"Huh." Bobby stared at Babbage's stomach.

"Indeed."

"So. . ." Danny interjected with as much of a sardonic tone as he could muster. "Some of them have their head up their butt?"

"Indeed they do." Maestro smiled. The Doohickey beeped again. "And now I set it to search. Doohickey, search database for. . ." He paused and raised an eyebrow. "Search for, 'How to enlarge a quantum field enough to move a planet from one solar system to another.'"

"Searching."

"Display search two-dee," Maestro requested.

A 2-D screen popped up on one side. Images and text raced past faster than Danny could read.

"Your Doohickey is that much bigger than Babbage?" Danny asked. "Future tech, right?"

"Hey, someone remembers I'm from the future!" He handed his Doohickey to Bobby. "My doohickey has a quantum memory app."

"Which means what exactly?" Danny asked.

"It has a quantum link to a miniverse storage unit." Maestro played with the 2D screen and called up a second one.

When he didn't seem likely to add anything more, Danny said, "Still waiting."

"Okay. . . you understand the idea that there are an infinite number of universes out there, right?" Maestro stopped working the screens and faced the boys directly.

Both boys nodded.

"Okay. . . It's like this, somewhere out there is a self-contained pocket universe whose sole purpose in existence is to power my

Doohickey and provide me with storage space, which means my hard drive is pretty much infinite."

"And they say size doesn't matter." Bobby chuckled and moved to stand next to his brother, nudging him with an elbow.

"That's because they don't have an enormous Doohickey," Danny rejoindered.

"That's actually a commercial two hundred years from now." Maestro shook his head and turned back to his screens. "Thirty-five billion entries? This crap is worse than Google. Okay. . . Doohickey, subsearch on blueprints *and* models." He played with the screens. "Okay. . . better."

Bobby's eyes asked Danny how he was doing.

Danny shrugged. "Maestro?" How could he possibly ask what he wanted to know? Babbage's comments had managed to worry him.

Maestro looked up from his work. His eyebrows raised. . . then fell, as if he knew Danny's thoughts exactly. "I don't know how many people I sent to their deaths," he said. "Probably billions."

Whoa. Not expected.

"How?" Danny asked.

"Time travel. I told you the Earth was taken over by aliens in my timeline." He'd told Danny as much earlier. "Barry and I traveled back and tried to fight them off."

"You didn't win?" Danny prompted.

Maestro shook his head. "No. . . and we kept going back further to try again. . . and again. . . and again. We lost every time. A few times, the Kla'arkians blew up the planet."

"But when you finally fixed things, it was like all those other battles never happened, right?" Bobby seemed to want to support the time traveler. "Wouldn't time reset itself? So you won and none of those other losses mattered."

"It doesn't work that way." Maestro shook his head. "Every time we changed the events, we created a new timeline. Each loss was locked in place in its own reality." He shrugged. "Not that it's an excuse, but we didn't know it worked that way."

"So why did you take *our* side against billions of lives?" Bobby's voice sounded small.

"I didn't take sides," Maestro insisted. "I refuse to believe there wasn't a way to save all those lives without putting you in danger. Babbage didn't even *try* to balance the good of the few against the need of the many."

Danny picked up a small medical doodad laying on a tray beside him and tossed it at Maestro, hitting him square in the chest.

Maestro caught it after it bounced. He gave Danny a quizzical look.

"Boss, you've been alive longer than anyone ever," Danny said. "I'm sure you've done a lot of horrible crap. You've had plenty of time for it. . . But you didn't go inside my head and make me do things against my will. You didn't use my thoughts against me. Maybe I'm completely self-centered and small-minded, but that makes it different to me. You told us we were going to be in danger and let us make the decisions." Maestro tossed the little hammer back to Danny, who caught it and replaced it. "I still trust you and am very glad you're in charge of this whole thing." Danny turned to his brother. "Brother?"

Bobby nodded.

"Any other confessions?" Danny asked.

Maestro shook his head.

"Once TJ and Torch are safe, I'd like to hear more about all that. . . really. But until then, all that matters is that I will follow you into the mouth of hell if you ask me to do so because I am convinced that you will save my friends." He raised a finger of one hand. "And if it all goes wrong, I will know that it's not because you lied to us but because sometimes things just go wrong."

The Doohickey beeped.

"Okay?" Danny asked.

"Indeed." Maestro took the Doohickey from Bobby. "Doohickey, remove stasis."

Babbage blinked a few times and looked around. "What the light?"

"I stopped you from killing yourself and found the data you need." Maestro waggled the Doohickey at him.

"What? How?" Babbage made a grab for the device.

"Space monkey from two hundred years in future," Maestro said with affected stupidity. He hit his chest with a loose fist. "What the shades? Do you people pay no attention whatsoever?"

"But. . . I. . ."

"It's already on its way to Peter." Maestro glanced at his wrist as if there might be a watch there. "He probably already has it since my Doohickey can send messages instantly to pretty much anywhere. I've already wiped the full data base from your memory core, although I left a backup of the blueprints in question and kept one on my Doohickey. . . just in case."

He folded his arms and regarded Babbage with contempt.

"Had you simply asked me in the first place, we could have taken a short trip to the Johnny Appleseed planet, and you would have had the necessary info days ago. No one would have been hurt and your compatriots wouldn't have had to break the very laws they wrote about protected planets. So what happens now?"

Three pairs of eyes watched Babbage. What would he do next? Most likely, he'd explode over the fact that Maestro had destroyed the rest of the database.

"Go ahead and prove me right." Maestro seemed to think the same thing. He grinned malevolently. "*Please* prove me right so I can vaporize you right now."

Babbage barely moved. "Thank you."

"Thank you?" Maestro wiped a hand across his face.

"It's the best of all possible solutions, and I wouldn't have been strong enough to do it." The EL found a chair and sat down. "That was probably the only copy of that database in existence." He shook his head sadly. "It's like losing a miracle, but it's for the best."

His contrite attitude sucked. The whole scene seemed anticlimactic: mission accomplished and no giant final battle. Nothing seemed to go according to the rules.

Fine. Whatever. More important fish to fry.

"We need to get Torch and TJ." Danny looked at Maestro. "The Shifters have the info to save their planets, now?"

Maestro nodded.

"Mission accomplished?"

Another nod.

"Then we go to phase three of your plan." Danny faced Babbage and rolled his eyes. "Are you going to help us on this one?" Would Babbage get how hard it was for him to ask that?

"You trust me to help you?" Babbage's surprise was obvious. "You look like you'd rather vaporize me."

"Of course, I would," Danny admitted, "but I'm not stupid. One, this is going to be *really* hard to pull off, and you can still make yourself useful. Two, we're better than you. *We* can look past our prejudices." He started to turn away from the robot but stopped and stared him directly in the eyes. "Once we no longer need you, my disposition toward your continued existence will be reevaluated." He turned his back and gave his full attention to Maestro. "What next, boss?"

"What?" Maestro held his hands up in supplication. "I'm supposed to have a plan for every little piece of this kardashian puzzle?"

"Karadashian?" Bobby asked.

"Oh. . . In my time it'll be a vulgar way of saying ridiculous and stupid, sorry."

"No way." Danny wasn't about to let Maestro return to the Hunter vessel alone.

"I am not putting you in any further danger," Maestro replied adamantly, adjusting a few weapons, "since it is in no way necessary." Babbage would stay to pilot the Galactic Police ship in the event a quick escape became essential.

Danny and Bobby would have to cool their heels while Maestro handled the tradeoff.

The whole thing sucked large apples.

"What exactly are we giving them?" Babbage asked.

"It starts with the plans I sent to Peter so it looks legit." Maestro held up a spare chip that looked exactly like the one in Babbage's head or. . . rather, stomach. "Then it goes into a viral version of the database that will load into the Hunter ship, crash it, and then erase every piece of data connected to the mainframe."

"You're giving them the database?" Babbage actually stammered as he said it.

"Not in any form they can use. The virus I'm using takes out the tech in twenty-five galaxies in 2235 before someone cracks it. No one here can touch it, and it will self-destruct utterly. Anyone who could crack it wouldn't need to because they'd already know what's in the database."

"You're positive?" Babbage demanded.

"Nope." Maestro grinned. "But pretty confident and ballsy."

"So what do we do while we wait?" Why should Danny be left behind with Babbage while Maestro went to help his friends?

"It should only take a few minutes." Maestro gripped Danny's shoulder. "I hand over the chip. They give me your friends. We teleport back and run away." He smiled. "What can possibly go wrong?"

"What have I told you about the laws of narrative causality?" Danny folded his arms for emphasis.

What Can Possibly Go Wrong.

The spar occurred in slow motion, more like a kata than a fight. Bobby wanted Danny to remember the moves correctly. From the look on his brother's face, Danny was probably playing the whole training session in his head as if it were a slo-mo fight scene in a movie.

Bobby didn't mind. With everything that had happened, it was nice to see his little brother acting like a kid again, even if just for a few moments. He kept Danny on the defensive, since any real fighting they might do would be mostly "avoid getting killed and run away."

The kid had some natural ability. If he actually applied himself, he'd probably end up better than Bobby. No worry of that, though.

Bobby had recommended a training session after Maestro contacted them to report a delay. The time traveler had assured them it was just the Hunters' way of asserting superiority.

The leader claimed to be indisposed and would not let Maestro see Torch or TJ until he was personally able to meet the one he called Tilda-food.

If Maestro *did* go up against the Hunters and won... Bobby would love to get some training from him. How could a human fighting hand to hand beat a giant bug in metal plating?

Working on their own skills was a practical use of the time and gave both boys a way to blow off steam while they waited. Bobby wasn't sure how much time had passed, but the black t-shirt stuck to his chest and back.

Danny had sweated up a storm as well.

On the other side of the giant glass wall of the observation window, the Hunter ship appeared as a small dot against the background of a massive nebula that shifted and expanded slowly but perceptibly. Checking it out every few minutes, Bobby had noticed changes. Like a cloud, it held different shapes to anyone who looked at it, but when Danny had pointed out what looked like an immense green dragon, Bobby had agreed immediately and dubbed it the Puffian Nebula, after a certain Magic Dragon.

The moves he showed Danny were so ingrained that Bobby didn't need to give his full attention to the exercise, and he was glancing out the window when Babbage's reflection appeared in the glass.

How long had the robot had been standing there?

Danny followed his brother's gaze, and his demeanor immediately changed. His moves grew more aggressive, and he sped up.

Why was his brother so angry with the robot? Maybe Bobby understood Babbage better. He kind of hated understanding both sides. How long until that blew up in his face?

"Keep it cool, Danny," Bobby advised.

But Danny moved even faster now and shifted into almost pure offense. He wasn't really any kind of danger to Bobby, since the older boy could keep up against just about anything Danny dished out as long as he wasn't distracted. But the fact that Danny's anger had the better of him was a problem since martial arts were about channeling aggression, not venting it.

Time to stop. Bobby took a step away and pulled his arms out of a fighting stance. . .

Unfortunately, Danny chose that exact second to throw a back-spin into a roundhouse and must not have noticed that his brother had dropped his defenses. The kick caught Bobby full in the chest, spun him around, and landed him on his face.

While Bobby examined the floor and caught his breath, his little brother cursed loudly and dropped onto his knees.

"Are you okay?" Danny said. "I am so sorry."

"Yeah, yeah, yeah, I'm fine." Bobby rolled himself over with Danny's unnecessary assistance and sat cross-legged. "But what does Dad always say about control? You totally took your crap with Babbage out on me. . . not cool."

"I'm sorry." Danny seemed pretty wrecked. "Really. I won't let it happen again."

"Yeah, you will. No one's perfect." Bobby snorted. "Now get over it. I'm fine." He looked up at Babbage who had moved closer.

"I was just watching," the EL said. "I'm sorry if I disturbed you."

"Don't." Danny stared at Bobby's face.

"Don't?" Babbage asked.

"Don't watch." The boy's expression told his brother that hurting Bobby was one more reason for him to hate the robot.

"Would it help if I let you smack me around a bit?" Babbage asked.

Danny offered Bobby a hand and helped him to his feet, then faced the robot directly. He stared angrily into the passive golden eyes for a long time. "No."

"But. . . since you're here. . . do you have any tips?" Bobby threw an arm around his brother's neck and pulled him closer in a move that often calmed him down.

"Are you a rabid hyena?" Danny threw his brother's arm away. Whoops.

"Dude, he's got *intergalactic* moves," Bobby insisted. "You're mad at him. I get it. But why pass up an opportunity to learn moves no one on our entire planet knows?"

"I don't want him touching me. ever. again."

"What?" Bobby took a step back.

"He was inside my head, Bigby. My *head*. . ." Danny held one arm out with one finger pointing mercilessly at Babbage's face. His own face was red, and he clenched his free hand in a tight white fist.

"And he lied to me and manipulated me. He *made* me pick up that stupid penny. He manipulated *Maestro*. . . a freakin' immortal time traveler, and he played him like a twenty-five cent video game. How do I know he didn't *make* me kill those dinosaurs? Maybe I had no choice in it. Maybe I did. Maybe it was all me. . . my own choice. I'll never know if I chose to commit murder or not."

It hadn't actually been murder; it had been self-defense, but Danny's rage would prevent him from accepting the difference. Bobby stared at his feet and tried to keep his mouth shut. Unfortunately, he was so busy preventing *that* idea from slipping out that he ended up muttering something almost as bad. "But no one actually died."

"And that makes it *better*?" Danny kept up with the finger pointing. "Bobby." Apparently, Bobby didn't look up fast enough. "*Bobby!*"

Bobby had never seen Danny this angry and vicious. It was scary.

"That sick *thing* made twelve-year-old kids think they'd killed people. He made us into killers, and none of it was real. . . or necessary. Okay. . . seriously, I am thrilled to learn I didn't kill anyone. I get all the 'how could he have known we'd help' crap. I get that. . . but he lied to us. He lied to us, and every one of us almost died. I just. . ." He paused to take in a couple gulps of air. "How can you trust him? *You* never lie about *anything*."

Bobby couldn't speak. His heart raced. Danny had no idea how wrong he was.

"You are unbelievable." Danny slouched and shook his head. "I really hope you aren't even *thinking* about asking me to cut him some slack. As far as I'm concerned, he's evil." He turned his full attention back to Babbage. "You," he said, jabbing a finger at Babbage's chest, "are an evil robot with mind control powers. You. . . are a science fiction cliché."

Bobby still hadn't recovered from Danny's comment about his honesty. His brother *couldn't* know about his secret. No one did. It was just a badly timed coincidence.

"Bobby?"

Bobby couldn't speak.

"Really?"

Bobby had no idea what Danny wanted to hear.

"Fine!" Without another look, Danny stormed past on his way to the door, passing close enough to hit his brother with one shoulder. "I need a shower to scrape off the stink of you *both*."

A long silence fell after the storm.

Babbage cleared his throat in a way Bobby thought people only wrote about but never actually did, unless they were British. "Bigby?"

"Big Brother. . . shortened to Big B and then Bigby." Bobby took a deep breath and let it go. "He hasn't called me that in years. . . not since he was a little kid."

"He still is," Babbage reminded him. "You both are, really."

"Not exactly endearing yourself to me, there."

"Why don't you hate me?"

"You have seventy-five billion lives to think about." Bobby couldn't tear his eyes away from the doorway through which his brother had just stormed. "We're just a couple of lame-ass space monkeys. I get it. I don't like it, but I get it."

Babbage only spoke after a long, awkward silence. "That's not the real reason." Of course, the robot was right, but he had "mind control powers" so he already knew Bobby's thoughts.

"Why do you make people say things you already know?" Bobby cocked his head to one side and regarded the robot.

"So we have an understanding." Apparently, he knew that answer was sufficient.

"Aliens are so complicated." Bobby shook his head and stuck his hands in his pockets.

He wandered over and picked up the little pile of shoes, socks, and belts that belonged to the Galactic Police but which Bobby and his brother had used for the time being. Huh. It wasn't really stealing, was it, since the Galactic Police—or at least one branch of them—had arranged the entire expedition in the first place?

"What you did sucks large grapes, but I'd be a hypocrite to

judge you." Bobby met the robot's gaze as evenly as he could. "You've been inside my head, Babbage. You're aware I know what it's like to have to keep secrets and tell lies."

Babbage said nothing.

Nope. Bobby wouldn't say another word about it. "I'll talk to him."

Fortunately, the robot was wise enough to keep his mouth shut as Bobby left the observation deck and padded the short trek to the locker room. As he did every time he entered it, Bobby wondered what it would look like configured for another species. What would a locker room for Hunters look like?

For humans, it looked pretty much like any of the locker rooms Bobby had seen before. It held four banks of lockers, a waist high wall separating the lockers from the showers, and a perfunctory bathroom in one corner: two urinals, two toilets and a couple of sinks with no stalls or dividers. As far as Bobby knew they only had the one locker room. What did they do when both men and women lived together onboard?

Oh. Did Shifters shift genders, too? That opened up an entirely new train of thought that Bobby forced into the file marked "too complicated." Where was Danny?

The sound of running water answered the question. Danny's locker stood open, and his clothes lay in a bundle against the knee wall, so he'd thrown them there in his anger. Big brothers knew those things. He picked Danny's clothes from the floor, folded them, and placed them on a bench before opening his own locker with the hand scanner.

Danny stood in one corner of the shower area with his head down in the water, dark bruises visible across his back and shoulders. As amazing as the doctor machines were, they didn't fix everything perfectly.

Bobby hated to think about the fights that had made those bruises. He should've been there to protect his brother, to keep him from having to fight. Instead, he'd been unconscious, and Danny had gone off to protect *him*. It was backward.

Bobby pulled off his shirt and checked out his own war wounds. They weren't as dark as they had been. He ran a hand over his bristly hair, suspecting the doctor machine had somehow artificially stimulated his hair growth. With a sigh and a knot in his stomach, he folded his clothes and padded into the shower area where he took the nozzle beside his brother's.

Danny ignored him.

Bobby took some soap from the dispenser and pretended to just do his thing.

Finally, he had to say something. "I'm sorry, Little B."

"For what?" Danny snapped.

"That I can't just hate him for your sake."

"You shouldn't hate him for my sake." Danny interrupted his ablutions to regard his brother directly. "You should hate him because he is the villain. He is an evil robot."

What could Bobby possibly say to that?

"Well?" Danny asked.

"Is there anything I can say that won't make you angry?"

"You can say you hate him and can't wait until we're rid of him."

"I'm sorry, Danny. I can't say that because it isn't true." If only he could, but he understood the robot's predicament.

"Unbelievable." Danny turned off the water, shook out his hair, and grabbed a towel.

With a sigh, Bobby followed suit even though he hadn't really finished. Some things were more important that hygiene.

While Bobby dried himself, Danny wandered into the bathroom.

"I'm not that naïve, Bobby," he called over one shoulder. "I get the whole needs of the many versus the needs of the few. Seventy-five billion people are more important than the five of us. True. I get it. If I die to save them, I consider it a worthwhile death. . . but the thing is. . ." He moved to the sink and washed his hands. "The thing is Maestro would have told us what was going on. He's just as worldly. . . or galactic-y or whatever the heck, but *he* would not have gone into my brain and changed things." He brushed past his brother and padded over to his locker.

Bobby sighed and dropped his towel in the hamper, following Danny. Just because Maestro *hadn't* deceived them didn't really mean he *wouldn't*. In all likelihood, Maestro was just as capable of deceit as Babbage, but Bobby shouldn't be the one to question Danny's loyalty to the space traveler.

The younger boy bundled up his towel and tossed it into the hamper from a distance. He pulled clean trunks from his locker and slid into them.

"I killed people, Bobby," he said, and Bobby could tell it was very important to him that his older brother understood and agreed. "I killed them, and the fact that they didn't die doesn't change the fact that I made the choice to kill them. I didn't *know* it was fake. I thought it was real. And those bugs, we killed *them* for real, and they were people, too. . . or almost people." He shook his head. "Are they people?" Danny pulled on his pants, picked up his belt and snaked it through its loops. "According to Maestro they were engineered by some other species to be nothing more than mindless killing machines. I mean. . . a species whose only word for other sentient species is 'food' can't be much more than talking bugs, right?"

Danny fell silent and stared at Bobby. Dang. How should Bobby know?

"Were they people or just bugs?" Danny sighed and sat heavily on the bench.

So much emotion waged a war on Danny's face, but what in the world should Bobby do? He'd somehow missed the YouTube video on how to help his little brother deal with the trauma of alien planet PTSD. Before Babbage, it hadn't been necessary.

Danny's lips pressed into a tight, white line, and Bobby's next job was obvious. He hurried to his locker and pulled on a pair of pants and a shirt, because that was the same expression Danny had worn after finding out he'd killed his goldfish by overfeeding them. Bobby knew what would likely come next.

"Out here there's no black and white," Danny said. "Everything

I believed is backwards or just plain wrong. . . It doesn't work here. Back home I had everything. . . a family, friends, good grades. . . I was set. . . Out here, I'm just a stupid little kid who's a pawn in someone else's game."

"Danny. . ." What should he say? Danny was so stupid smart he sometimes seemed older than Bobby, and then some days he threw a tantrum like a five-year-old. Sometimes, the best thing to do was just hold out his arms and be there for him.

Danny's eyes grew wet with tears on the edge of pouring out.

"No! I'm not a little kid anymore. Not after all this." He pulled into his shirt angrily and backed away. You can't give me a hug and make it all better." He wiped his face on his arm. "I'm not going to cry over this." He took a deep breath. "I'm not."

But Danny was a little kid. And he should have a good cry over it. But Bobby couldn't say that. On the one hand, he wanted to shake the little guy's hand for acting so brave and on the other he just wanted to wrap him up until all the bad men went away.

But it wasn't like when Danny had been scared by horror movies years before he should have watched them. They couldn't turn off the TV to make the bad men go away.

They weren't even men, were they? And they wouldn't just go away.

"Once we're safe and we get rid of the evil robot. . . then I'll lose it." Danny took a deep breath. "Then you can hug me all you want. . . but not—"

"Guys, you need to come to the bridge," Babbage's voice said over the PA.

"Not a good time, Babbage." Bobby really wanted to find some way to make things right with his brother.

"No. . . it's not a good time," Babbage said darkly. "We're under attack, and Maestro and the others are fighting the Hunters on their ship."

Oh, crap. What the heck did that even mean?

Danny's eyes opened wide, and Bobby's likely did the same. Had Maestro gotten tired of waiting for the Hunters to let him see

TJ and Torch? Danny wiped his face one last time and was the first out of the locker room.

Dressed but barefoot, they rushed through the ship.

"I'm putting them over the com," Babbage's voice said.

Sounds of battle filled the corridor, confusing and chaotic. Well, that was Torch shouting profanities, which meant he was still alive, but the sound of guns and lasers and small explosions overlapped with the chittering of Hunters.

"Should I return fire?" Babbage's voice cut through the confusion.

"Well, we are on the ship in question," Maestro said over the com, "so I would prefer it if you didn't vaporize us."

"I wasn't planning on that."

"Good to hear. Good to hear."

The Galactic Police ship had to be under fire but how were they supposed to know what was happening? The lack of shaking and rocking made sense, but it was really hard to know what was going on.

"Any suggestions, Maestro?" Babbage inquired.

"Well, evasive maneuvers seem like a reasonable idea," Maestro said. "You might try to take out their engines or their scrambler so you can teleport us off this thing. Look out, TJ. There's one behind the barrel there!"

The boys reached the bridge with its usual peaceful scene. Babbage stood with his hands calmly behind his back looking up at a hologram of two ships racing and darting through the nebula, bright green and blue gases drifting away from them in slow-motion turbulence.

"Are TJ and Torch okay?" Danny called out, a bit more loudly than necessary, but where were the audio pick-ups, anyway?

"As well as can be expected." Maestro paused for gunfire. "They're both pretty handy with a weapon, which is a bit of luck. I will never again disparage the playing of videogames." He cursed loudly.

Danny and Bobby stood shoulder to shoulder at the railing,

watching the firefight they could not feel. The Police vessel spun and whirled through the layers of gas, using the particle fields and interference as cover. If he hadn't been so worried about his friends, Bobby would've found the tour through the nebula a pretty amazing experience in a collection of amazing experiences.

"We're taking some pretty heavy damage." Danny pointed at the red areas of their own ship. "How tough is the Hunter vessel?"

"Fairly tough," Babbage said. "Ours is so old. I don't know what I was thinking." Babbage glanced at Danny, who was pointedly not looking his way. He glanced at Bobby, who shrugged. "Hunter tech is pretty poor by today's standards. . ."

"But a far sight better than this old bucket of bolts, right?" Bobby hoped his enthusiasm might be catching.

Okay, wrong approach. His brother didn't even glance at him, although at least he didn't move away.

"Maestro?" Babbage called out.

"Still alive."

"I can't trace your Doohickey back to you," Babbage said, "so I have no way to teleport you out. I'm trying to break the shields and disarm the scrambler without vaporizing the ship. If you fire a shot through the outer hull, I can locate your approximate location."

What? Both boys turned to stare at the robot.

The brief silence and quiet voice Maestro used to break it told Bobby that the space traveler was as taken aback as he had been.

"You want me to run the risk of explosive decompression so you can send us a bouquet of roses?"

"Use a pinpoint energy beam and get close to a bulkhead." Babbage grabbed the rail with both hands. "It's too small to do any damage, and we can read it no matter how narrow the beam. The ship can track it back into the vessel itself." He glanced at the boys. The red sections of the Galaxy Police ship were more numerous than the corresponding sections of the Hunter nest. "I don't know how things are on your end," Babbage said, "but we don't have a lot of time over here." A very loud barrage of gunfire followed then the sound of TJ and Torch cursing at the tops of their lungs.

"Fine. I'll do it," Maestro shouted. "Gotta focus now. Out."

"What's the situation?" Danny's voice was small and tight.

"The ship isn't built for a sustained firefight with a modern vehicle," admitted. "And we weren't at one hundred percent after our. . . fight with the Saurians."

"I can't get used to how quiet battles are." The ships whirled and dove and whirled and dove. Bobby tried to feel the movement, but the ship stayed steady as a rock.

"Here in the nebula," Babbage continued, "we can't use the quantum drive. Too much ambient radiation. We could end up in the heart of a star, which would be bad. I need a fix on Maestro and the boys so I can teleport them, but I'm having a devil of a time because of the Hunter scramblers and the nebula itself." He pointed at a tiny white line attached to the image of the Hunter ship. "Laser pointer spotted, enhanced, and fixed in space." The line stayed attached to the ship.

A small explosion rapidly mushroomed away from the Hunter ship centered on the point where the white line touched the hull. . . then the translucent orange glow that had represented the ship's shields flickered and vanished.

"What the heck?" Something deep inside Bobby started to worry.

"Not to worry," Babbage said. "Maestro and the boys were directly below the shield generator. That's a bit of luck, then. Now I can find them easily." His look of concentration intensified.

Real space battles would look lousy on the big screen since there was no racing from computer to computer or hectic manipulation of computer screens, holographic or otherwise. . . just a rather intense look of concentration on a robot's face.

Another explosion wracked the Hunter ship, this one closer to the center.

"Are they okay? What's going on?" Danny nearly flipped over the railing to get closer.

Bobby grabbed him around the shoulders; he would have been lying if he'd said it wasn't as much for himself as for his brother.

"These are good things." Apparently sensing their fears, Babbage put as much calm assurance into his voice as he could. "Ships aren't shielded internally the same way they are externally."

Several sections of the Hunter ship flashed red. Unfortunately, its weapons seemed unaffected, and the Police ship glowed more red with every passing second.

"Maestro's Doohickey has an incredible app that oscillates the laser in a way that renders most current shielding about as impenetrable as wet toilet paper." Babbage had to be buying time. He should've already located Maestro and the boys and teleported them home.

Something was wrong.

"He shot directly through the nest's shield generator," Babbage said. "It blew and appears to have started some kind of minor cascade... And there's ambient radiation in their area, which is making it a little hard to see... but I'm sure the nest will contain everything to a small—"

The ship exploded.

Boom!

Boys and robot froze as the expanding cloud of gas, heat, and debris filled the area of the hologram that had once contained the Hunter nest.

Their own vessel came to a halt nearby, the shrapnel neatly deflected by its shields.

Utter silence filled every nook and cranny of the bridge.

Danny was the first to try his voice. His first attempt was little more than choking croak. He tried again. "Tell me they got off the ship."

Babbage didn't respond. He stared wide-eyed at the rapidly dissipating explosion.

"You teleported them, right?" Danny ducked under the railing and raced directly through the hologram. He grabbed Babbage and turned him so they faced each other. "Tell me they're okay." He shook the robot to get his attention. "Tell me they're okay!"

Babbage blinked once... twice. Finally, he looked down at

Danny's ashen face and shook his head in a tiny, horrified little movement.

"I can't, Danny. I can't" He turned back to the horrifying hologram. "I don't know. I really don't know."

The blast expanded into space and dissipated.

Wait a minute. Ten or so distant specks grew rapidly as they approached from the other side of the nebula. Had the Hunters called for reinforcements?

Thirty Minutes Ago

Before Maestro teleported to the Hunter ship, he'd pulled Babbage aside.

"I am responsible for the other two. If anything goes wrong over there, get *these* two back to Earth. Do *not* put them in danger with senseless heroics, okay? Let me handle anything that happens there. *Anything.*"

Babbage had agreed but hadn't seemed happy about it. And now, after an hour of cooling his heels without even seeing TJ or Torch, Maestro wasn't happy, either.

His Doohickey told him the boys were finally on their way. They'd been stationary for the past hour in the same holding cell they'd enjoyed the first time on the Hunter vessel.

Maestro had tried to hijack the security cameras to get a peek at the boys, but the Hunters must have figured out the Doohickey frequencies somehow because they blocked him. All he knew was that they were alive and sticking to each other like glue.

As they finally made their way to the bridge—where Maestro stood wishing that more extraterrestrial species used furniture—six Hunters escorted them. Apparently, the leader wasn't taking any chances. Maestro smirked. It was nice to make an impression.

Shortly before the boys appeared, the leader strode casually onto the bridge, all four feet thumping loudly as he moved. Maestro wondered, and not for the first time, why they insisted on metal decking in their vessels. Sneaking around would be almost impossible if they were boarded. Although perhaps that was the point. Why would a Hunter ever need to "sneak"?

"I was beginning to think you'd been deposed by an underling," Maestro said.

"It is not so easy to rile me, Tilda-food." The leader chittered and chuckled. They took their place in the center of the room and regarded Maestro with disdain. "You have the database?"

"Indeed, I do." He faced the doorway before the boys entered, telegraphing his knowledge of their movements to the leader. "And my larvae have had, I trust, a pleasant visit?"

Oh, drat. Something had gone wrong. Horribly wrong.

The boys were dirty, disheveled, and covered in blood. TJ leaned heavily on Torch, avoiding any weight on his right leg, which was covered in black cast plasma. His pants were gone as was Torch's shirt.

Maestro scanned them with his Doohickey.

"Maestro!" Torch called out with a flush of joy then composed himself. "Er. . . hey. . . Dad. Good to see you."

The look of relief on both dirty faces brought a lump to Maestro's throat. They hadn't been positive they'd ever get off this vessel. Torch only had a new collection of bruises and minor cuts, but TJ's leg had broken badly. The Hunters had set it well, and it was already partly mended, but he shouldn't put weight on it until he saw the doctor machine in the Police vessel. How had the Hunter's doctor machine even known how to deal with mammalian physi— oh. One of the boys must have thought to hook his Doohickey into it. Brilliant, but the injury complicated things.

Maestro threw an arm around each boy, which wasn't hard since they clung together. He pushed his head between theirs and pulled their faces close.

Although they seemed rather startled by his display, neither of them protested.

Listen fast, and don't react to what I say in your head. While he did hope his affection filled them with a little courage, the real reason for it was the need to be that close to send a message to them both. *I apologize in advance, but I need to punish you because of the broken leg. It will be an act. It's the only way I'm going to get you out of here as anything other than hors d'oeuvres.* He kissed each of them on the temple. *I will get you out of here.*

He was about to release them, but the Hunter's next words convinced him to hang on longer.

"Such affection is a sign of weakness, Tilda-food. Perhaps you wouldn't even need to be tenderized before consumption."

"Just tasting to make sure you haven't poisoned them." Maestro looked them carefully in the eyes and even gave a cursory brush through their hair for effect. "How do I know what you might have done to them while I was gone?" He sniffed.

Be strong. Before backing away he held their gaze for a moment.

They each nodded barely perceptibly.

Maestro strode up to the Hunter leader with all the courage he could muster. The cannon fodder twitched but held their positions.

"Since you seem to have no problem harming my larvae," Maestro shouted, "who knows *what* you might have done to them!" He halted less than a foot from the leader, his eyes boring into the Hunter's largest left eye, which was usually the dominant one.

The soldiers didn't seem certain whether they should intervene or let the leader handle this mammal by itself. Good to know.

Trying to prevent Maestro from noticing what he had already noticed, the leader waved the cannon fodder away before they could move, as if implying that Maestro was no threat.

"Why did you let this happen?" Maestro smiled at the leader so they would know Maestro already knew their motives.

The Hunter regarded him levelly. No. This was not going to go well.

Maestro held his position with the Hunters by sheer force of will and by convincing them that he had a procreative member of substantial size. TJ's injury could be the death of them all. Any sign of weakness would be fully exploited.

The leader gestured at a pair of Hunters, little more than larvae, really, smaller than the rest, with shiny new copper carapaces. They were barely battle-tested.

Maestro worked hard to prevent showing his dismay. As far as the Hunters were concerned, his boys had allowed themselves to get beaten up by a couple of toddlers. Of course, as far as the rest of the galaxy was concerned, they'd been assaulted by six-foot metal-covered monsters with pincers like steel vices. Unfortunately, the rest of the galaxy wasn't around to comment.

"Your larvae were sparring and invited mine to join them." If they had had the mouth for it, they would have likely grinned like the rapsoloid that ate the distressi. "Apparently, yours lost."

Here we go, Maestro sent. Hopefully, TJ heard him.

"Are these the Hunters you let injure you?" Maestro turned his wrath on his "sons." He pointed at the two Hunters who had assaulted the boys.

TJ's face fell blank. "I. . . don't know."

Maestro backhanded him hard enough that Torch had to take his full weight to prevent him from landing on his broken leg. Maestro had been careful to smack him in the right direction to push him onto the good leg.

"Don't lie to me. You were beaten by infants!" Hmm. Could he turn this to an advantage? He gestured at the Hunter leader. "This unfortunate leader has such pitiable troops they are reduced to guarding you with their larvae, and you not only pick on them like the bullies you are, but you let one of them break your leg?"

A loud chittering filled the air from the normally well-behaved bridge crew. The Hunters moved closer, likely assuming this confrontation could have only one outcome since such a reprimand would normally lead to death and, of course, the injured mammal was too much for the other two to eat on their own. Snack time had to be on its way.

They seemed to miss the subtlety of Maestro's tirade, though.

The leader, apparently, had not. They held up one claw and the chittering immediately ceased.

"You dare insult my crew?" Their voice faltered.

Maestro faced them directly. Had his trap worked? If the leader chastised Maestro for insulting the quality of their troops, they'd be forced to admit they had *intentionally* sent undeveloped larvae, hoping to cause trouble and to embarrass the mammals. That would look like the actions of a coward and a cheat. No Hunter could live with the shame of such actions. The Hunter sense of pride was a terrible thing to navigate, even for the Hunters themselves.

"I hold you responsible." Maestro squared up against the Hunter. "My son was damaged while in your care. He will slow us down."

"Eat them now," the leader suggested.

"What? Before I've had a chance to tenderize him?" Maestro threw it out to distract the crew, who chittered again.

The boys exchanged worried glances, and, fortunately, they would never know the Hunter process of tenderizing.

"I see you know our ways well, Tilda-food." The leader chuckled softly. They held one claw out toward Maestro, who was glad he knew better than to shake hands with a Hunter. "Let's put these unpleasantries behind us and conduct the business at hand. I brought you to your ship. You will give me the database. Yes?"

With a great show of righteous indignation, Maestro pulled the chip out of a coat pocket. Thanks to every god he'd ever met, he'd managed to save the boys from what could have turned into a horrible, violent bloodbath.

"It's the EL's brain." He held the chip out to the leader. "I'm afraid there's no way for you to get at the data without interfacing this time." He took the chip to the science station and dropped it onto a small table littered with tools. Any chance they might wait until returning to the Hunter homeworld to explore it?

Nope. The science officer picked it up with a probe and slid it into its station.

"Well, I guess it's time we transported back to our ship." Maestro clapped his hands and made a show of returning to the boys' sides and throwing an arm around TJ. "It has been great fun working with you, but we have a walkabout to finish, and I need to find a new planet."

"Surely you'd like to wait until we know we have what we expected." The leader gestured at the console.

Not especially, Maestro thought. "Of course. . . although I really need to get my son here hooked up to a doctor machine."

"In due time." They stared at the science officer who chittered with delight as data filled the console. "I wish to make certain we have made a fair exchange."

Silence filled the bridge while the Hunter's computer analyzed the database, and Maestro slowly put his hand into his pocket. He hit the node on his Doohickey that would send a signal to Babbage to extract the team.

Nothing happened.

He hit the node again.

Nothing happened once more.

Oh, drat.

Get your Doohickeys ready, boys. I have a bad feeling about this.

"Tilda-food?" The leader had taken a few steps toward the humans. "You bring up an interesting point. While we wait for my crew to analyze the database, why don't you explain how a protected planet, such as yours, can have an interplanetary walkabout as a deeply held tradition."

"I told you I'm from the future." Maestro put on his most nonchalant face. Drat. "In my time, walkabouts will have become standard."

"And your larvae are from the future as well?"

Did they have any kind of temporal sensors?

"Their mother is from this timeline," Maestro said.

He and the leader bantered back and forth like that a few times while Maestro marked the location of each soldier and bridge crew member. The exchange took far too long. The chip would go viral any second, at which point the feces would smash the turbine.

Maestro set his Doohickey to vaporize and mentally sorted through his spells while he bickered with the Hunter.

An alarm rang. Ah. The vessel's computers had noticed the aggressive virus assaulting it. Bother.

The leader approached the science officer's station, and Maestro used the split second their back was turned to blast them into dust.

"Boring conversation anyway." Maestro dragged the boys to the floor.

A dozen shocked Hunters stared at the spot of dissipating vapor that had been their leader.

Maestro called out the words of a rather aggressive spell. His eyes glowed a bright purple and crackled with electricity as he drew an arcane symbol on the floor with one finger.

The letter glowed green.

Maestro covered the boys with his body and intoned a shield spell. A green globe covered them as a violet pillar shot up from the glyph he'd drawn. It splashed against the ceiling, orange flames sliding up and down its length.

All eyes, and there were eight apiece on each Hunter, stared at the coruscating pillar. Without a direct order, they seemed unable to act. Excellent.

Maestro muttered a single word, and the pillar flashed out, filling the room and throwing every Hunter in it against the wall and vaporizing them.

Maestro's shield sputtered and died as loud sirens filled the air.

"How did. . ." Torch was the first on his feet. "What the heck *are* you?" He hoisted TJ to his one good foot while Maestro struggled to get to his knees. The spell had just about wiped him out.

Hopefully, Torch was up to supporting his friend.

"We're going to have company." Maestro pushed to his feet but couldn't quite hold it and dropped to one knee. Blast.

The air smelled of barbecue.

"Are you okay?" Torch grabbed Maestro under one armpit and pulled him to his feet. "How did you do that?"

"I'm a time-traveling witch from two hundred years in the future, okay? That spell took a lot out of me, and this place is about to be crawling, literally, with bugs. There has to be an escape pod in the leader's quarters. We should head for it in case the virus in the database doesn't shut down the scrambler, and we can't teleport out." He waited for annoying questions or hesitation, but the boys exchanged quick glances and shrugged.

"Okay, get us out of here." Torch gestured for Maestro to take the lead and got a good grip around TJ's torso.

"Excellent." Maestro left the bridge, let the boys pass him, turned to close the bulkhead, then shot the mechanism to lock it. He heard the tell-tale sound of metal feet on metal floors. "Shoot anything that chitters!" He dashed forward to take the lead and started firing even before the first of the bugs rounded the corner.

He pulled the boys into an open doorway then rolled across the hall to the opposite door and set up crossfire. He prayed that this nest had two close contenders for the recently vacant position of leader. If two Hunters had to fight it out, the odds of escaping increased dramatically. Hunters were so used to following orders that they would have a hard time organizing any kind of attack without a clear, decisive voice.

Hopefully, the virus would take out the scrambler soon. He'd really rather be on the Galactic Police cruiser.

"Babbage, you evil son-of-a-peasant, tell me you're getting this." He laid down a blanket fire and dashed down the hall to the next juncture so they didn't get pinned down. "Let's go, boys!"

They rushed to follow, firing wildly and screaming bloody murder.

The bugs at the next corner—there were only two of them— turned and fled. Torch stopped for a split second to aim. He nailed both of them easily.

"Once again," Maestro said, "excellent."

"I do my best," Torch drawled. He blew over the top of his Doohickey as if it were a six-shooter.

Laser fire sprayed the walls and floor around them, forcing them to duck behind a counter near one wall. As they hit the floor, Babbage's voice called to them. "Maestro? What's going on over there?"

"Negotiations were not as amiable as we had hoped."

Torch and TJ did a decent job of laying down fire and keeping the Hunters at bay, so Maestro gave his full attention to the conversation. "We're trapped with a shipful of really annoyed bugs, and I would guess they're going to attack you as soon as they figure out who's in charge."

"I'm willing to bet they figured it out," Babbage said.

"Why?"

"They're firing on us."

"Drat."

The lasers shooting back and forth in the corridor sent up a dreadful smoke and the chittering of a dozen Hunters filled the air.

"Uh. . . Maestro?" Torch nudged him with one foot.

Maestro peeked over their cover.

A large contingent of Hunters had arrived.

A stray beam hit a panel in the wall, which promptly blew. Some of the bugs used projectile weapons and the gunfire was loud and stank of gunpowder. They must not have enough beam weapons with short distance options.

"Should I return fire?" Babbage asked over the com.

"Well, we are on the ship in question, so I would prefer it if you didn't vaporize us." Maestro fired.

"I wasn't planning on that." His voice was frustrating in its calm.

"Good to hear." Maestro attempted to outdo the cool. "Good to hear."

The door behind them was locked. Maestro put the Doohickey against it and hit a tab. The door opened and he shoved the boys into the small storage room beyond. It contained a few crates, but most important was what was absent: there were no bugs firing at them.

Maestro hit a tab and fused the door.

"We're kind of trapped now, boss," Torch whispered.

Maestro shook his head and aimed at the wall opposite.

"Any suggestions, Maestro?" Babbage persisted.

"Well, evasive maneuvers seem like a reasonable idea." Maestro set his beam on cutting and sliced a hole into the far wall as the door behind them glowed bright white. "You might try to take out their engines or their scrambler so you can teleport us off this thing."

He shoved the boys forward into the next room, which was another storage room. "Look out, TJ. There's one behind the barrel there!"

They all dove into a heap behind a crate. They needed to get through this room fast or they'd be trapped with a squadron of bugs on both sides. Maestro took a deep breath and pressed his back into the crate and turned to get the boys attention. *On three, okay?*

They nodded.

He held up one finger, then two—

The floor shuddered beneath them.

The boys' eyes opened wide.

It's just Babbage firing at the ship. The bugs' stabilizers aren't as good as ours.

The boys nodded, and Maestro could tell they remembered his words that they shouldn't be able to feel an attack. Another shudder.

THREE! ...and up they jumped, Torch and Maestro supporting TJ, spraying a heavy barrage of fire across the room. TJ took his arm from around Maestro so he could fire, too.

Maestro led them across the hallway, the trio trapping the Hunters with a sustained salvo from three Doohickeys.

The door to the first storage room blew open.

Maestro grabbed the boys and pulled them behind a large crate near the far door, just shy of their goal. With a questioning look at Maestro, Torch settled TJ on the floor as the Hunters in the room filled the air with lasers.

Torch would understand in a moment. Hopefully.

The squad of Hunters poured in from the first storage room, guns blazing, laying waste to pretty much all of the Hunters who had had Maestro and the boys pinned.

A brief silence ensued, during which Maestro held the boys down to keep them from interrupting or getting themselves noticed.

Was he right about—

"We must discipline ourselves for our error!" a bug cried out.

The others chittered agreement.

The sound of automatic weapons and lasers was music to

Maestro's ears. He peered over the crate. Yep. He and the boys were the only living creatures left in the room.

"Stupid bugs."

"Are TJ and Torch okay?" Danny's shouted voice over the com startled Maestro after the brief respite.

He nodded in the direction of the far door, unwilling to waste their good luck by hanging around. He grabbed projectile guns and passed them around. They were nearing the outer hull where beam weapons could actually be a liability.

"As well as can be expected." Maestro held his gun around the doorway and fired at random, just to check. Nothing fired back so he chanced a peek. Clear. "They're both pretty handy with a weapon, which is a bit of luck. I will never again disparage the playing of videogames."

He chanced a glance at the boys who grinned from the adrenaline and praise. He nodded at the hall, and the boys hurried into it. He sealed the door. Gunfire sliced across the corridor and slammed into Maestro's leg, tripping him. He cursed loudly, regained his balance, and pushed the boys ahead of him into the doorway across the hall.

Torch tried to push past to engage the Hunters, but Maestro held him back with one arm. He held his other palm up and wiggled his fingers, muttering under his breath.

A golden light, thin as a human hair wove its way around his fingers, quickly growing into a golden sphere of shifting, oscillating light.

He dropped to one knee—ignoring the horrific blast of pain in his thigh—and rolled the ball of light like a bowling ball. As it slipped off his hand, it grew to something the size of a watermelon.

TJ and Torch peeked around the corner above him, but Maestro yanked them inside the room before the spell detonated. The shrieks of burning Hunters filled his ears.

Maestro chanced a peek into the hall, but when he put weight on his injured leg it gave out completely, and he landed on his back with a grunt.

TJ and Torch appeared above him, eyes and mouths wide in horror. Maestro was the only chance they had of avoiding dinner with the Hunters, and from their faces they didn't want to find out how the bugs "tenderized" mammals.

Blast. Had he passed out? So many powerful spells so close together had left him weak. They didn't have time for that.

"Maestro?" Torch said.

"Still alive." He winked and reached up to Torch, who helped him to his feet. Gambling that they were close to their destination, Maestro closed his eyes, intoned a healing spell and felt another drag on his energy, as if he'd just run a marathon in seconds.

Magic always exacted a price. Since Maestro was immortal, he could pay a much heavier toll than most and he recharged faster as well. . . but even he had limits and the spells he had used were magic of the highest and most expensive order.

He tested the leg. It hurt like heck but supported his weight, now. According to his Doohickey, the door at the end of the hall led to the former leader's quarters. Their room would be the only one with an escape pod since they were the only member of the crew worth saving.

He waved the boys to follow and broke into a jog.

Babbage's voice returned, still infuriatingly calm. "I can't trace your Doohickey back to you, so I have no way to teleport you out. I'm trying to break the shields and disarm the scrambler without vaporizing the ship." Rumblings and shaking confirmed the report. "If you fire a shot through the outer hull, I can locate your approximate location."

Maestro stopped so abruptly, the boys barreled into him. Both Maestro and TJ grunted in pain. Absolute silence descended on them while Maestro contemplated the maneuver.

"You want me to run the risk of explosive decompression so you can send us a bouquet of roses?" He spoke as quietly and with as much restraint as he could manage.

"Use a pinpoint energy beam and get close to a bulkhead. It's too small to do any structural damage, and we can read it no matter how narrow the beam. The ship can track it back into the vessel itself." Which would probably allow the sensors to penetrate the scramblers and locate them. Probably.

A new burst of gunfire hit Maestro out of nowhere.

And time slowed down.

TJ and Torch pushed back against the wall behind the scant cover of a bulkhead frame.

A torrent of bullets lifted Maestro off his feet and tossed him, riddling his torso and legs with horrible pain.

TJ and Torch cursed loudly and returned fire.

"Fine. I'll do it." Maestro coughed blood, but one lung kept working. "Gotta focus, now. Out." He cut the feed. "Stay there," he shouted before the boys could dash out to help him. "Doohickey, close the dratted bulkhead." The bulkhead dropped, and the sound of gunfire rattling against it sounded faint and far away. Hopefully that was because it was a good, stout door and not because Maestro was passing out.

Well, so much for the risk of explosive decompression. He aimed straight up, told the Doohickey to go atomic on the beam width. . . and fired. He held his breath as the boys dropped down beside him, which was a stupid maneuver for TJ, who would have a heck of a time getting back on his feet.

Explosive decompression failed to happen.

Maestro blew out a breath, which brought up more blood. When he could breathe again, he held a hand out to Torch.

"Torch, buddy, looks like you get to help both of us to our feet."

"But you're. . . You're bleeding all over the place," Torch insisted.

"I've had worse." Which was true. . . although it still hurt like heck. "Get me up. TJ, too. Now!"

The shaking of the ship increased. Since they weren't immediately transported out, something had gone wrong, and an escape pod very far away from the Hunter nest might be an excellent place to be.

Torch did as he was told, and they hobbled to the end of the hall. Overriding the room's lock with the Doohickey took a matter of seconds. During those short seconds, time slowed down again.

TJ leaned against the wall beside Maestro.

Torch covered them both in case anything came at them down the hallway.

A loud ticking and a deep base rumble above them indicated a failing shield generator a level above. Maestro had heard them fail before. He must have hit it with his desperate signal to Babbage.

Torch cursed as a fireball blew down from the ceiling a few yards away. He turned his back to it and closed his eyes, spreading his arms and shielding his companions with his body. The boy's weight hit Maestro, and together they plowed into TJ as the door slid open.

The trio crashed into the leader's quarters and slid across the floor.

"Close the door!" Maestro shouted at his Doohickey, hoping to block any further blast and all the shrapnel that was bound to follow. He cursed again. The situation was going from bad to worse.

He pulled out from beneath Torch.

"Whoa, that was a punk-ass ride." The boy's eyes were open and only slightly glassy. "Let's do it again."

"You'll live." Maestro pulled the boy to his feet, but Torch staggered and moaned. He stumbled against Maestro, who stumbled against TJ, who screamed in pain as they all fell together to the floor in a heap. . . again.

"What's wrong?" Maestro demanded of Torch.

"His whole back's like this." TJ was the one who put his hand against the back of Torch's head and pulled it away covered in blood and ash.

"Yeah, but head wounds are a lot worse than they seem, right?" Torch asked.

Maestro spun him for a look. Drat. Even on his best day, Maestro would have a hard time healing that. How was the boy even standing?

And where was the blasted teleport?

A second explosion rocked the floor beneath them.

"I thought we weren't supposed to feel stuff like that," Torch muttered thickly, rising to his hands and knees.

"We're not," Maestro said.

They had one chance. As it was, they'd never get to their feet, let alone reach the escape pod in time.

Just one room to cross but it might as well have been a galaxy.

"Okay guys, I'm going to use a hardcore healing spell that will give us five seconds of feeling like kings, and then lay us flat worse than we are now, so we have to get into the escape pod fast. . . *really* fast."

"Worse?" Torch swayed in place.

"All magic comes with a price."

"Why just five seconds?" TJ asked.

"Anything more, and I'll pass out here and now." Hopefully, it wouldn't happen, anyway. With any luck he had enough juice to make this work. If not, they were all dead.

He muttered the spell.

Exhaustion hit him so hard he almost threw up.

He drew a symbol on Torch's forehead. It glowed blue.

He drew the same symbol on TJ's forehead.

"Here we go. Follow me and don't stop for anything." He muttered a final word, and the spell hit them all.

5. . . *Time slowed down and they pushed to their feet like sprinters at the sound of a gun. Maestro raced to the escape hatch in the corner of the room.*

4. . . *He told the Doohickey to open the pod and prep it for evacuation. "I feel great!" Torch called out, his voice deep and slow in the magical field of the spell. "Why don't we. . ."*

3. . . *The escape hatch released as the floor dropped several inches, and Torch's suggestion was lost as he stumbled from the force of the vessel's vibration.*

2. . . *Maestro threw TJ in first then grabbed Torch by his belt.*

1. . . *He threw Torch into the pod, where he landed squarely on top of TJ, who was going to be in a heck of a lot of pain in a second.*

0. . . The spell faded as Maestro dropped into the pod.

"Launch! Launch! Launch!"

The humans huddled in a tangled heap as the pod door closed and the full effect of all that deferred pain smashed into their abused bodies.

They screamed.

The Hunter ship exploded.

His Eyes Betrayed Amazement.

A lonely escape pod shot through the variegated mists of the largest nebula in the galaxy, leaving a wake of ripples and eddies behind. Blackened and scorched, it resembled a short, fat sausage left on the grill wa-a-a-y too long. Dents and dings covered the metal as if it had survived a barrage of shrapnel from a huge explosion, which, in fact, it had.

It had hatches on each end. The hatch that had once connected to its mother ship had melted solid. That entire end had flowed like water for a brief moment before the icy cold of space crystallized it into a fragile, rippled puddle. Anyone seeing the pod from a distance would think, *Melt the bugger down and make something useful, all right?*

Inside lay three people who would rather no one liquefied it just yet.

Maestro watched the boys as they slept, huddled under a fire blanket he'd found in a small locker. The blanket had to be a leftover from the original owners of the Hunter vessel, rest their souls whoever they were. Bugs didn't really *do* blankets, fire or otherwise.

Two pairs of legs lay draped across Maestro's lap because that's how small the pod was. It had been designed for one. . . maybe two. For three it was. . . cozy.

Maestro had been in tighter spots.

As the boys slept, he thought of his own children and family trips with them. . . and the grandchildren. . . and the great-grandchildren. . .

TJ's bare foot pushed out from the cover, and the boy muttered in his sleep. "No. . . no. . . it's a bicycle. . ."

Chuckling, Maestro took TJ's foot and rubbed it absently the way he had thousands of times with his own progeny.

As the horrifying explosion had rendered the Hunter vessel down to its constituent particles, the pod had ejected and leapt into space, barely avoiding utter annihilation. Even at a distance, the three passengers had been tossed about like ping pong balls in a bingo tournament.

Once the pod's stabilizers finally counteracted the violent, random tumbling, the three survivors untangled themselves to the sound of TJ's screaming. His leg had rebroken.

Maestro had reset it with one quick motion.

The boy screamed curses in three languages.

"This is going to suck more than you can imagine," Maestro had told him once the screaming subsided, "but your leg will be completely mended at the end of it."

TJ nodded.

Maestro had spoken to Torch, next. "Get behind him and hold him tight, especially his head."

The boys exchanged glances that communicated three paragraphs worth of dialogue, at the end of which TJ nodded, and Torch moved into the recommended position.

"You need to hold him steady, so he doesn't hurt himself worse," Maestro instructed. "Magic always costs something."

Torch nodded. He pulled a dirty black rag out of his pocket and shoved it between TJ's teeth.

Maestro cast the spell, and TJ screamed and screamed. A golden light surrounded his leg.

"Stop it!" Torch demanded as TJ writhed in his arms. "You're killing him!"

"It's infected and shattered." Maestro gritted his teeth against the sound of the boy's pain. "If he ever wants to walk again—" Shiny lights flashed in Maestro's sight. "I'm sorry, TJ. . . it. . ."

TJ's pain slammed into him, and he almost cried out. That was one consequence of his craft. He felt his patient's pain. If more doctors had to suffer the same thing, there would be fewer doctors and more pain medications. The bones in Maestro's right leg unknit themselves as the bones in TJ's slowly mended. Maestro sucked in a shallow breath and intoned the last part of the incantation.

His accelerated healing allowed him to restore others by simply drawing their injury into himself and then letting his body take care of business. It was the fastest way to get the job done.

As many times as he'd done it during more wars that he could possibly remember, he'd learned to keep working in spite of the pain.

It was done. TJ sucked in a deep breath, relaxed against Torch, and fell into a peaceful slumber.

"He's okay?" Torch's eyes searched Maestro's face.

Maestro nodded and used every ounce of his own strength to avoid passing out.

"Thank you, sir." Torch held his friend protectively. . . fiercely.

"He'll be fine when he wakes up," Maestro said. "He's just resting, now."

"What about your gunshots?" Torch asked. "You gotta be feeling some pain there."

"It hurts, but my body will heal itself."

"How?"

"It just does. I'm not sure how it works." Exhaustion poured through every cell, and Maestro wanted nothing more than sleep, but Torch's back needed attention, no matter how well he seemed to ignore the injury. "Turn around so I can heal your back."

Torch hesitated. "No offense but you don't look in much shape to heal a boo-boo, much less what happened to my back."

"I appreciate your concern, but I can handle it. Let me see."

"You sure?"

"I'm immortal. I can take whatever price the magic expects and pay it out over time. I'm lucky that way."

"Lucky? Sounds kinda sucky to me, but whatever." He turned his bloody and burned body.

Maestro placed his hands on the boy's ravaged skin.

"Is this going to be like what you did to TJ?" Torch winced before steeling himself to the experience.

"Not nearly as bad. That was infection and broken bones. . ." He drew arcane symbols into the boy's flesh. They glowed blood red.

"Dude, that tickles!" Torch wriggled.

"Give it a minute." He spoke the spell and Torch gasped, arching his back away.

"Okay. . . No more tickling. . ."

He held up well. Maestro had expected some screaming. It wasn't as painful as TJ's healing, but Torch still proved himself a brave trooper.

Maestro gritted his teeth against the fire and lacerations that opened up on his own back. The pain always felt ten times worse when the wounded were so young and when Maestro himself had been in charge of their safety. Two more lives torn apart by his mistakes.

He finished his work and pulled away.

"How can you—" Torch sucked in a deep breath and turned to Maestro. His eyes betrayed amazement. "You're crying."

"Sorry. I know how much it hurts." Maestro wiped his face with one sleeve. Trying to change the subject, he slid out of his long-sleeve uniform shirt. "Here. You need this more than I do." He still had the black t-shirt.

Torch just stared.

"What?" Maestro asked.

A long silence fell between them.

Torch took the shirt and pulled it on. It hung on him like a loose sack. There was much more in that seemingly flippant head than the boy normally let on.

"Sir. . ."

Maestro let the silence play out while Torch gathered his thoughts.

The boy looked down, then at the wall only a few inches away before finally bringing his gaze back to Maestro's face.

"Thanks."

Maestro pulled out the fire blanket, gesturing for Torch to get under it with TJ.

"You both need to sleep," he said, "and I. . . I need to rest."

Torch wrapped himself around his friend and pulled the blanket over the two of them. He fell asleep in seconds.

Maestro chuckled. Boys. How funny.

Pulled back to the present, Maestro tucked TJ's foot under the blanket and patted it. Would someone would find them before they ran out of oxygen? What would it be like to die of asphyxiation again and again until someone found the pod? He'd managed to avoid that one so far.

The pod shuddered.

Maestro held his breath. Space was so mind-numbingly vast that the chances of getting hit by something dangerous were small, even after an explosion since all the shards and shrapnel would have shot away from each other more quickly than a divorced couple at a cocktail party. However, collisions could happen.

The pod shuddered a second time then settled into a steady movement. Ah. A tractor beam had hooked them. Unfortunately, he had no way to tell who'd discovered them. A massive EM pulse from the exploding Hunter ship had scrambled the Doohickeys.

"Hey, guys. I think someone found us." As much as Maestro hated waking the boys, they might need to face a boarding party. Drat.

"Good guy or bad guy?" Torch woke up first.

"Not sure."

Torch shook TJ. They scooted into crouches that were the best they could do given the cramped space.

Maestro positioned himself between the boys and the only working door. He pulled out his Doohickey and set it for vaporize. . . but it was scrambled. Drat. He held it out anyway to give the boarding party something to think about.

Chances were anyone who'd found them would mean at least as much trouble as the empty reaches of space. The Galactic Police cruiser had been in rough shape, and the most likely folks on the other end of the tractor beam were Hunters following a tracking signal.

The pod floated along silently for several seconds then shuddered and clanked loudly as it docked.

"Okay, boys," Maestro whispered. "Get ready."

"To do what?" Torch muttered. "Bleed all over them?"

Well said.

The screen on the door flashed and flickered as the two vessels communicated, but Maestro couldn't read the language.

"Not everyone out there can want us dead," TJ said. "Can they?"

The ship clanked loudly again then rocked a bit, forcing all three to grab the nearest handhold.

Air hissed into the pod as it equalized pressure.

The door ground metal. . . then opened.

Dazzling light filled the dark pod, blinding Maestro. Blast. How could he be so stupid? He shielded his eyes with one arm and searched the light. Would the boys be dead by the time his eyes adjusted?

A slight figure crouched into silhouette in the doorway and reached out one rather skinny arm.

"Hey guys," he said, emphasizing the outstretched hand. "It's Danny Decker. I'm here to rescue you."

A Half-Remembered Dream

In a nutshell: the ships Bobby had spotted shortly after the Hunter nest exploded were Shifter vessels. Peter Test had scrambled them upon receiving one tiny part of the database instead of the entire thing. Something had gone wrong, so he enlisted every ship he could enlist.

When they rendezvoused with the Galactic Police cruiser originally "borrowed" by Babbage and Maestro, Danny and Bobby screamed at the EL, since the shot that had ultimately led to the destruction of the Hunter nest had been his idea.

"Someone needs to erase this evil robot's hard drive." Once he'd met the rescue crew, Danny had grown very quiet. "Someone else can get us home."

But Peter revealed that a faint distress beacon in a Hunter frequency had been discovered.

"Is it them?" Danny had demanded.

No one knew for certain.

"That's the problem with certain nebulas," Peter explained. "Massive ambient energy."

Once they'd ascertained that the pod indeed carried their human friends, Danny had insisted on leading the welcoming committee.

"Please feel free to quote rescue protocols to me," Danny had said, "Mr. Galactic Police officer who orchestrated Babbage's abduction of innocent children from a Protected Planet." He must have worked hard to so clearly enunciate the capital letters.

Danny's dramatic entrance at the escape pod led to hugs and tears, but only briefly since the medics insisted on checking Torch and TJ. In spite of Maestro's healing, they still looked like they needed attention.

"And pants," TJ insisted. "I really need pants."

Maestro and Babbage had been pulled away to answer questions, but Danny and Bobby refused to allow the doctors to separate them from their friends. All four boys physically latched onto each other and when someone recommended sedation, Danny favored Peter with a withering glance that would have generated applause from Wednesday Addams.

"The fact that you haven't left our side means you're afraid we can end your entire career," he said. "Handle this."

Peter held Danny's gaze for less than ten seconds before giving in. "Just fix them up."

"What planet are they from?" a tech asked.

"Just fix them up!" Peter repeated before retreating to one side of the room. "And don't ask any unnecessary questions."

"Bloody obstinate species, whatever they are," another tech muttered. He pulled an array of arms and gadgets from the ceiling with one of eight pseudopods.

Danny smiled.

Torch raised a fist.

Danny bumped it.

After doctor machines, showers, and clean clothes, the boys found themselves at the door to an observation deck.

"Wait in there," Peter told them. "Someone will be along to deal with you shortly."

He turned on his heel.

All the boys had Doohickeys again. They chimed to indicate a text received.

So did Peter's.

Tell him Elizabeth says hi: Maestro.

"Elizabeth says hi!" the boys shouted in chorus.

Peter stopped, his hands clenching into fists.

But he didn't turn.

He walked away.

Danny Decker was fairly certain that his adventure had almost concluded. He'd long since ceased to think in terms like "absolute certainty" or "utter impossibility."

"Horribly unlikely" was about as definitive as he would think in the future.

He stood on the observation deck of a Galactic Police cruiser that made every other ship he'd seen thus far look like tinker toys. The deck stretched a hundred yards across and bustled with dozens of different species of extraterrestrial origin. They stood around snacking or chatting or simply enjoying the view and relaxing.

Apparently, the cruiser held a complement of a thousand and this was one of several break rooms. This was what a spaceship should look like.

A few feet away, Bobby spoke with a young Aquarian with blue skin and gills who hailed, not surprisingly, from a planet with no major land masses. The two seemed to be comparing notes on their respective martial arts. The Aquarian's water-filled helmet didn't seem to inhibit his moves at all.

Torch was trying to make the moves on a very pretty girl who looked mostly human except for the extra arms. And she was almost naked. Torch had leapt so far out of his league he was playing the wrong game entirely.

TJ had connected his Doohickey with someone who resembled nothing more than a wandering cactus of indeterminate gender.

"I think he's related to a species in Texas!" TJ grinned. "Can you even imagine?"

Danny couldn't, but he gave TJ a thumbs up. Yeah. He really needed to spend more time with that friend.

Since everyone who mattered seemed to be having fun, Danny explored the view out the observation deck window. The nebula rolled and drifted in gold, green, and purple, and over a dozen Shifter vessels glided through the luminous fields in tight formation.

Some of the ships were little more than metal cigars. Many of them billowed with enormous solar sails that scooped up the gaseous matter and converted it to fuel. Some of them were delicate and beautiful and some of them were dark and formidable.

Danny could watch them drift for weeks and never tire of the view.

"After everything that's happened, there are usually two reactions," a familiar voice told him. Maestro had managed to sneak up while Danny's attention had been focused on the scene beyond rather than on the glass itself.

Danny smiled. Just having Maestro nearby made him feel safer.

His friends gathered around.

"One sort of person just can't wait to get home to be reunited with familiar faces," the time traveler said. "The other wishes they could stay out here forever and never had to go back."

"First sort," Torch declared.

"Definitely the first sort," TJ agreed.

"Planet Earth, here I come," Bobby added.

All eyes turned to Danny.

"I miss Mom and Dad. . . and our other friends." He gazed out the window again. The tiny vessels shuttling from one of the big ships to another held his attention. "But look at it out there." He turned to include the activity surrounding them, the myriad shapes and sizes. "And in here."

As if to emphasize his point, a tiny female sprite only one foot tall with huge catlike eyes and dragonfly wings buzzed the little group on her way to a collection of flowers in one corner of the room.

"Our world seems so small after all we've seen," Danny admitted.

"And Danny Decker comes full circle." Maestro laughed and threw an arm around his shoulders. "From craving adventure to dreading it and back to craving it again."

"Not adventure. . ." After everything that had happened, he'd likely never crave adventure again. "But there's so much to understand that we'll never learn on Earth, and I don't see us officially reaching out to the galaxy in my lifetime." He sighed then broke into a grin and punched Torch in the arm. "Of course, I didn't get shot or exploded or have my leg broken. . ."

"Yeah, you had a day at the spa while the rest of us did all the work." Torch punched him back.

Everyone laughed.

"So what's next, boss?" Torch asked.

"We use a quantum shift to take us home, and you boys try to get on with the business of having ordinary lives." Maestro clapped his hands and rubbed them.

"What about Babbage's planet?" Danny asked. As much as he hated the robot, he hoped the end game saved those in need.

"All efforts are being undertaken to rescue the planets," Maestro said. "An appropriate star is about to receive its new complement of satellites. We saved 'em all, I guess."

"Which brings up a point," Torch suggested brashly. "Who gets credit for this? The Shifters can't admit that they involved monkeys from a protected planet, can they? Will anyone know *we* were the ones who helped make this possible?"

"We'll know," TJ said.

"Yeah, yeah, and that makes me all warm and fuzzy inside, but we can't tell anyone back home." Torch rolled his eyes. "No one'll believe us." He opened his arms expansively. "Shouldn't there be a freakin' statue of us out there somewhere?"

"It'll never happen," Maestro said. "A small group of Shifters orchestrated this, but they acted with approval closer to the top than I like to ponder. There's a central council of Shifters instead of a president. I'm sure they'll get the credit."

"Great." Torch harrumphed. "And we get a warm sense of satisfaction over a job well done. And me with all these deep emotional scars that could use a little salving."

Danny elbowed him and shook his head. Torch had to be angling for some kind of reward.

"Those won't be a problem." The voice was familiar by now, but almost completely without emotion.

Oh. Danny had thought it was Peter, but this was a tall, Asian man in a trench coat and fedora.

"Peter." Maestro's face changed to cold and angry. Right. Test was a Shifter.

"You recognize me in this outfit?" His eyes registered surprise.

"Elizabeth taught me how to see through what you wear." He crossed his arms and moved to stand between the Shifter and the boys. "What do you mean, 'Those won't be a problem?'"

"I'm sure you know exactly what I mean." The Shifter raised an eyebrow.

"You will not wipe these minds." Maestro's voice relayed just how factual he knew his words to be. Considering the animosity involved, how strange that Peter had arrived alone.

"We don't have a choice, Maestro." The Shifter showed no emotion. He spoke as if they discussed removing a Band-Aid. "They come from a protected planet."

"And whose responsibility is that?" Maestro barked out a single sharp laugh. "This goes too deep for mind wipe. There will be scars, even if I do it myself. Magic works a lot better than tech, but there will be too much cognitive dissonance here. I will not permit it."

"You will not permit it?" Peter smiled. It was a small smile, a mere hint of amusement, but it betrayed even to Danny and his young friends the depth of this Shifter's arrogance. He shook his head and shrugged as if to imply that it would be foolish for Maestro to think he could stop them.

"Doohickey?" Maestro said with a smile of his own. "Please connect that call, now."

A garishly dressed, feline humanoid appeared, the badges at her shoulder indicating that she was a hologram. A sweeping mane of orange and red hair streamed down her back, shifting as if it had a life of its own. Velvety brown fur covered her skin, and she purred all of her Rs.

"This is Vesta Prima coming to you *live!* from only the shades know where, since I am talking blind with my good friend Maestro who assures me he has the biggest scoop since I spilled the beans on the Alpaca Consortium's slave trade in Kho Wah." She looked around, obviously waiting for Maestro's hologram to appear. "Maestro? Babaloo? Are you there? Do I get a scoop?"

Wordlessly, Maestro raised an eyebrow at Peter, who glanced around uncomfortably at the gathering crowd. From the delighted expressions on the myriad faces around them, Vesta had quite a following. A celebrity?

"Vesta, my dear…" Maestro's enthusiasm bubbled over. "Thank you so much for holding. It's wonderful to have you here… well, I'm not sure if I should tell you where…"

"Maestro… You *are* there…" She cast about for him dramatically.

Peter stepped forward and cut one thumb across his throat.

Maestro held a hand up to his ear as if he couldn't quite hear.

Peter employed sign language to avoid speaking.

Maestro replied.

Peter responded very emphatically and at length.

Maestro gave his final answer using a single digit in a sign Danny clearly understood.

Torch sniggered.

Peter, no longer appearing smug, turned on his heel and strode off into the crowd.

"Sorry, Vesta, but I'm afraid my little trick worked, so I don't get to provide you with a scoop today." Maestro faced the hologram.

The lovely feline woman turned to look directly at Maestro and gave him a very definite wink before disappearing.

The boys hooted, clapped, and jumped on Maestro.

The crowd drifted off to other entertainments.

Danny patted Maestro on the back one last time as he extricated himself from the pile of hooting monkeys.

The time-traveling space witch stared each boy in the eyes, as if he were about to say something of the utmost importance.

"It is going to be hard for you," he said. "You *can't* tell anyone what happened, and no one would believe you anyway. You'd end up institutionalized or worse." What could possibly be worse? "As far as they're concerned a house burned down and some friends joined you on a little holiday to recover from the loss. That's all. Your other friends will want to know where you've been. And they'll probably know that you're lying. Your teachers will want to be helpful with enough seemingly innocent questions to drive you mad." He shoved his hands deep into his pockets. "Stay together. You're the only ones who know the truth. You'll keep each other sane."

"What about you?" Danny had to ask. Would they ever see him again?

"I went insane more than a thousand years ago." Maestro smirked. "I got better." He ruffled Danny's hair and produced a small stack of business cards.

```
Maestro
Tell me your tale of woe.

Mysteries solved.
```

The back had a phone number. "If you ever really, really need me. You know how to reach me."

"You do this sort of thing for a living?" Torch read the card out loud.

"It's mostly finding lost cats and missing spouses, but we save the world from invasion every once in a while so it doesn't get boring."

Torch whistled. "Where's the guy recruiting for *that* sort of job on career day?"

Danny read the card over five times before shoving it in a pocket. Could he call without an emergency? This amazing man had said he was Danny's friend, but he had adventures all the time. Would he just ride off into the sunset without a second glance?

"I just might check in from time to time," Maestro said as if reading his thoughts. Wait. Could he? Most likely.

Maestro's smile mellowed a little. He held one hand in the circle.

One by one, the boys each placed a hand on his.

Maestro set his other hand on top and squeezed them all together.

"Go team," he said very quietly.

"Go team," the boys chorused.

Danny and his friends made their way to a shuttle that headed through the nebula without the least sense of movement. Even this tiny vessel made the Galactic Police cruiser seem like the Model-A it was.

"Make ready for quantum shift," a voice said over the PA system. "Quantum jumpers may wish to medicate at this time."

"Drat!" Maestro said then muttered something else.

The space between Danny and his friends expanded exponentially.

The universe expanded... all of it.

Danny fell unconscious... again...

Someone held Danny on his feet as he regained consciousness. Bobby stood on one side and Torch on the other.

"Danny?" Bobby adjusted as Danny tried to hold his own weight.

Didn't work so well. Bobby held him fast.

"And he's back." Torch patted his shoulder.

"What happened?" Danny got his feet under him, and Torch let go, but Bobby kept an arm around his brother.

"Dude, you went all CG again like the first time we did a quantum travel," Torch said. "It was totally *Altered States*."

TJ nodded.

"What is that about?" Bobby asked, but Danny had no idea.

"Since you'll likely never leave the planet again..." Maestro held Danny's head gently and searched his eyes one at a time. "It doesn't much matter. Some people are sensitive to quantum drive tech. I am, too, but I've made enough jumps that I can control the effects."

He released Danny.

"He didn't puke this time," Torch offered helpfully.

"That's because I knocked him out," Maestro explained. "If you're unconscious, the effect is fairly minimal."

And that was all he would say on it.

A viewscreen displayed the earth, and the boys finally saw the sun rise over the planet the way Torch had mentioned the first time they set foot on a spaceship. Had that just been days ago? It seemed like a lifetime.

But wow, what a view.

"Uh-oh," Torch muttered.

"I wanted to let you know the data Maestro sent was exactly what we needed." Babbage stood in the doorway to the bridge. "We should be able to transport the planets in a few days."

Spit. It had to be an excuse to see them off, as if Danny would want to see the lying, evil robot ever again.

"We knew that already," Danny said.

"I guess I just wanted to say goodbye." The sorrow in Babbage's inhuman, glowing eyes was easy to read.

"So you've said it and now you can leave." Danny turned his back to the robot. This man. . . this *robot*. . . had betrayed them, had tricked them and nearly killed them all. How could he hope there was any coming back from that?

A trio of technicians stood together near the wall on the other side of the deck. One woman seemed human. Red hair.

Red hair. . .

What was it about a red-haired woman?

"Are you in my head?" Danny snapped.

"No. . . no. . ." Babbage startled. "Of course not."

"He can't," Maestro threw in. "There's a scrambler active."

Never mind then. That moment of fear at a new invasion settled it. Danny turned to the viewscreen. Would they please just transport them down so he could get away from the traitor?

With a shaking hand, Danny dug into his pocket and pulled out the coppery "penny" that had been the beginning of his adventures. He placed it on his thumb and flicked it back over his shoulder. It clattered against the floor.

He turned.

Babbage crouched and picked it up.

"Find a penny, pick it up," Danny said with scorn.

Babbage rose and searched deeply into Danny's eyes for a moment, then the robot nodded, guilt and pain etched in his face. He turned to go, slipping the memory chip into his pocket.

Red hair. . . Wait a minute. There'd been a dream, hadn't there? That first night. A beautiful red-haired woman. Who had she been?

Oh, spit. Danny's stomach clenched and churned.

"Wait a minute." He'd never live with himself if he didn't ask.

Had he been wrong about Babbage all along?

Babbage stopped and turned back.

"A woman with red hair," Danny asked. "Who is she?"

"No one." All emotion drained from Babbage's face, and he closed his eyes for a brief moment. "No one you need to worry about." He turned to go again.

But Danny was almost certain who she had been. Why would Babbage hold back?

"You owe me this much, Babbage." Suddenly, everything the robot. . . no, everything the man had done started to make sense. "Is she your wife?"

Babbage stopped with his back to the boys and his head dropped.

"What? Wife?" Bobby demanded.

"But how can he. . . I mean, he's just. . ."

Just a robot.

Shame filled Danny with nausea. How had he never thought of it before? All his talk about Babbage being a person, being his friend, and Danny had never considered he had personal reasons to save the star system.

"Where is she?" Danny asked, dreading the answer.

"The answers change nothing, Danny Decker." Babbage shook his head. "I did what I did. You should go home to your family and try to forget about me."

But Danny couldn't do that, now. As much as he would hate himself for it, the answer to his question might change everything.

"Where is she, Babbage?" And Danny was more surprised than anyone to hear tenderness in his voice.

The EL looked back over one shoulder, tears shining in the golden glow of his eyes, a glow put there by his organic creator to ensure that anyone who saw Babbage would know he was an engineered life form and not a real boy.

Babbage didn't speak, just shook his head with a jaw clenched so tightly he likely *couldn't* speak.

"She was on the planet that died, wasn't she?" Danny spoke as kindly as he could. "That planet was your home. . . and you weren't there when. . . when she died."

"I should have been there." His voice was small and sad and defeated. "I should have been with them."

Them.

Danny's friends held their breath. Even Maestro closed his eyes and slumped.

"Who else?" Danny asked, his voice almost cracking.

Babbage stared at the ceiling, shaking his head slowly, his arms tight around his strong chest, his breath in short quick pants.

"You had children?" Danny asked.

Babbage opened his eyes and stared at Danny directly.

The boys around Danny muttered surprise at that as well. How could a robot have children?

We have been engineered by scientists rather than born randomly by nature,

Babbage had told them, *but I am just as real as any of you. And we're more than just an intelligence, we have emotions and personalities, too.*

And families. And why not?

How could Danny have been so horribly stupid and arrogant? He had thought they treated Babbage like a person, like a man doing a job. . . but there are times when a job is much more than just a job. . . when the man does things out of grief and loss he might not otherwise ever consider. Hadn't Danny almost gotten Torch killed out of his grief when Bobby was hurt? What Babbage had done was worse, certainly, but he had lost so much more, as well.

At the end of the day, Danny hadn't actually lost anyone.

"How many children did you have?" Danny asked.

Babbage swallowed and coughed. "One. . . a daughter."

A lump grew in Danny's throat for the lost family of the engineered life form he wanted so desperately to hate. But he just couldn't do it anymore.

"What. . . what was her name?" His voice broke.

Tears ran down Babbage's face and his shoulders twitched. He snuffled loudly before he spoke. "Delaney."

"Why didn't. . . why didn't you say?" Maestro asked.

Babbage stared.

"Why didn't we ask?" Danny answered for him. He couldn't stand it anymore. He closed the space and threw his arms around Babbage's middle, hugging him close. A heart pounded in Danny's ear and breath sucked in and out in shaky fits.

After a moment, Babbage's strong arms closed around Danny.

"I'm sorry," Danny told him. "I'm so sorry I never thought to ask."

And then all of Danny's companions joined in a huddle.

Horrible pain and anguish are never fun or entertaining to read unless you're messed up in the head, so it's time to let the boys and Maestro support Babbage through the first time he let himself really feel the loss. We'll check in on them a little later.

A little later, Danny once again stood on the sidewalk in front of his grandparents' house. The sun shone, the squirrels chattered in the trees, and the birds sang a melancholy song. As far as this neighborhood was concerned, nothing at all had happened.

And now Danny had to return to that life.

"I want to hear all about your family, Tin Man." He hugged Babbage one last time.

"Of course, friend Danny." Babbage seemed to like the nickname. "It's only fair since I already know so much about yours."

"Will I really get the chance?" Danny took a step back.

"It's utterly impossible," Babbage admitted, "but you know how well that worked out for you the last time." He glanced at Maestro then met Danny's gaze again. He shrugged.

"I think I'll miss you most of all, Scarecrow." Danny grinned then threw his arms around Maestro.

"All right, Dorothy, you've milked that reference about as far as it'll go." Maestro hugged Danny tightly then set him back a step. "And don't ask."

Danny opened his mouth to ask.

"Don't," Maestro insisted, "ask. Asking ruins it."

Danny closed his mouth and nodded.

So it was goodbye then. For real.

The other boys hugged the adults in turn, Babbage and Maestro stepped closer together, and then they were gone. No fuss. No fancy effects. Just gone.

The boys faced Grandma and Grandpa Decker's house. It had a new front door, but otherwise it hadn't changed. Danny, however, felt remarkably different, even though, to the casual observer, the changes might be invisible.

"So. . ." He took a deep breath.

"So. . ." Torch looked from him to the house.

"*Donc. . .*" TJ took his place in line.

"Geek." Bobby scoffed.

"It looks so small," Danny said. "It's not supposed to look small until after we grow up."

"Maybe we did grow up," Torch suggested. "Maybe we just didn't get any taller."

"You should come in with us." Danny turned to his friends. "Our folks were out there, too. They'll understand and want to hear all the stories."

His friends smiled and nodded. As Maestro had said, they needed to stick together now.

All four stared at the house. Once they crossed the lawn, the whole adventure was officially over.

Bobby put an arm around his little brother's shoulders. There would likely be a lot of that for a while. Stellar.

"*Were* your parents out there?" TJ asked quietly.

What?

"Was that really a hologram of your folks you saw," TJ elaborated, "or was that just part of the act?"

"Well, I guess this might prove more interesting than we imagined." Danny exchanged a look with his brother.

"Bobby?" a voice carried to them from across the street.

A tall, muscular Asian teenager with straight black hair hurried toward them from across the street. Bobby's friend Nax. He stopped uncertainly a few feet away, checking out the foursome and not-so-subtly checking out their matching outfits. He stared at Bobby's buzz cut for a moment but refrained from comment.

"Hey, Nax," Bobby said a trifle uncertainly.

"Hey." Nax sort of shuffled one foot.

Awkward. They hadn't spoken in so long, and now, after everything that had happened. . .

"Are you okay, Bobby?" Nax asked at last. "I've been hearing all kinds of crazy stuff." He glanced at Danny and his friends, as if uncomfortable. "I was. . ." He paused then sucked in a deep breath. "I was worried, okay?"

Bobby startled. "Really?"

"Yeah." He shrugged. "Duh."

Bobby stared stupidly at his friend, as if uncertain what to say. Remembering how angry with Nax Bobby had been, Danny gently lifted Bobby's arm from his shoulders and patted his brother's back.

"What my reticent older brother wants to say is that he is grateful for your concern and would love to tell you where he's been."

Bobby's face became a mask of confusion.

"Whatever happened between you guys doesn't really matter anymore, does it, Bigby? Really?" Danny had Torch and TJ, his two best friends who'd been out there with him. They would always understand if he jumped at a loud noise or steered clear of large bugs. Bobby didn't have anyone his own age who would understand. Why not bring Nax into the circle? In spite of Maestro's warnings, Danny suspected they could find a way to convince Nax they weren't insane.

Bobby looked from Danny to Nax. A slew of emotions crossed his face: frustration, fear, anger and hope. Then everything relaxed.

"No," Bobby admitted, shaking his head. "I guess it's no big deal after all."

"No?" Nax's smile could have lit up a major nebula. "It's. . . we're cool. Right?"

Danny turned and started up the sidewalk, sweeping Torch and TJ into his wake.

"We're cool," Bobby said behind him.

"So. . ." Nax said quietly as if testing the waters. "What's up with the basic training haircut?"

Bobby chuckled, and Danny slowed down so he could hear the answer. "It got shaved off after I was smacked in the head with shrapnel from an exploding control panel on a Galactic Police space cruiser."

Yep, that would be an interesting conversation.

"Whatever he tells you is the God's honest truth, Nax," Danny called over a shoulder without really turning. "After you guys talk, you should come in for food and we'll corroborate what he says."

Wow, food. When had Danny last eaten? Hopefully, Mom would be willing to make her famous meatloaf.

"Dude. . ." Torch stopped dead in his tracks and his head fell back. "Tell me you can talk your mom into making me-e-e-at lo-o-o-o-af."

"Torch, my friend, you absolutely read my mind." Danny pulled his friend forward to give his brother some privacy.

As he reached the front door, Danny glanced back. Bobby was showing Nax one of the moves he'd learned from the Aquarian.

Danny grabbed the doorknob and turned—

It was locked tight.

He jiggled it as if that might somehow help.

"It's locked?" He jiggled it again. "It's locked."

TJ and Torch laughed as Danny banged on the front door to his grandparent's house.

"Mom? Dad?" He banged louder.

"Hello?" He banged some more. "Hey! We're home!"

Across the street, two men stood in the shadows, watching the scene. The five little humans regrouped and headed to the side of the house where one of them pulled a rope ladder out from under a bush.

"Why did the monkeys get to leave the planet, Phineas?" The tall, skinny man pulled an apple out of a coat pocket and popped it into his mouth, swallowing it whole.

"I don't know, Bogg." The shorter, stout man watched the boys with feral intensity.

"It doesn't seem fair that we're stuck on this stupid little rock, but the monkeys get to leave." Phineas pulled a second apple out of his coat and popped that into his mouth as well.

"No, it doesn't seem fair at all."

"What are we going to do about it?" The tall man pulled a live bird out of his coat and swallowed that whole, too.

"I'm not sure, Bogg. But I'm certain I'll think of something." The shorter man scrutinized the boys' activities. They climbed up to a balcony and made their way into the house. Why they would be allowed to ignore the protected planet status was a mystery to Phineas, and he didn't much care for mysteries.

Bogg pointed at an alley cat eyeing them from a nearby sidewalk. When he smiled, his grin grew more than a trifle larger than a human's. "Here, kitty, kitty. . . kitty. . .

Acknowledgements

Thanks to Byron and Blake, who helped me learn that, yeah, boys really can be that smart. And awesome. They were two of my best friends the 2.5 years I lived in Virginia Beach. I miss them. Thanks to Ryan and Hope for giving me refuge while I brought my writing skills to the next level, and thanks as always to Lauran for helping me write gooder. Drafts of this novel benefitted from the kind interference of Jennifer Wenninger Neidfeldt, Amanda, and Jace Toronto who helped me work Maestro into a new universe. There are others, as always, and if you see this without your name, please contact me so I can add you.

About the Author

John Robert Mack lives and breathes in Franklin, NC today. He splits his time between teaching dance and inhabiting parallel universes. His spare time (which he has hijacked from one of the aforementioned dimensions) is spent with his friends, trying to live up to the hijinks in his novels. He has written numerous novels, plays, screenplays, magazine columns and other sundry stories. He doesn't believe in the Oxford comma but understands that some folks need to cling to tradition in a turbulent world.

Please enjoy this selection from another novel with Maestro.
Also available on Amazon.

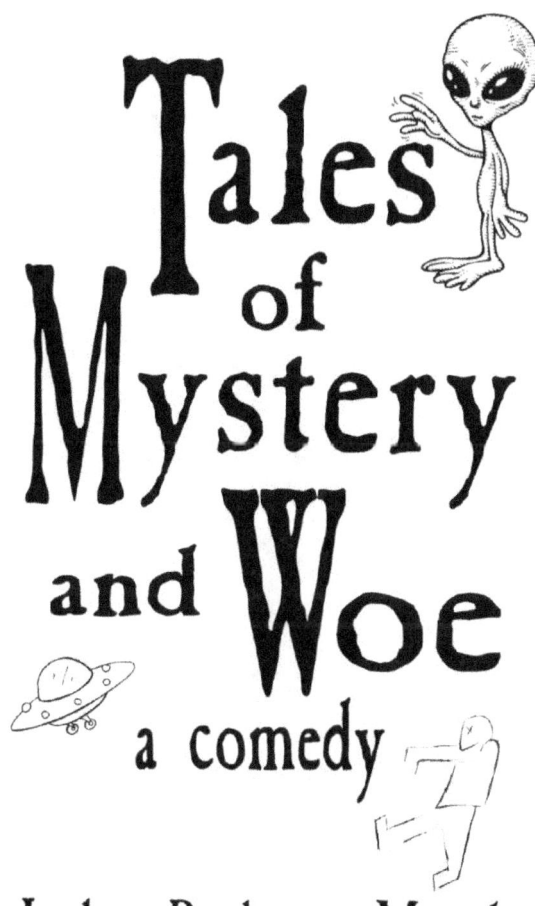

Tales
of
Mystery
and Woe
a comedy

John Robert Mack

Channel

Channel was dead.

He'd been killed back in 1961 at the age of seventeen but never stopped walking around and shooting off his mouth. Or so his brother, Ross, liked to say. For the record, Channel hated the word "zombie."

He stood in his basement, arms raised and eyes closed, reciting a spell of demonic summoning. *"O Fortuna. . . velut luna. . . statu variabilis. . . semper crescis. . . aut decrescis."* Dust motes sparkled in the light of a hundred blood-red candles and swirled inside the arcane containment circle painstakingly inscribed on the bare concrete floor.

Channel's "Ye Olde Booke of Shadows" had called for "thee blude of a styll-brything mongrel poured unto the colde, colde stone whilst it screamed its fynal cries of terrour after its throat was verily slitte." But that was impossible, since an animal with its throat slit couldn't cry out in terror anymore. Channel had a deal with the butcher down the road who sold him farm animal blood at cost, just to get rid of the stuff. Close enough.

He continued his spell as he dribbled the cow's blood into the concrete, which ate it up greedily with faint suckling sounds.

Channel hung out with a Goth crowd that'd taught him how to dress the part at a place called Bitter Sweets on Austin's east side. All these years of spell casting and hunting creatures of the night, and Channel had never realized the importance of image. His short black hair rose in a spikey mess. His normally dark, Mexican skin was made up pale and kohl surrounded his eyes. He wore black leather pants, black boots, a black velvet shirt and a burgundy cowl with the hood down so it wouldn't muss his hair.

Who'd have known it'd take so much effort for an actual life-challenged American to blend into the death-becomes-us crowd?

He opened his eyes and raised his voice. "*Vita detestabilis. . . nunc obdurate. . . et tunc curat. Ludo mentis acie. . .*" His voice dropped an octave and reverberated with a cavernous echo. "*Egestatem. . . potestatem. . . dissolvit ut glaciem.*"

The dust motes swirled into a vortex within the protection circle and a column of light ignited, bright enough to drive away the shadows and expose the clutter in Channel's basement, pushed to the walls to make room for spell casting.

The illumination revealed the usual assortment of old—but still perfectly serviceable—chairs and tables, a collection of demon banishing swords and daggers laid out for easy access, boxes of clothes bound to come back into fashion someday, a standing mirror of soul capturing, and a Hello Kitty lamp.

An ethereal breeze stirred the various flags, banners, and drop cloths. Faintly, in the background, a chorus in three-part harmony rose up to support Channel's voice.

The spell was working.

He could feel it.

The power started as a tickle at the base of his spine and spread through his nervous system, which was nothing more than a conduit for magical energy since his death and reanimation. Warm. Tingly.

Oh yeah, it was working.

"*O Fortuna. . . velut luna. . . statu variabilis. . . semper crescis. . . aut decrescis.*" Soon, the gate would open, and his own personal demonic companion would step through the dimensional rift and shuffle up this mortal coil to—

A happy violin riff cut through Channel's chant. Someone had rung the front doorbell.

He faltered, as did the unearthly chorus. But only for a moment.

Ignoring the distraction, he raised his voice and focused. The chorus rejoined him, and the spell continued. "*Vita detestabilis. . . nunc obdurate. . .* damn it."

The violin music broke in again, joined by a heavily accented little girl's voice. "Hello Kitty, come outside and play!"

"*Et tunc curat Ludo mentis acie. . .* crap."

The theme song interrupted itself to start over.

Person at the door impatient much?

The chorus cut out. Channel lost his place in the spell. "Blast!" His voice still held all the reverb and echo of a demonic overlord.

The maelstrom in the center of the room suddenly and rapidly swirled down into a tiny spot on the floor like water down a toilet in fast forward. The last of the magical energy disappeared into the concrete with a pathetic "thwip."

The Hello Kitty theme repeated itself.

With a disgusted snort, Channel glared at the ceiling in the direction of the front door. He pulled at his sleeves and headed for the stairs.

"That had better be pizza."

As he tramped up the stairs, his Goth boots thundered to suit his mood at the interruption.

He burst through the door into a kitchen obviously decorated entirely from Ikea and headed toward the front door. A more traditional doorbell replaced the bright melody from his downstairs alarm. "If there's no pizza. . . there will be heck to pay."

Unfortunately, the soft and well-padded carpet in the front hall spoiled the heavy tread of his boots, but he managed two heavy stamps on the hardwood of the foyer to get his steam back up. When the doorbell rang two or three times in rapid succession, Channel yanked the door open as abruptly as he could.

"You better have pizza!"

A middle-aged man in a grey trench coat stood with his back to Channel for a moment before turning quickly to face him, his mouth already open to speak. He did not have pizza. His mouth hung open for a split second before closing as if he'd forgotten what he was going to say or had changed his mind.

Holy Columbo!

He looked Channel up and down, and then his eyes settled on Channel's face with an expression so utterly blank, it was worse than scorn.

In the bright light of the front hall of a two-story, mid-century modern home and surrounded by furniture from Ikea, the burgundy coat and knee-high boots were possibly a trifle excessive. And how much make-up had Channel actually applied?

Emotionless, the stranger extended a business card. "I just happened to be passing through your neighborhood and thought you might need some help controlling the demon you're trying to summon."

Channel sucked in a quick breath. How did he know? He grabbed the card. It read:

```
              Maestro
       Tell me your tale of woe.

          Mysteries solved.
```

Channel glanced from the card to the man. "What. . . demon. . . what?" He floundered. "Do I look like someone who would try to conjure—?" He glanced at his reflection in the hallway mirror, suddenly embarrassed at the get-up. With the crowd at Bitter Sweets, it had seemed restrained. Hadn't it?

The stranger, Maestro, spoke gently. "You look like a reject from a Goth Hello Kitty convention."

Channel wanted to disagree but searched Maestro's eyes. He was definitely a fellow mage. Sorcerer? Witch? A powerful one, whatever he was, from the complete sense of control he radiated. Other than the power in the man's eyes, though, he was so bland he'd be nearly invisible in a crowd.

Oooh. Was that just how he liked it?

Channel drew himself up. "How did you know I was summoning a demon? Could you sense a disturbance in the ethereal realm? Ripples in the—"

Maestro snorted. "You are such a little girl." He pointed up.

Channel looked at the ceiling. Nothing there apart from a few cobwebs. Time to call the maid.

The man grabbed him roughly by the arm and dragged him across the porch and onto the front lawn. He was stronger than he looked.

The front lawn needed mowing. Time to call one of his grand-nephews—

Maestro pointed up again. "Actually, the giant hellsmouth over your house was my first clue."

"Holy spit!" Channel stumbled as Maestro released him.

There, above his home, raged an enormous, swirling tornado of smoke and fire and lightning lit from inside by a sickening green radiance. Spirits and demons flew in and out of it, for all the world like fireflies swarming a lantern.

In almost sixty years of hunting supernatural evil, Channel had seen *nothing* like it. Nothing even close. He was so ultimately screwed.

Maestro smacked him on the back of the head. "Close your mouth before something evil and smelly flies in. You look like a tourist." The man calmly turned away from the giant funnel of interdimensional power as if it were nothing more than a backed-up sink. "Tell me this isn't your first ride on the merry-go-round."

Channel ran to catch up to the stranger who had already opened the back of a green and white VW Microbus.

Maestro dispatched an apepi as it slithered toward one of the myriad bystanders too stupid to realize they should run in terror. As his banishing sword sliced the giant snake in two, the slimy creature exploded into a ball of smoke. One handy thing about most demons: when banished, they popped back to their personal hell without leaving behind an enormous mess. Made it easier to deal with the local constabulary. Also meant they occasionally hunted down their killer for revenge.

Speaking of which, Maestro spun and skewered one of Azidahaka's three heads, pulled the blade free, and sliced off the other two, sending her back to a very, very hot place.

How had the kid managed to create a dimensional portal *this* bloody powerful? Maestro knew the "kid" had been born in the forties, but nearly everyone held in magical stasis at a particular age maintained the maturity of that stage. Channel would be seventeen forever.

Assuming he learned to watch his own back and managed to survive the night.

Maestro sliced through a ghast behind Channel, who spun quickly enough to see it evaporate with a high-pitched scream. He glanced at Maestro in embarrassment at letting down his guard and threw out the first thing that came to mind to cover his humiliation. "And you just happened to have a couple of banishing swords in the back of your Mystery Machine?"

His surface thoughts were easier to read than stereo instructions.

"And you don't?" Maestro raised an eyebrow.

Behind Channel, a ghoul chased a middle-aged woman in a housecoat. Maestro intoned a spell. The ghoul evaporated.

Channel stared like a groupie. "Your eyes. . ."

Maestro grabbed him by the shoulders and turned him around just in time for his rising blade to slice a ghost in half. "Yes, yes, yes," Maestro muttered. "They glow purple when I cast that spell. It's very cool. Now you need to get centered and *close that portal.*"

Suddenly, Channel spun out of Maestro's grip, stabbed forward into a ghoul and then quickly flipped his blade backward into a second as it zoomed out of the hellsmouth. "Yeah. . . centering here. Totally peaced-out and chill." He pulled a dagger from his belt and tossed it into the center of a cresil chasing a dachshund with obvious lascivious intent.

Maybe the kid wasn't utterly hopeless, after all.

Then he grinned like a puppy eager for a pat on the head, which completely ruined the effect.

"We're kind of on a clock here," Maestro reminded him. "Reporters and cops on the way."

Channel frowned and turned his back to Maestro, bringing his hands together. "Not helping."

With a quiet mutter, Maestro banished the giant hellworm inching toward Channel. "Civilians gonna start dying soon." He let his sword drop to his side for a moment and watched the energy swirl and collect about Channel.

"Helping even less," the lad complained. But he did focus better. His energies stabilized into a gentle globe around him.

Channel needed someone directing him. Not good. He'd spent so many years as part of a team, who knew how badly he'd screw up on his own? And the fact that he'd tried to summon a demon in the first place meant he'd started down a dark and lonely path.

Which, although Channel would never know it, was the real reason for Maestro's intervention. He'd seen what he needed to see. Channel couldn't be left alone as much as Maestro would like to remain aloof. He'd watched him from a distance for years. It was time to step in.

"Tourist," Maestro teased. He raised his banishing sword and tossed it from hand to hand in a rapid figure eight. "*Lorem ipsum dolor sit amet.*" He spun twice, whirling the sword over his head. "*Duo nonumy legimus dignissim.*"

He grabbed the pommel in tight fists as it glowed bright white, switched his grip so the point faced the ground. With a guttural shout, he drove the sword up to the hilt into the pavement, dropping to one knee as he did so.

"*Quidam!*"

Lightning crashed into him. A sphere of white light, centered on the quartz crystal in the hilt of Maestro's sword, expanded in a flash a hundred yards out, instantly banishing anything supernatural it touched. Dozens of creatures exploded.

Stupid bystanders applauded.

Maestro focused hard to keep the spell from destroying Channel as well.

The kid staggered as the hydra he'd been fighting suddenly ceased to exist. He turned to Maestro with shock and awe all over his face. "Who are you, and how have I never heard of you?"

Maestro's grip on the sword tightened as the blade began to vibrate. Uh-oh. "Kinda hoping you'll hurry up." Sweat trickled down his forehead and into one eye. The ground trembled.

"Oh. . . right." Channel raised his arms and the echo returned to his voice. "*Sicsercedtau. . . sicsercrepnessilibairavutats anultulevanutrof o!*"

Maestro closed his eyes. Please let it work. He could do it himself but didn't want to play that card just yet. Please let Channel be able to handle it.

The clouds churned.

The demons screamed.

The giant cyclone of arcane energy swirled into the roof of Channel's home like water down the drain of a toilet. Great billows of smoke and lightning sucked into the house, and Maestro opened his third eye and shifted his gaze to Channel's ridiculously cluttered basement.

The entire maelstrom whirled into the center of the summoning circle on the floor and vanished with an anticlimactic "thwip" that barely managed to blow out the ridiculous and unnecessary assortment of candles.

Maestro loosened his grip on the sword and let himself breathe. The giant glowing bubble faded like so much steam. With the thunderous roar of a demonic gate silenced, the car alarms, the weeping, and the distinct sound of police and fire sirens rose to fill the void.

Damn. No rest for the wicked.

Before Channel could start in on some foolish "we saved the day" ritual he'd no doubt had with Percy and Ross, Maestro left the sword in the road and rose to his feet, motioning the lad closer.

Channel wiped his forehead and hurried forward, smiling.

Maestro reached for the boy, who grinned even more and opened his arms for a celebratory hug.

Maestro snorted. "Don't be ridiculous." He spun Channel so they were back to back. "Don't move. Our work isn't done."

Maestro pulled out what most anyone would mistake for an iPhone. When he touched the screen though, a 2-D hologram popped up above it. He tapped the image.

"*Harkle barkle Beelzebub.*" Hopefully, his words were good enough to fool Channel into thinking this was spellcasting. Sometimes alien technology just worked better, but he couldn't let the little ghoul know about it. He wouldn't make that mistake twice.

A faint light pulsed out of the device and flashed across the neighborhood, blanketing the block in something not unlike the vapor from dry ice.

Maestro closed his eyes and sent his gaze outward and upward to look down on his handiwork.

In a slowly blossoming wave, every person, animal, and insect settled to the ground as if needing a nap. Cars crawled to a halt. A cat about to pounce on a mouse gently fell asleep, the mouse dropping only an inch from its paws.

Opening his eyes, Maestro clicked his tongue at the eerie muting of sound from this particular app. He shoved the device into a pocket before turning to Channel, who walked away and spun a slow circle. Disgusted with Channel's touristy amazement, Maestro slipped his sword from the pavement and hurried to relieve Channel of the second banishing blade.

"That's why you haven't heard of me," Maestro explained. "Cells have been blocked the whole time, and they won't remember a thing."

Channel gestured at the spouting fire hydrants, the crashed cars. "But how do you explain all this?"

Maestro yanked open the back of his van. Damn, it did resemble the Mystery Machine. "A gas main blew up and knocked everyone out." He returned the swords to the interior and slammed the doors.

"Gas main? Really? You expect people to buy that?" He tapped a sleeping mailman with one toe.

Striding directly behind Channel, Maestro reached over his shoulder and pointed at the nearest yard. "Abracadabra." He tapped the device in his pocket.

The lawn exploded in a carefully controlled ball of fire. Before ringing Channel's doorbell, Maestro had set the explosives against just such a necessity.

"Jeepers!" Channel rocked back into Maestro.

Maestro pushed him gently but firmly away. "I do expect them to buy that."

People woke up, and the sirens roared back full volume.

How did everything look? Mayhem and destruction, yes, but no one had been seriously injured. The hellsmouth had been closed. No civilians would know how close they'd come to the Apocalypse. And Channel would never guess why Maestro kept an eye on him.

This incident belonged in the "win" column.

"You. . . are a rock star." Apparently, Channel agreed.

Without offering him the satisfaction of a response, Maestro dragged Channel back into his house, released him, and wandered into the living room. Channel would close the door behind them.

Channel leaned against the closed front door.

What. the. heck?

His unusual visitor wandered around the living room. He seemed to dismiss most of the furniture but paused to touch the ratty afghan over the back of Ross's old recliner, the only piece of furniture that wasn't new.

Channel's brother loved that chair. He'd passed out in it a thousand times over the years after nights of cocktails when he was too drunk to drive home to Lana and the kids. It'd been Percy's before, well, before he'd died... and that old man had been the closest thing to a father Channel and Ross had ever known.

Now Ross was an old man, and he would die, too, just like Percy.

Maestro moved to the fireplace and examined the photos on the mantel.

Channel left the safety of the foyer and joined his guest in the living room.

Standing there in a rumpled overcoat, the man radiated nothing. As average and boring as anyone on the street, but the power he'd shown had been incredible.

Was there any chance he'd be willing to work with Channel, train him further? Channel had been alone longer than ever in his afterlife. It blew.

Maestro turned his disquieting gaze on Channel. Okay. Kinda intense.

Russ's recliner called Channel, so he moved to it and worried one corner of the afghan. "Don't the cops ever notice there's a VW microbus at an awful lot of gas main explosions?"

"I change cars fairly often." He didn't look away, and his eyes held no emotion. Geez.

Why was he still here if he was just going to be Mr. Standoffish? There had to be some way to connect with this guy, but he was so intensely distant.

"Why the demon?" Maestro demanded.

Wait. What?

"What?"

Maestro didn't respond.

"Oh..." Channel wasn't about to admit the truth, so he stalled. "Why does anyone summon a demon? Power."

Maestro finally broke eye contact. "Seems like you have a pretty nice setup here." He glanced around the room before leveling his laser beam gaze on Channel once more. "Why the demon?"

"I told you. . ." Channel smoothed out the afghan. "I wanted more power."

Maestro shoved his hands into his coat pockets, cocking his head to one side. He needed a fedora.

"If I thought that were true," he said, "I'd have let my banishing spell take you out as well. People could have been hurt tonight. They could have died. If you were delving into the dark arts just to satisfy a craving for power, you'd already be lost." He adjusted his coat. "Why the demon?"

"You won't believe the truth." Channel fled the safety of Russ's afghan and moved to the fireplace. A photo drew him: Ross, Channel, and a very perplexed-seeming Santa Claus. Ross had been much older than the dime-store fat man.

Maestro plucked the photo from the mantle. "This was taken recently, and I note a suspicious lack of ridiculous Goth apparel. Something changed." He handed the photo over. "Why the demon?"

Geez. What was his deal?

The photo felt heavy in Channel's hand. "There's nothing ridiculous about Goth apparel." Ross had grown so old.

"Ordinarily, I'd agree with you, but on you, it's preposterous." Maestro leaned against the fireplace. "It's like Elvis Presley drag. Not everyone can pull it off. I ask one last time, and then I simply walk out the door." He took the photo from Channel and replaced it. "Why the demon?"

Channel stared at the photo. What could he say? It seemed idiotic now that he needed to explain it. When he'd been on his own last night, looking up spells and drinking Jim Beam, the plan had seemed logical. Tonight? Under the scrutiny of a mage who made Channel's ability seem feeble? Idiotic.

With a grunt, the other man pushed away from the fireplace and headed for the foyer.

Damn it. He'd leave forever if Channel didn't tell him the truth.

Was he that desperate? Yes.

"I was lonely."

Maestro stopped but didn't turn around.

"Ross was the one who found me after. . . after this happened to me." Channel picked up the photo. "We were seventeen." Those first days had been full of terror and despair, and Ross had held Channel together through it all. "He's not. . . biologically, he's not my brother, but we fought supernatural evil bastards for so many years. We sort of adopted each other." Even after Ross had married and had kids, the two of them would go off together whenever Percy found something to kill.

Then Percy died.

"Then Ross got old." Channel replaced the photo and faced Maestro. "One day, he'll die. And so will his kids. And his grandkids."

"But not you?"

"I'm already dead."

"So you summoned a demon to keep you company?"

"At the time, it made a certain kind of sense." Channel shrugged. How long before Maestro started laughing? "I told you you wouldn't believe the truth."

"Oh. . . I believe you all right. I mean. . ." He gave Channel a very pointed and critical perusal. "Have you looked at yourself in a mirror?"

Channel glanced at the foyer mirror. Sweat had ruined his make-up. In the sharp light of the overhead lamp, he was a caricature of a zombie pretending to be a real boy playing at being the undead. Ridiculous.

"I don't pull it off, do I?"

Maestro regarded him and, against all probability, he showed only the merest hint of judgment.

"Teach me. Please!" Maybe Channel didn't need to do this all by himself after all. He took a single step closer. "I've been fighting the supernatural a long time, but I've never known anyone who can do the kind of stuff you did tonight. . . well, except for a couple of evil demons. . ." That was one possibility he hadn't considered. "You're not an evil demon, are you?"

Maestro didn't visibly react. "I'll help you on two conditions."

"Anything."

"Don't be so quick to make promises." The scary man crossed his arms. He stared at Channel for a long time. "Condition one: get rid of the makeup unless you're going out on a Friday night. You look ridiculous."

"Done." He wiped his face with the back of one sleeve.

"Condition two: don't ever try to hug me again."

"Agreed." Channel grinned. This would be easier than he'd anticipated.

"I mean it." The man's face had returned to that spooky lack of expression worse than any amount of disapproval. "You ever try to hug me again, I will sever your soul from your body and send it to spend an eternity in the deepest circle of Hell."

Whoa.

"Can you really do that?" Channel asked.

Was Maestro going to smile?

Nope. No response.

Channel swallowed. "Agreed. For reals."

The other man's hand came up so fast Channel jumped.

"Okay, there's a third condition," Maestro said. "No catchphrases. I don't ever want to hear you say 'for reals' again." He grabbed the doorknob and yanked the door open.

"Hey!" How would Channel find him? He pulled out Maestro's business card. "Your card. . . there's no contact info." He held it up as if Maestro didn't already know what was on it, or, more importantly, what was not.

Maestro met Channel's gaze. "I thought you said you'd been on this merry-go-round before." He closed the door between them.

Channel grinned. "Brass ring."

He ran up the stairs three at a time to get his laptop and start googling.

www.ingramcontent.com/pod-product-compliance
Lightning Source LLC
Chambersburg PA
CBHW070917180626
46817CB00003B/1097